The View From Here ...

The Short Fiction of

Russ Heitz

Published by Aabra Publishing
Copyright 2019 by Russ Heitz

ISBN: 978-0-9882240-3-2

Dedication

To Lee, of course.
My wife, my treasure, my best friend.

Table of Contents

Forward

As some of you know, I've been writing most of my life. Sometimes as a student, sometimes as a staff writer, sometimes as a freelancer, and now as a semi-retired word mixer. Much of the time I have written simply because I enjoyed it, and because it gave me—and still gives me—a lot of personal satisfaction, whether anyone else reads what I write or not.

What you might *not* know is that much of my published work, with the exception of the two Jesse Eichenlaub novels and a nonfiction book about Florida wildlife, has been written under several different pseudonyms. I used pseudonyms mainly for marketing reasons and also to keep the various genres separate from one another. Unlike some writers who keep writing the same kind of novel, in the same kind of style, and aimed at the same kind of reader, I have consistently branched out in many different directions. Throughout my writing career I have used whatever style is appropriate for whatever genre in which I was writing. And I write in whatever genre appeals to me; and there are many that do.

There is another reason I write in different genres. Like most people, I get bored when I do the same thing over and over and over again. With my writing, I don't have to be bored. All I have to do is change topics, change styles, change genres, change point of view, etc., etc. You get the picture.

Over the years, however, there have been a number of pieces that I've been particularly pleased with but have, for one reason or another, never been published. Some of these pieces fit into the category of "short stories." Some are even shorter than that—the "flash fiction" pieces for example, which are very short pieces indeed, usually less than one thousand words. On the other hand, some of these pieces are somewhat longer than short stories but not long enough to be called "novels" or "novellas." One might call them "novelettes." The longest and last story in the collection—*A Bird That Flies, A Bird That Soars*—can rightly be called a novella.

At any rate, regardless of length I finally decided before it's too late to make these stories available myself, collected all in one place in a paper book form. The book is also available as an ebook. Each story in this collection includes a short blurb about the story itself or about how I came to write it. Each story, in its essence, is a character study. Whether you like the characters themselves, or the life they led, or the words they used, each is an accurate and realistic sketch of a real person. At least they are real to me.

Some of these stories are sad. Some are humorous. Some are scary. Some are tragic. And some are painful. But they are all mine. And now they are yours, too. I hope they will touch something inside of you as all of them have touched something inside of me.

Please feel free to contact me with any comments about the stories—or about your reaction to them—at russheitz@yahoo.com. Be sure to write "View From Here" in the subject line. Your comments are too important to end up in the spam folder. Thanks!

Russ Heitz

PS: For anyone interested in my two Jesse Eichenlaub suspense novels—CROSSHAIRS and DYING IN DEER COUNTRY—they are still available on Amazon as ebooks. You can find them by searching either for my name—Russ Heitz—or Aabra Publishing. My only non-fiction ebook—FLORIDA'S AMAZING WILDLIFE—is also available on Amazon and has been updated with new photos. Additionally, all of my pseudonymous novels are available as ebooks on Amazon under Aabra Publishing.

Silence and the Wind

(This is a novelette about isolation and how it can affect a lonely child.—rh)

To the north was Monument Pass, gateway to Arizona's Monument Valley; to the south, Agathia Peak. Between those two misshapen stony breasts was nothing but sand, rocks, crumbling buttes and a hot dry wind that never died. In the middle of the emptiness, between two house-sized boulders, was an ancient Princess mobile home. The trailer's white aluminum skin had been sand-blasted by the wind to a dull slate grey; the only thing left of the once-colorful trim panels was a few streaks of faint turquoise. A small crudely-built deck extended a few feet on both sides of the pock-marked aluminum door. Paint-less metal steps descended from the deck to the stony sand. Next to the steps was a sagging faded sofa, upon which sat eight-year-old Luke McKlister.

Luke's narrow face was tanned, his blond hair sun-bleached and fluttered by the wind. He wore faded brown shorts and a woman's pink blouse that was much too large. On his feet were beaded grey moccasins, also too large. On his lap was an open well-worn Bible, its gritty pages wind-blown beneath his grimy hands.

Luke frowned at the fluttering pages and shook his head. He had been trying to read for nearly an hour and he didn't understand. When his mother used to read from the Bible, the words always sounded soft and good and gentle and clean. But when his father held the very same book and jabbed at it with his finger—his eyes black and fierce—the words came out like sharp-edged quartz, hot and fiery. The stories she read were about love and peace and forgiveness. His were about death, damnation, and endless pain. And all from the same book!

Luke struggled again, trying to understand the words that sometimes swirled before his wind-teared eyes. But he had to stop often. There were words he'd never seen before, not even when he was going to school. He stopped going to school when he and his parents moved to Arizona. But for a while, he and his mother would sit alone in the kitchen before his father woke up in the morning—sometimes before his father came *home* in the morning—and his mother would read to him. Then she would have Luke read to her. Not only from the Bible but from other books, too, books about coyotes, rocket ships, wars, Indians.

Once, when his father had heard them reading in the kitchen, he had gotten very angry and called Luke stupid, called him a dummy, said he couldn't even tie his own shoes. But his mother had held Luke close. She covered his ears; but he heard her anyway, telling his father that their son was *not* stupid, that it just took him a little longer to learn things. Then she uncovered Luke's ears and told him he was precious in God's sight whether he learned fast or not. It didn't matter to God. But his father said it sure as hell mattered to him, and he wasn't sending no skinny little white dummy to an Indian school so all the redskin kids could laugh at him. His father didn't want any Indian father laughing at him, either, for having a dummy son.

Luke unfolded his hands and lifted them into the air. He didn't like thinking about his father. He would rather think about the hot gusty wind which immediately caught the Bible pages and began flipping them rapidly, one slithering after another. When Luke put his hands back down, the pages stopped moving, except for the edges. When he lifted his hand again, the pages flapped and fluttered.

Luke began to smile, delighted with his own power. He could make the pages stop. He could make the pages go. And he could do it over and over again. He wished his mother was here so he could show her.

Luke's eyes caught a movement off to the left and he forgot about the pages. He thought at first it was the shadow of a bush, tossed by the wind. He used to be afraid of shadows until his mother told him a secret: shadows were moved by the breath of angels.

What he saw now, however, was definitely *not* a moving shadow. It was a moving creature, a creature his mother had also told him about. She had even shown him a picture of one in the Bible. Serpents were demons in disguise, his mother had said. Serpents could bite and kill. So if one ever gets close to you, she had said, you had to run away as fast as you could. If it was not so close, all you had to do was wait, and if you waited without moving, without even breathing, it would go away.

Luke sat very still for a long time and sure enough his mother was right. One minute the serpent was there, stiffly curled like a fat quivering S. And then, with an amazing arching sideways movement, the snake simply slithered out of sight, behind a rock, perhaps, beyond a bush, or maybe into a rock-ledge hole.

Luke's head suddenly jerked around, abruptly drawn to a cloud of dust, coming fast. He recognized the sight immediately and his heart began to pound; fear leaped into his belly and started to grow. The closer the cloud came, the larger the fear grew. Minutes later a battered and colorless pickup truck slewed to a sideways stop in front of the sofa, less than ten feet away. A choking cloud of dust enveloped Luke, making him squint and cough, making the pages flutter again. But even after the cloud had dissipated, his father continued to sit behind the wheel, staring straight ahead, toward the empty horizon.

"Daddy?" Luke said softly.

He could hear his own heart thumping in his ears. But his father hadn't heard the boy. Nor did he appear to see him. James Joyce McKlister simply stared ahead, through the dust-encrusted windshield, his eyes empty. Finally, he touched his hand to his forehead and then pushed the door open with a loud oil-less squeal. He swung his Levi-covered knees out first, then the scuffed and dusty cowboy boots, and then the rest of him. When his heels hit the sand, he heaved himself out of the truck and immediately collapsed in a heap.

Luke was on his feet, panic in his pale blue eyes. "Daddy?" he cried again, louder now. But he didn't run to his father. To do so would have brought a lightning storm of rage. He had learned that much. All he could do was stand there, swallow the terror, and wait.

Finally his father began to move again, clumsily, awkwardly, like a marionette trying to erect itself after all of its strings were cut. Hands and knees in the sand, head lolling, shoulders drooping, spittle stringing from nose and mouth; he began to crawl slowly, jerkily toward the metal steps. Halfway there he stopped and rested for a moment, panting. Then, still on his hands and knees, he crawled up the steps and across the small deck. After resting again, he placed one hand on the door knob, carefully levered himself into a crouching position and then pushed himself upright, wavering. He pulled the door outward and almost lost his balance, nearly toppling over backwards. Somehow he recovered and managed to lurch around the out-swung door and then lunged into the trailer.

After hearing a loud thump, Luke slowly mounted the same steps; he crossed the deck and peered inside. It took a moment for his eyes to adjust from the glare of the sand and the sun to the gloom of the dark wood-paneled walls. Gradually, he made out the boot heels, then the long legs, then the shoulders. His father was lying face down on the faded and well-worn living room carpet. He was snoring loudly.

Luke watched the rise and fall of his father's chest for a moment and then backed out of the trailer, tip-toed down the steps. He stood at the bottom, glanced back at the trailer's open doorway and then went to the pickup. After another furtive glance back at the trailer, Luke climbed up and onto the gritty vinyl seat. He grinned at the tiny television set that his father had duct-taped to the pickup's dash. A cord ran from the TV set to the cigarette lighter of the old truck.

Luke punched the on/off button and then twisted the channel knob until he found the snowy black and white images of a cartoon coyote. The coyote was flying through the air with a large firecracker strapped to his back. Luke watched and laughed until his eyes got heavy, until he fell asleep.

* * * * * * * * *

Luke woke to the sound of whimpering. He pushed himself upright and rubbed his eyes. The sun had slid down behind one of the round smooth house-sized boulders but there was still enough afterglow to illuminate a large brown dog. It was standing on its hind legs, its paws on the seat of the truck. It appeared to be smiling at Luke. Delighted, Luke reached out with both hands and the dog began to lick his fingers. Luke giggled. The dog *woofed* softly, his long tail thumping against the truck's open door.

"Where did you come from?" Luke said, looking around. There was nothing to see but the trailer and the shadow-filled empty desert. He looked back at the dog. "Are you hungry?" The dog *woofed* again and Luke laughed. "Me, too. Let's go see if Daddy's awake."

Luke started sliding underneath the steering wheel, pushing the dog gently backwards, when his father suddenly loomed behind the dog. Face warped and twisted by the evening gloom, his father shoved the animal roughly aside.

"How many goddamned times do I have to tell you, Luke? Keep your fuckin' hands off the goddamned TV." He stretched an arm across Luke's lap and yanked the adapter plug from the cigarette lighter. Then he grabbed the pink blouse Luke was wearing and dragged him out of the truck. He shoved his son toward the trailer. "Goddamned dummy," he muttered. "Probably drained my goddamned battery. Then what do I do? Huh? Out here in the middle of fuckin' nowhere!"

James Joyce McKlister scowled at Luke and then slid behind the wheel, turned the ignition, and pumped the gas pedal. The starter protested weakly at first but after four groaning tries the engine finally fired up. It ran unevenly but it ran. McKlister pressed the gas pedal firmly, the unevenness evened out, and then he let the engine roar for nearly a minute. Satisfied, he killed the engine and heaved himself out of the truck again.

"Goddamned moron," he said, shoving Luke again toward the trailer. He glanced down at the dog which was prancing happily beside the two of them. McKlister kicked out at the dog but the dog just grinned and leaped away, wanting to play. "Can't afford to keep no dog, neither," McKlister grumbled. He looked down at Luke and poked him in the hollow of his chest. "You hear me?"

Luke winced and nodded, his pale eyes wide.

"What's he doing here anyway?"

"I think he's hungry," Luke said timidly. "I am, too. You weren't here to fix breakfast."

McKlister grunted. "Time you learned to fix your own goddamned breakfast. I ain't no fuckin' maid, you know."

The two of them mounted the steps to the deck, Luke in the lead. The dog started to follow after them but McKlister made a loud noise and kicked at it again. This time the pointed toe of his cowboy boot caught the dog just behind the shoulder. It yelped and leaped away. Luke started to run after it but McKlister grabbed the collar of the pink blouse and jerked him back.

"Either that dog goes or I go, you understand?" He glared at Luke for a moment and then he laughed. The sound was cold and mean. "You know what I think? I think maybe you *want* me to leave, just like your momma did. You want me to leave you out here all alone, don't you? Just you and that mangy dog? Is that what you want?"

Tears welled up in Luke's pleading eyes. He grabbed his father's horseshoe-shaped belt buckle. "Please, Daddy. Please don't leave me. I'll be good."

McKlister snorted and turned away. He stomped into the trailer, Luke half-trotting behind him. "Good?

You're too goddamned dumb to be good. You're too goddamned dumb to be anything." He turned and glared down at the boy. "And stop calling me Daddy."

Luke stared up at him, open-mouthed. "But why? You are my daddy. Momma said so."

McKlister snorted again. "Your momma was a lying bitch. She was also a whore. Look, nobody knows who your goddamned daddy was. I just know it wasn't me." He jerked his head toward the table. "Now sit down and shut up while I make us some supper."

McKlister opened two cans of refried beans with a manual can opener. He used a table knife to scrape the contents into a scorched pan and then lit the small two-burner camp stove with a wooden match. He poured a cupful of water from a plastic jug, dumped the water into the beans, and then set the pan on the burner. After pouring some more water into a brown plastic tumbler, he pulled an amber vial from his pants pocket. He flipped off the cap and washed down a misshapen white tablet with a gulp of water, made a face, and then stood by the sink, waiting. He glanced back over his shoulder.

"What're you gawking at?" he said.

Luke looked down at the floor. "Nothing," he said.

"Good. Because you ain't seen nothing, okay? And take off that goddamned blouse. You look like a fuckin' queer."

"This was Momma's," Luke protested.

"I know whose it was. I said take it off."

Luke got up from the table and padded across the living room. The moccasins made a slapping noise as he disappeared down the hallway. When he returned a few minutes later he was wearing a New York Jets tee shirt. Like the blouse, the tee shirt was several sizes too large.

As Luke sat down at the table again, McKlister glanced over at him but said nothing. Instead, he lit a brown misshapen cigarette, pulled a can of beer from the fridge and ripped off the tab. Sipping the beer, he waited and smoked by the little stove until the beans were hot. He spooned the steaming mounds onto two yellow plastic plates and pushed one of the plates across the table toward Luke.

"I don't know why I'm doing this," he mumbled, sliding a spoon after the plate. "Not my goddamned responsibility."

They ate in silence. When his plate was empty, McKlister lit another brown cigarette and stared out the window. His face began to soften slightly, the deep-cut grooves were less distinct. His eyes were beginning to take on a hollow empty look. When he glanced across the table again he seemed surprised to see the boy. "What?" he said.

"I said when is Momma coming home?" Luke said, his voice barely above a whisper.

McKlister stared at the boy. In an instant, the softness disappeared, the deep grooves came back and his eyelids squeezed together almost to the point of being pinched shut. He took another drag from his cigarette and let the smoke shoot out of his nose.

"She ain't never coming home, boy, so you might as well forget it. Okay? Forget it."

"But where did she go?"

McKlister catapulted to his feet, knocking the chair over backwards. Leaning over, his knuckles bridged on the table top, his flushed face was inches from Luke's.

"How the fuck do I know where she went?" he yelled. "She's gone, that's all I know. And that's all you need to know, too." He glared at the boy and then swept his bean-smeared yellow plate off the table and across the room. It bounced off the wooden panels and fell to the floor. "I gotta get the fuck outta here," he muttered. "Before you drive *me* crazy, too."

McKlister grabbed a denim jacket off the back of a chair and whirled it over his shoulder. He stopped at the door. "And if that dog's still here when I get home I'll shoot the fucker. And God will know it's your fault, and He will send you to hell. You got that?"

Luke was trembling violently, his voice shaking. "But … he's … he's hungry."

"To hell," he said again. "That's where you'll go. And no one *ever* gets out of hell."

He hurled the door open, clumped out onto the deck and down the steps. Moments later, the engine roared to life, stones clattered in fender wells. The truck sped away and the silence returned; the silence and the wind.

* * * * * * *

Luke scraped the rest of the refried beans out of the pan and onto his yellow plate. He took the plate outside and set it down in front of the dog. The dog gulped down the beans and then tried to lick off the smears. But the more he licked, the more he pushed the plate away.

Luke laughed out loud as the plastic plate scooted across the pebbly sand. It finally butted up against a rock and the dog finished licking it clean. He followed Luke up the steps and into the trailer.

After finding a cereal bowl and filling it with water, Luke carried the bowl outside and set it by the sofa. The dog lapped at it noisily. The two of them sat there until the sun went down and the stars came out. A sprinkling at first, the points of light soon turned into a stream, then a river, and then a flood of diamonds that seemed to arch from one horizon to the other.

Luke stretched out on the sofa and the dog stretched out beside him. He tried to remember a story his momma had told him, a story about stars and about a brave sea captain who sailed around the world with nothing but the stars to guide him. He wondered if his momma was looking up at the stars, too, right now, thinking about him. He wondered if she was still wearing that dark blue blouse that he liked so much, the one with the stars on the collar. He cried for a while and then fell asleep.

* * * * * * * * *

He awoke in an instant, terrified. The dog leaped off the sofa and stared at him, his ears up, his brow wrinkled. Luke shielded his eyes from the harsh early-morning sun and scrambled to his feet. He looked out across the open flatness and could see the cloud of dust. It wasn't coming as fast as it usually did but it was coming. And the dog was still here, still with him. Luke began to whimper. He didn't want the dog to die. And he didn't want to go to hell either.

Luke looked around wildly, searching for a place to hide the dog but all he could see was rocks, and low dried-up bushes, and more rocks, and more dried-up bushes. Frantically, he ran around behind the trailer, calling the dog to follow. The dog crouched for a moment, watching the boy, and then leaped after him. But instead of following Luke around the back of the trailer, the dog raced away to the right, swung around and then ran back again, barking wildly, enjoying the new game. Then he ran to the left and did the same thing, swinging back, barking loudly.

"No!" Luke cried. "You must hide! You mustn't let him see you!"

But the dog refused to give up the game: crouching, jumping, leaping sideways, and running wildly back and forth, barking and barking. The more Luke pleaded and ran after him, the more the dog barked, and the more he wagged his tail. By the time Luke finally grabbed the dog around the neck he heard the thump of a car door. And then a voice. A woman's voice.

"Hi, there," she called out. "That's a mighty nice dog. What's his name?"

Luke turned around and stared at the woman as she walked toward him. She really didn't look like his mother but she was smiling like his mother smiled, and the sunlight turned her hair to gold, too.

Luke felt suddenly shy. "Doesn't have a name," he said. He squatted down beside the dog and hugged it around the neck, not looking at the woman. But he could hear her footsteps crunching closer. Then he felt her shadow falling over him.

"Well then, what's your name? I'm Patti Klein."

"Luke," he said, not looking up.

"Luke is a very nice name," the woman said. "I have a brother named Luke. Isn't that something?" When Luke didn't respond she said, "Is your mother home?"

Luke shook his head.

"How about your father?"

Luke shook his head again.

"I see," the woman said. "Brothers or sisters? Surely you're not out here all by yourself."

Luke looked over at her car. There was a big sign on the side of the door. "What does that say?" he asked.

The woman glanced back over her shoulder. "It says Navajo County. I just started working for the Navajo County Government and I'm afraid I've gotten lost. Do you know when your parents are coming home?"

Luke hugged the dog tighter. "Daddy says Momma ain't never coming home. Ever. He comes back at night, sometimes. Sometimes in the morning."

The woman's smile faded. "Don't you go to school?"

Luke shook his head again, still hugging the dog. "Daddy says they only have Indian schools around here and the Indians would all laugh at me if I went to their school. He says they'd call me a skinny white dummy. He says I can't learn anything. But Momma used to teach me. I know how to tie my shoes," he said, looking up at her for the first time. "And I also know my left and right."

"Oh, my," the woman said. She sat down on the sofa and patted the dusty cushion. Reluctantly, Luke sat down beside her. "Can you tell me your last name, Luke? Or your father's name?"

"Daddy's name is James Joyce McKlister. Momma said he's named after a man who wrote poems. Momma's name is Mary. That was the name of Jesus' momma, too."

The woman looked at the boy for another moment and then looked up at the trailer. "The battery on my cell phone went dead," she said. "Do you think your father would mind if I used your phone?"

"Don't have a phone. Daddy said we don't need one."

"I see." She thought for a moment. "Luke, do you know what a map is?"

Luke nodded and smiled. "Momma used to show me maps. In books."

"How about your Daddy? Does he have any maps?" Luke nodded. "Do you know where they are?"

"There's one in the kitchen. You want me to get it?"

The woman got to her feet. "That would be awesome. Maybe it would help me get back to town."

"Maybe," Luke said eagerly. He pushed himself off the sofa and started up the steps. The woman and the dog followed. When she stepped through the open doorway the woman stopped and looked around. She took a breath and let it out with puffed cheeks.

The bean-smudged plate was still lying on the floor by the wall. Several newspapers were crumpled on a stained brown recliner that seemed to be strapped together with duct tape. A blue rocking chair was missing an arm. Beer bottles were scattered everywhere. Dishes and cups were stacked in the sink. And the acrid smell of marijuana hung in the room like a pungent dirty cloud.

Luke came to her with a tentative smile. In his outstretched hand was a geodetic survey map that had obviously been folded and refolded countless times. "This is Daddy's map. He said it told us how to get here."

The woman smiled. "Thank you, Luke. In that case, I *know* it will help me get back to town."

She unfolded the map gingerly, trying not to tear the well-worn folds. After pushing aside several empty beer bottles and a collection of dirty glasses, she spread the map on the table. She found an X in a circle and assumed it marked the location of the trailer. With an index finger she traced a faint dotted line that led to a thicker solid line. That line connected to a numbered county road, which went through the city.

The woman reached out and squeezed Luke's shoulder. "Thank you, sweetheart. I'm sure I won't have a bit of trouble now."

She looked around the room once more and then slid a thin silver case from her pocket. She clicked the case open and handed Luke a business card.

"When your daddy comes home, tell him I was here, okay? Tell him I want to help both of you. And tell him I'll be back tomorrow. Can you do that for me, Luke?"

* * * * * * * *

It was after midnight when McKlister came home again. Luke was waiting for him. The boy's eyes widened when his father came through the doorway, his arm in a sling, bandages across his cheek and neck.

"What happened?" Luke said, alarmed.

"What happened?" McKlister mimicked in a high whiney voice. He grunted. "Goddamned bitch nearly killed me, that's what happened. Practically ran me off the road. And then the cops tried to say it was my fault. A lot they fuckin' know; bunch of stupid fuckin' Injuns. She didn't know where the hell she was going, that's what happened. Goddamned government car." He laughed. "But she got hers all right. Dead as a fuckin'—"

He glanced at the table and saw the card. He went to it quickly and picked it up. "What the hell is this?" he demanded.

"A lady was here today. A nice lady. She was lost. She said she could help us. She said—"

McKlister was around the table before Luke could say another word. He grabbed the boy by the arm and jerked him hard. "We don't need no goddamned help," he shouted. "You hear me? We don't need no god-damned busybodies snooping around here either. No bleedin' heart do-gooders. Goddamned government peo-ple." He grabbed Luke by the shoulders with both hands and shook him violently. "We don't need any of them. You hear me?"

Luke was too terrified even to cry. His father shook him once more and then thrust him away. "Anybody else comes around here you run away and hide. You got that?"

"Where?" Luke managed.

"Where? How the hell do I know? Those big fuckin' boulders out there, I guess. There's got to be some kind of cracks or caves you can crawl into. Use your fuckin' head. You're a kid for Christ's sake. Kids can always find a place to hide."

* * * * * * * * *

Hidden in the shadowed hallway, Luke watched his father swallow several more of his little broken pills. He washed them down with a few gulps of beer and then lit a cigarette, dragging deeply, holding the smoke in for a long time and then letting it out slowly. When the cigarette had burned down to a tiny brown nub he pinched it out and dropped the nub into a small blue plastic box. He stood by the kitchen sink drinking the beer until the can was empty. He opened another can and drank that one empty, too. Crushing the last one in his fist, he tossed the can with his one good hand. It clattered around in the sink as he walked gingerly toward the living room, swaying slightly. His right arm still in a sling, he lowered himself slowly onto the duct-taped recliner and tipped it back. The dim light from the nearby kerosene table lamp fell across his bandaged face, etching the lines more deeply. After a lengthy sigh, McKlister began to snore.

Luke knew his father would sleep for many hours now so he could do whatever he wanted to do. And he didn't have to be careful about making noise. His father never heard anything after he swallowed his pills.

Luke retrieved the flashlight that he'd kept hidden under his mattress since he found it in a closet the week before. He flicked it off and on several times and the batteries seemed strong, the light still bright, but he didn't want to use the flashlight unless he had to. Daddy always said batteries cost a lot of money. He also said they die if you kept the light turned on. Luke didn't want the batteries to die. He didn't want anything to die.

It was full night now and the kerosene lamp cast a warped patch of light through the open doorway and out across the deck. The desert beyond looked black and endlessly deep. Luke paused for a moment and listened. But there was nothing to hear, nothing but the faint sighing of angels.

By the time he reached the bottom of the steps his eyes gradually became aware of the giant looming boulders, one to the left and one to the right of the trailer. He started moving away from the trailer as soon as he could see the much larger, much higher, and much farther-away lumps of blackness on the horizon. Momma had names for those two mountains but he couldn't remember what the names were.

When he was some distance from the trailer, Luke wondered what name his momma would have given the dog. It should have a name. How could you call it if it didn't? But what name?

As he walked, he began to think of the men his momma used to read about in the Bible. They all had good names, names like Joseph, and Benjamin, and Paul, and Daniel, and Moses. But after thinking about each one of the names he decided he liked Joseph the best. He tried it out.

"Jo-seph," he called. "Can you hear me? It's Luke. Jo-seph."

The wind had cooled slightly and it seemed to blow his words away. He slid the flashlight partway into his pocket and then stuck his two pinky fingers into his mouth like his momma had showed him once. He blew mightily. At first, nothing came out. But after several tries he managed a shrill breathy whistle. He called again, louder this time. "Jooooo-seph."

For a moment, Luke took the flashlight out of his pocket and turned it on. If he aimed it down he could see the rocks and the sand that surrounded his moccasins. If he aimed it straight ahead, the darkness seemed to swallow up the puny beam. But Luke wasn't worried. The stars were bright and a creamy glow was starting to spread upward from the horizon. He knew the moon would soon be lighting up the whole world. When that happened, he wouldn't need the flashlight at all.

He called again. "Come on, boy. I know you're out here." But there was no answering *woof*. No bark. No sound. Only the wind curling around and into Luke's ears. "Joseph? Joooo-seph."

Luke continued walking for several minutes and then glanced back at the trailer again. He could still see its outline and the faint light from one of the windows but he suddenly realized it didn't look quite right. When he had brought the dog out here that afternoon he had done the same thing. As he walked, he kept looking back at the trailer so he could tell which way he was going. But now the trailer didn't look like it had that afternoon. So maybe he *wasn't* going the right way. Maybe he should walk more to the left.

Luke suddenly stumbled and nearly fell down. He quickly switched on the flashlight and aimed it at the ground. What tripped him was a rock. But it wasn't just one rock. There was a pile of rocks. Most of them were together in a kind of row, but several looked out of place. Small holes had been dug, sand had been kicked into little piles. Luke frowned at the holes and wondered what had made them. Coyotes? Something smelled bad, too.

He glanced back at the trailer again. He was certain now; it wasn't very far to where he had tied Joseph to a small tree but he would have to walk more to the left.

He walked on as the moon crept above the horizon and began to spread its pale glow across the stony sand. Luke was still whistling, still calling, and he didn't understand why Joseph didn't bark back at hm. Then he saw a patch of something dark and light, swirling along the ground. It had come from behind him, blown by the wind.

Luke hopped sideways, trapping it under his moc-casin-covered foot. He reached down and picked it up. It was material of some sort, dark with white spots on it. The spots were almost like stars. As he stuffed the scrap of material into his pocket he looked ahead and finally saw the small leafless tree that he'd tied Joseph to. And there, finally, was Joseph, lying in the tree's moon shad-ow.

Luke ran forward wildly, joyfully, calling the dog's new name. But as he got closer the joy quickly turned to confusion. Joseph wasn't jumping up and down. He wasn't trying to get to Luke. He wasn't trying to break the rope. And he wasn't barking. He wasn't doing any-thing.

Luke lurched to a stop and stood for a moment, un-certain, fearful. Softly he said the name again. But the dog didn't move.

Luke's confusion turned to fear as he stepped for-ward slowly and pulled the flashlight out of his pocket. He was afraid to turn it on, and yet he knew he must.

"Joseph?" The name came out in a whisper as the beam shot out and then down.

When it lit the dog's twisted face, Luke let out a yelp of fear and pain and then he began to cry. Joseph was lying on his side. His eyes were still open but they were dull and lifeless. His body was swollen grotesquely, the lips pulled back in a snarl-like stiffness. Between the teeth was the crushed remains of a rattlesnake, its body nearly bitten in two.

Luke whirled around, dropping the flashlight, and began running wildly, blindly back toward the trailer. Several times he tripped on unseen rocks. Several times he felt the earth skinning his knees, scraping the palms of both hands. But all he could feel was the pain inside. The black terror. The whirlpool of panic that was trying to suck him down and into the earth.

He could see the trailer: a low flat hulk nearly lost in boulder-shadow. The surrounding desert was flatter still, splotched and pocked with shadows of rocks, shadows of spread-arm cactus, shadows of broken gullies, all smeary and blurred by the burning tears.

By the time he reached the trailer the word was coming out automatically, choked and harsh. "Daddy! *Dadddeeeee!*"

Luke ran around the end of the trailer, his face and hair albino-white in the moonlight, the bloodstains black on his hands and knees. His breath was coming in gasps. A sharp pain tore at his side.

The pickup truck was still there, the door still open. The door to the trailer was still open, too, and the skewed square of dim light still fell outward across the deck.

Luke scrambled up the steps and bounded into the trailer. "Daddy! Daddy! Joseph is hurt," he cried. "You must wake up and help."

He ran to the chair and grabbed his daddy's hand. The skin felt dusty and dry. "Please wake up. Please! Don't let Joseph die!"

Luke ran around to the other side of the lounge chair and grabbed his father's other hand, twisting the fingers back. He was sobbing now, pleading for his father to wake up.

Frantic, he climbed into his father's lap and hugged his father's chest. Breathless, terrified, he cried, "Hold me, Daddy, please. Hold me."

But his father didn't move.

A Golden Ride in Silver Snow

(In snow country, one of childhood's greatest winter-time joys is sledding down the highest hill in the neighborhood on a clear, cold, and snowy day. The joy is compounded when that very first ride of the year is done on a brand new Flexible Flyer sled that still has traces of green paint on its runners—especially if that brand new sled was the Christmas gift you'd been dreaming about since July. Does anyone besides me remember that joy, that thrill, that inexpressible delight?—rh)

It wasn't just a sled. It was my first Flexible Flyer, lacquered and new, a Christmas gift with a bright green bow. It was also the most beautiful, the most perfect, the most rapid form of transportation then available to any eight-year-old anywhere. Of that I was certain.

There were other gifts beneath the tree. Sensible gifts. Things I needed. Underwear. Sox. A blue and grey flannel shirt. A winter coat for Sundays only.

All paled before the gleaming magnificence of that sled.

Like all other Christmas Days, however, that one too was hemmed in by certain obligations that even children had to meet. But after the wrappings and ribbons

had been ripped off and then stuffed unceremoniously
into a large Sears, Roebuck carton; after the turkey and
dressing and cranberries had been crammed relentlessly
into the circle of bulging stomachs that surrounded the
table; after all of that was finished and out of the way, me
and the Flyer quietly escaped to Dad's work bench.

Originally slicked with a leaf-green skin of paint
that matched the trim on the lacquered wood, the sleek
Flyer's up-curving runners had to be thoroughly sanded
by hand. Then they were scraped and sanded some more.
And then they were sanded again.

After a while my fingers and nails and most of my
hair were all coated with light green dust. Like war
paint, the smudges of green also covered most of my
face. The runners, however, were clean and smooth and
buffed to a silvery sheen. There wasn't a doubt—they
were ready to go. So with everything finished, me and
the Flyer rushed back to the house.

My uncle Chester said: "3-In-One-Oil is best. It
keeps the runners free of rust."

My brother Tommy: "A thin coat of Vaseline will
prevent rust *and* increase downhill speed, both at the
same time."

Grandmother MacSweeny insisted: "Candle wax
was the only thing *my* grandmother *ever* used on sleigh
runners."

Just to be safe, I used all three magical potions, generously.

When morning came, the firmly attached and end-knotted rope felt stiff and new and excitingly coarse. It scraped and clung to the palms of my brown Buffalo Bill gloves, the ones with the fringed wrist cuffs. As I looked back every few steps to make sure the rope was still knotted tightly, I could see the runner tracks following me, sharp-edged and glistening with just a hint of oil and wax. I could feel the snow creaking beneath my black buckled galoshes.

When I finally crossed the narrow snow-plowed road and reached the path, I stopped for a moment and looked back at the house. Even though everyone had ducked out of sight behind curtains and blinds a second before, I knew they were there, watching me now.

I glanced at the rope again and then at the Flyer. And then with my eyes I followed the path that wound its way like a frozen snake, all the way up to the top of the hill.

The path was narrow. It grew narrower still as it twisted and turned its way toward the crest. It was a hard well-packed path, glazed with melted snow that, overnight, had turned to a glitter of ice.

The path gave my stomach a funny shake.

I sneaked another glance back at the house. I thought I saw several faces pull away once more from several windows. There was no turning back now. No matter what the risk, no matter what the danger, I had to make the run I'd been dreaming about all night. And everyone was watching so the choice was gone. All I could do was take a long, slow, and a very deep breath. And then, reluctantly, I plunged ahead, up the perilous slope.

The climb itself was an arduous task, a breath-stealing chore that filled my chest with a thumping drum. Clouds of steam gushed from my mouth and nose. My legs got weak, my arms got tired, my shoulders ached, my fingers burned. The summit appeared to be light-years away, spinning beyond my reach.

I began to suspect—and then I knew for certain—that my heart would surely give out long before I reached my goal. I knew, too, that everyone who was watching me—uncles, cousins, sisters, brothers, even my parents—would remember how strong, how brave, how deter-mined I'd been to reach the very apex of this previously unchallenged and unconquerable peak.

Then, when I didn't die a sudden and very brave death, something else pushed up beneath my ribs. At first it was a small swelling thing that quickly grew larger

and larger. It continued to expand until it had formed itself into a huge sparkling globe.

What filled my chest of course was a bulging
world of anticipation. It was a world shaken to its very
core by waves and waves of thrilling quakes, quakes so
fierce they threatened to split my heart. The closer I got
to my goal, the wilder the quakes became.

Somehow though, miraculously, I finally reached
the top of the hill. And despite the endless strenuous
struggle that preceded it, the pause I allowed myself was
long enough only to catch my breath, hoist the Flyer, and
aim it—arrow-like—down the glittering slope.

The fear that suddenly crushed down on me was
too heavy to bear, the anticipation too glorious to deny. I
couldn't wait an instant longer. It was definitely time to
fly.

A second later, breathless and shaking, my feet
sent me rocketing off on a giddily wild and stumbling
run. Wool scarf flying, cotton fringes flapping, fingers
clenching the slippery wood. The growing orb of fear
had suddenly transformed itself into a universe of terror.
In the same instant, the anticipation had exploded into a
nova of elation.

My galoshes crunched the snow, my gloved fingers
grasped the wood as I galloped forward and down. As I
ran, the cold black steel of the Flyer's nose was bouncing

before my face. It framed the steering bar, the house, the valley, the church steeple, the whole incredible blue-drenched world. I saw myself schussing an Arctic crevasse, blurring with speed, trailing flames of frozen fire.

An instant later the entire universe slammed through my brain as the Flyer took off with a bounding, weightless, and fearful leap. And then …

Coat-cushioned slam of ribs against wood.

Gloved hands clutching the guider bars.

Snow-clumped rubber soles flat to the sky.

Eyes wide, nose and mouth gulping frost.

In an instant, the ice-glittered speed increased so quickly, so precipitously, I thought I'd been shot from a puffed rice gun.

Runners jolted on hidden icy bumps, knifing through miniature drifts. The freezing wind was burning my face. My nostrils and throat instantly turned to frozen pipes.

Cheeks numb. Eyes streaming. World blurring. Whizzing. Bouncing. Shrieking. Burnished steel flashing through white. Toes dragging. Shoulders leaning. Tree stumps barely avoided. Snow humps gut-slammed.

And then—much too soon—the wild careening sideways-lurching slide exploded into clouds of billowy white snow-powder as I leaned and pulled sharply to the left to avoid the plowed road. The snow sprayed up like a skier's frosty rooster tail. The Flyer *fumped!* into a snow bank and the joy was so great I could scarcely breathe. I let out a shriek instead.

Then: *woof!* I rolled off the sled and flopped in the snow and onto my back. I tried to catch my breath. The air was sharp and cold and pine-tangy. The sky was immense and endlessly deep. I tried to drink it all in. Then, with a jolt, I suddenly realized that I understood everything. The world, school, Mom and Dad, life, even my little sister. *Everything suddenly made sense!*

Although they are immeasurably sweet, epiphanies, however, are also immeasurably brief. An instant later the joy was gone, replaced by a harsh bold truth that still remains, seared in my brain: golden rides will always end entirely too soon.

But even that flash of truth was mercifully short. Silver snow was dusted off, eyes wiped, galoshes stomped, shrieks stowed. Lofty thoughts had suddenly vanished. I heaved the sled around, jerked the stiff new rope, and the long joy-rebuilding trudge began again. And then again. And then again.

It went on like that till the sun went down, the stars came out, and the sound of the dinner bell floated away.

Waiting

*(This is a prose poem about how much the inconvenience of "waiting for something to happen" can change drastically during the brief interlude we refer to as a Lifetime.
—rh)*

It is something everyone knows about. It is something everyone experiences, countless times throughout their life. And yet, like everything else in life, waiting changes with time.

When we are young and/or are lucky, waiting comes mostly in the form of petty annoyances. We wait impatiently for a red light to turn green. We roll our eyes at the sagging sky, waiting for the rain to stop. We twist and crane our necks, wondering where the hell the waitress went.

Any one of these waits can make us pout, sigh, tap a foot, or groan. Don't they know we have other places to go? Other things to do? Don't they know this waiting is wasting my precious time?

When we are old, and/or are not so lucky, waiting can surround itself with a completely different atmosphere. It can be bathed in a much darker, much more ominous color.

We wait for a test result that may tell us the rest of our days will be different, *very* different. We wait for a light in the eastern sky that will tell us an endlessly swirling night of pain and turmoil will soon be over. We wait for a phone call that will tell us a life that has lingered on much too long has finally, finally, come to an end. We wait for a car that will take us away from a place we once called home. Now, that same place is nothing more than an empty building owned by strangers.

Waits grow longer as time moves on. They erect fragile walls of shifting sand. They turn clock hands into motionless stone. They convert the sounds of life into a silence that grows and expands like frost on steel.

But like everything else controlled by time, sooner or later, waiting, too, will come to its last and final end.

The Phone Call

(This is a story about the special love and devotion one mother had for her first born son.)

Maribel Zeiss woke up long before her alarm was set to go off at six-thirty. Despite a restless night, her heart was a sunny balloon, floating free, filled to the brim with hope. Even her gnarly arthritic knuckles felt loose, their motion fluid, as she slid into a faded blue robe that matched her faded blue pajamas. After maneuvering three buttons into fraying buttonholes, she eased her chubby white feet into fuzzy blue slippers. Then she heaved herself up from the bed.

It was going to be a good day, a very good day, because today was the day Robbie would call.

Maribel wasn't exactly sure when the certainty had come to her. Maybe it was when she let her well-thumbed Schofield Reference Bible flop open on her lap before she went to bed last night. She often let the Bible flop open by itself. That way God could decide what He wanted her to read. Last night the pages split apart at the prodigal son and she thought of Robbie right away.

She knew her first born son would not be coming home like the prodigal son. That would take a fully

fledged miracle for sure. But she was just as certain—
stone-cold certain—that Robbie would call her today.
God Himself had told her that. She could hear His
words, loud and clear, deep in her heart.

Minutes later—while inky coffee percolated noisily, filling the small kitchen with its rich burnt odor—
Maribel pressed her pudgy belly against the sink, pushed
aside a yellow curtain and examined her small corner of
the outside world.

Night was giving way to day but day had not yet
filled in all the shadows. The sky overhead still had the
gray hazy look of dawn. Rosy fingers toyed with a gauzy
collection of mare's tail clouds. Near the horizon, a
broad streaky swath of pink had back-lit a five-acre wood
lot that lay just beyond Mike's house. The tree trunks,
the spindly limbs, and the fresh leaves all looked black
against the wash of rose and gold.

Maribel's eyes came to rest on the house itself. It
was small, two stories, and plastered with white stucco.
Its roof was covered with green shingles. Kitchen windows made up most of the wall to the right of the front
door.

Through the windows, Maribel could see her
daughter-in-law moving about from sink to stove. Bethy
was going through her normal early morning routine:
making coffee, setting out bowls and silverware, pulling

cereal boxes out of cupboards, feeding a pair of blue-gray parakeets, and opening cans of dog food.

Soon, Mike and Bethy's two sons—fourteen-year-old Karl and twelve-year-old Elliot—would amble into the kitchen from a closed set of steps that led to their second floor bedrooms. Mike's car was already gone. He had to be at Dusty's Garage every day at seven, six days a week.

Maribel's eyes focused closer still. A gravelly driveway circle lay between the house and Maribel's single-wide mobile home. In the center of the circle was a young maple tree. An early robin hopped beneath the tree. Each time the hopping stopped, the robin cocked its head first to one side and then to the other, listening.

Maribel's puffy face crinkled itself into a slit-eyed Clint Black smile. Like the robin, she, too, would be listening today. But instead of hearing the hushed soil-crumbling sounds of a worm tunneling through dark earth, Maribel would hear the joyful sound of one heart tunneling through to another.

Maribel let the curtain drop as the percolating coffeepot issued its last and final burble. Still smiling her secret smile, she turned around slowly and then padded between the copper-tone sink and stove.

Standing on slippered tiptoes, she stretched her stubby torso and short arms. One hand pulled open a walnut-veneered cupboard door. The other hand lifted down two fragile cups that had pink and silver rosebuds delicately painted along one side. They were the last of a set of dishes that had been bought many years before. Maribel then lifted down a pair of matching saucers.

Temporarily, she set the chinaware on the sun-yellow counter top that ran along three sides of her kitchen.

An extension of the counter served as a small narrow desk that was cluttered with doctor bills, Medicare statements, an ancient telephone, and a jumble of white-capped amber vials that were filled with a muted rainbow of pills.

Also on the corner was her husband's breathing machine. It was little more than a small grey metal box that had several switches and dials on its front panel. Hoses went into one end of the back panel and came out the other end. The black paint on the dials had been worn away by several years of thumb and finger adjustments.

Maribel positioned two pink plastic placemats on the round table that nearly filled the tiny kitchenette. After she transferred the cups and saucers to the placemats she poured herself a cup of steaming coffee and sat down at the table.

Glancing at the telephone again, she felt the deep satisfying peace that fueled her smile and kept it warm.

She couldn't remember when she had felt so happy. He could be calling any minute.

As she sipped her coffee, Maribel could hear her husband's labored breathing and random bumping noises as he struggled to get out of bed. Sounds moved freely through the cramped mobile home and through the thin panel walls that separated his room from the living room. No wall separated the living room from the kitchen, only an upright lattice divider that was trimmed with amber plastic panels.

Sounds also flowed easily in the other direction, from his room, through the bathroom, and into Maribel's bedroom. Her sleep had been shattered many times, many nights by her husband's startled cries and pain-filled moans. His sleep, too, was often broken, but by nightmares of suffocation.

Once, he had told her, he'd been trapped in a pit of sucking mud, his head tilted back at a painful angle. An avalanche of smothering white sand suddenly started pouring out of the sky like a grainy waterfall. The sand slowly filled his nose. It filled his mouth. It poured into his throat. And then it began to fill his lungs.

He had retold that nightmare many times, to any-one who would listen.

With Ted forever fighting for breath, Maribel's nights were seldom restful either. But now—with the blackness of night gone and the sunlight angling in like a wedge of gold—even her husband's nightmare gasps seemed far away and not so bad. Robby's call was certain to make everything else seem not so bad, too.

A special bond had always existed between Maribel and Robbie. She had been so young when it happened. She didn't know anything. She didn't even know what Ted was doing to her, until it was too late. And even then she didn't know for sure. All she knew was that it hurt. It hurt a lot.

But something good had come from something bad. A beautiful baby was born with dark sad eyes. The instant those eyes met Maribel's eyes, a bond was formed as pure as the golden sun and as strong as a band of steel.

When she touched Robbie's pink and wrinkled skin for the first time—and blew on his tiny fingers and toes—the bond became a welding torch that melted two hearts into one.

There were other connections of course, with Mike and Dovey and Ronald. But those were connections, not bonds, and they were never as strong, never as pure as the weld that fixed her to Robbie.

Maribel often felt guilty about that. She even prayed that God would help her overcome the selective kind of bonding that even she could see. She prayed that

God would help her love the other children, if not more than she loved Robbie, than just as much.

But for reasons known only to God, her ties to the others had never matured, never strengthened, never thickened.

Finally, internally, Maribel had thrown up her hands. Robbie was her special child. He would always be her special child. And that was that.

Maribel sagged inside and her memories got jostled when her husband came coughing into the living room. Ted was a skinny fragile-looking man who appeared a decade older than his seventy-five years. His sunken chest, covered with wiry grey hair, was visible through the brown wrinkled unbuttoned pajama top. His chin was also stubbled with several days' growth of coarse grey hair. Only the hair on his head, now spiky and sleep-matted, was the same sandy color it had been when Maribel met him years and years ago.

He still called her Mari then and even awkwardly hugged her now and again. Once, and only once, he told her he guessed he loved her, although he guessed he wasn't sure he really knew what love was. And Maribel had guessed that that would have to do.

Ted's rattling phlegm-filled cough made him pant and curse as he padded into the kitchen. The cough also triggered a series of short squeaky farts that filled Maribel's face with momentary annoyance.

"Do you have to do that?" she said.

Ted's voice, between gasps, was hurt and whiny. "I can't help it. They just come out."

Maribel pursed her lips in resignation and then glanced at the phone. "Well, never mind," she said, not looking at her husband.

She went to the breadbox, pulled out a partial loaf, slid it onto the table next to a chrome-lidded butter dish. She retrieved two eggs from the refrigerator and placed them on top of the stove. She watched the eggs wobble briefly and then she sat down again.

Ted kept coughing and squeaking as he shuffled barefoot toward the stove. Maribel sipped her coffee and ignored him as he found a battered frying pan and set it clanging onto a burner. There was a quiet pop as a circle of blue flame swirled up to meet the blackened pan.

Ted turned the flame as high as it would go. Using a misshapen rubber spatula, he smeared butter around the quickly warming pan. Then he cracked the two eggs and let them plop onto the scarred surface. The broken shells were tossed into the sink and the gelatinous egg mass was blackened with pepper.

In less than two minutes, the yokes had turned into solid chunks of yellow rubber. The thin sheet of egg white surrounding the yokes had become a curly brown crisp. Ted scraped the stiff mass onto a plate and then sat down to eat.

"Robbie's going to call today," Maribel said, her smile almost saintly.

With his mouth full of soft white bread and stiff yoke, Ted mumbled, "You're crazy, you know that? He's not even thinking about us. He never thinks about us."

Maribel stiffened. "He doesn't think about you," she said. "That's for sure. Why should he? You never thought about him when he was little. All you could think about then was getting drunk."

Ted grumbled, not looking up from his greasy egg-cluttered plate. "What are you talking about? I thought about him as much as anybody. Including you," he added pointedly.

"A lot you know about it," Maribel said. Then she went on, as though talking to herself. "I'm his mother and a mother has a special bond with her children."

Ted scoffed. "With Robbie, you mean. You always treated him like he was one of those glass trinkets your mother stuck in every nook and cranny. You didn't treat the other children like that."

Serenely, Maribel said, "You don't know what you're talking about." She got to her feet, went to the stove and returned with the coffeepot. She automatically filled Ted's cup, carried the pot back to the stove and then sat down again.

Ted picked up the cup and looked at the curl of steam coming out of the black liquid. Carefully then, he poured the coffee out of the cup and onto the saucer. Some of the coffee dribbled down the side of the cup and splashed on the tabletop. Setting the cup down he picked up the saucer, blew across the surface of the coffee, and then slurped the dark liquid noisily off the saucer. Maribel looked at him disapprovingly.

Ted glanced at her for a second. "Well, what am I supposed to do?" he said, his voice hurt and angry. "It's too damn hot."

"You don't have to swear about it," Maribel said mildly.

Twenty minutes later Ted was back in his tiny room with the radio turned low. Maribel couldn't understand the thin tinny words. But she knew by the rise and fall of the voice that Ted was listening to the same radio evangelist he listened to every morning.

They both had their own ideas about radio evangelists. The one's Ted liked, she didn't. The one's she liked, Ted didn't.

After sliding back the curtain, Maribel glanced through her kitchen window again as she washed the dishes and frying pan. She saw two happily bounding mixed-breed dogs burst through Bethy's front door. Like brown blurs, the dogs gamboled around the side of the house and disappeared into the wood lot.

Minutes later, Maribel watched her two grandsons come out of the house and trudge down the steep driveway toward the narrow winding two-lane road. Each boy had a book sack slung over one shoulder. The lane was so steep the boys quickly descended below her line of sight.

A few minutes after that, Maribel watched her daughter-in-law come out of the house and start across the driveway circle.

Bethy was wearing a red and blue triangular-shaped bandana that was folded across her brown hair and secured beneath her chin. She was also wearing a threadbare pink sweater over a multicolored dress that had faded from many washings.

Maribel could hear the clinks of Bethy's footsteps as she climbed the metal steps. The clinks turned into clunks as Bethy crossed the narrow wooden porch that Mike had built along one side of the mobile home. There was a knock on the door and Maribel called out, "It's open."

"Just thought I'd drop in for a second before I go to work," Bethy said, pausing in the open doorway. "You and Daddy okay?"

Maribel shrugged. "He had a bad night. You know, nightmares."

Bethy nodded. "Are you okay, Momma?"

"I suppose," Maribel said doubtfully. Then she smiled, remembering. "Robbie's going to call today."

Maribel's daughter-in-law stared a her. "Today's Friday," she finally said. "Robbie will be at work."

"I know," Maribel said. Her voice was light. Her eyes almost sparkled. "But big executives can make phone calls any time they want to."

Without conviction, Bethy said, "Maybe. But I don't want you sitting around all day, waiting. You know how disappointed you get when you think he's going to call and doesn't."

Maribel's smile brightened even further. "This is different," she said happily. "He'll call. I just know it. God led me to the prodigal son last night," she said, as if that settled everything.

"Well, maybe," Bethy said again. "But it might be better if you didn't get your hopes up." She stood in the open doorway a moment longer and then said, "So if you don't think you need anything I guess I'd better be going. Our supervisor has a fit if anyone's late."

As she watched Bethy's big green Buick slowly disappear down the driveway, Maribel leaned the last saucer in the drainer and draped the dishcloth over the faucet.

Ted's voice called out. "Who was that, Momma?"

"I'm not your Momma," Maribel called back, annoyed. "It was Bethy. Who else would it be at this hour?"

Maribel refilled her coffee cup and sat down at the table again. She wondered if Bethy was right. Why would he call her from work on a Friday?

She pondered the question for a few minutes before the answer popped into her head. Robbie was probably getting promoted today. And he'd want to tell *her* about it first. What else could it be?

Anyway, she assured herself, it was always easier for him to call from the office. That way his wife, Connie, wouldn't know about it.

Maribel didn't know why Connie hated her and Ted so much. Well, maybe she didn't hate them exactly. But she sure didn't like it when Robbie called them on the phone. She probably didn't like it when he wrote them letters either. That's probably why they never got any from him. Well, hardly ever.

Maribel supposed it was jealousy, even though it didn't make much sense for a wife to be jealous of her mother-in-law. It didn't make any sense at all, in fact. Maybe, Maribel thought, Connie couldn't stand the fact that Robbie loved his mother more than he loved his wife.

Between cups of coffee, Maribel checked the phone several times. The dial tone always sounded strong and definite. The phone was working fine.

At eleven o'clock, Maribel heaved herself to her feet. She rinsed out her coffee cup and dried her hands on a frayed blue hand towel. She glanced at the phone again.

As she moved down the hallway she could smell the stale stuffiness coming from her husband's room. It definitely needed a good airing but she could never get Ted out of the room long enough to do it.

She glanced in as she walked by. Ted was lying on top of the beige thermal blanket that covered his narrow cot. He was fully dressed. His wrinkled long-sleeved shirt was dark brown, his wrinkled work pants were dark blue. His bare feet looked pasty white, the skin almost transparent, the veins blue.

"Brown shirts don't go with blue pants," she informed him as she walked by.

Ted grunted sarcastically. "Nobody cares what I put on except you. And you don't like anything I put on."

She didn't answer him as she continued down the hallway, past the bathroom, and into her own bedroom.

Her room was slightly larger than Ted's but it seemed much smaller. There was barely enough space to wiggle between the double bed, the four walls, and the pair of mismatched chest of drawers. One of the four walls was a sliding faux wood closet door. But the door was always open and pushed out of sight, revealing a closet that was jammed with skirts and blouses, sweaters and coats.

Each item of clothing dangled from a wire hanger. Shoes, boxes and plastic bags were heaped on the closet floor. At one end of the closet was a small hot water heater, barely visible beneath the clutter.

Maribel made sure the gaudily-flowered curtain that hung from the room's solitary window was tightly closed. Then, with some difficulty, she shrugged out of her robe and pajamas and laid them across the bed.

Slowly she extracted several blouses and pullover sweaters from the tightly packed closet. In their turn, she tried on each one, glancing at herself in a long mirror that her son, Mike, had screwed to the bedroom door. Then she tried on three different skirts. One was flowered, one had wide green stripes, and one was solid blue with a white patch pocket on either hip.

She finally settled on the blue skirt with pockets and a white blouse that buttoned all the way up to its flouncy blue collar.

When she walked past Ted's room again her husband called out maliciously. "All dolled up for Robbie, hah? Well, you might as well forget about it. 'Cause he ain't gonna call."

Maribel kept walking, her shiny pumps clattering on the linoleum-floored hallway. "Don't be silly," she said. "I just like to look presentable that's all. It wouldn't hurt you to fix your own self up every now and then. You never know when someone might decide to drop in."

Twenty minutes later, sitting again at the kitchen table, Maribel felt a wave of cramps coursing through her lower abdomen. She pressed the flat of her hand against the soft rolls of fat and pushed in firmly. She could hear a gurgling sound as the cramps seemed to move about.

Glancing at the phone, she waited as long as she dared while the cramps intensified. Then, reluctantly casting another pleading look at the silent phone, she hurried toward the bathroom.

"Tell me if the phone rings," she called as she clattered by Ted's open door. "I'll be in the bathroom."

"You'll hear it," Ted grumbled. "You can hear everything in this tin can. And I do mean *everything*." He frowned, shook his head disgustedly and then turned the radio louder.

As she started to wash her hands in the bathroom a few minutes later, Maribel heard the raucous jangle of the phone. "I'm coming!" she called out frantically. "I'll get it!"

She quickly blotted her hands on a thick green towel. Then she tossed the towel over a wooden bar that had been fastened crookedly to the wall above the toilet tank. Her heavy footsteps clattered down the hallway.

"See," she said with pomp and certainty. "I told you he'd call."

The whole mobile home seemed to vibrate slightly as Maribel hurried across the living room and into the kitchen, a girlish twinkle in her chestnut eyes. She snatched up the receiver and brightly said, "Hello? Robbie?"

But it wasn't Robbie. It was her sister. "Oh. Hi, Minna," Maribel said, her voice clearly disappointed. "I can't talk long. I'm expecting a call from Robbie and I don't want to tie up the line."

"Oh," Minna said. "Is he still playing the fiddle in that country music band?"

"Oh my goodness, no," Maribel said with a chuckle of superiority. "Not much anyway. Just weekends. He has a full-time job now, you know. With this big oil company. Did I tell you?"

Without waiting for a reply, Maribel rushed on.
"He still plays the fiddle on television, of course, once or
twice a week. But he'll probably have to give that up,
too. He's getting a big promotion. That's what he's calling me about."

"Oh my," Minna said, sounding impressed. "He
must be making pretty good money then."

"I suppose so," Maribel said airily. "People who
do don't usually talk about it and Robbie never talks
about money. But they give him a lot of time off at the
oil company," she rushed on. "To play his fiddle. So
he'll probably be going to Nashville pretty soon. All the
big country stars want him to play for them when they
make big records. Did I tell you he played on several
Merle Haggard CDs? 'Course that was a couple years
ago when Merle was still alive."

"I think you did tell me that, yes," Minna said
slowly. "Well, I'm glad he's getting along so good. My
son, Nick? He's not doing so good. He's been sick, you
know. And now his wife, Dina, wants to leave him. I
just don't know what's going to happen to him and the
kids. Why, just yesterday Dina told him—"

Maribel cut her off. "I'm sure things'll work out,
Min. We'll talk about it some other time, okay? Like I
said, I'm expecting Robbie's call any minute now. And I
don't want to tie up the line."

When Maribel hung up the phone she called out to Ted. "Is Robbie still playing his fiddle with that country music band?"

Grumpily, Ted yelled back. "How the hell should I know. He never tells us anything. His kids are probably all grown up by now. Probably got kids of their own."

"You just don't remember what he tells us, that's all," Maribel replied haughtily.

"What's to remember?" Ted said. "He hasn't written in what? Two years?"

"Oh, don't be silly," Maribel said. "He writes all the time."

Sarcastically, Ted shouted," You just check the postmark on his last letter, if it hasn't rotted away. It's been two years all right. I'd bet money on it."

At twelve-ten Maribel heard Bethy's green Buick roar up the driveway. Five minutes later she heard the slam of Mike's car door. At twelve-fifty both cars were gone again, back to work, and the sky was no longer blue. It had a washed-out look that was nearly white. A stiff breeze was turning the young maple leaves inside out.

Maribel could feel her stomach sag a little. As the morning waned, she had been certain Robbie would call during his lunch break. She looked at the clock bleakly.

Abruptly, her back straightened. It suddenly dawned on her that there was a time difference between here and Oklahoma. But she could never keep it straight. Was it two hours? Or one hour? And what about daylight saving time? Wouldn't that make it even earlier out there? If that was the case, Robbie hadn't had his lunch yet. So there was still plenty of time.

She nodded to herself, smiled, and settled back in her chair again, her fingers around the coffee cup.

At one-twenty Ted padded into the kitchen again, still in bare feet. "Ain't we getting any dinner today?" he complained.

Maribel said it was time for lunch, not dinner. Dinner was later in the day. And she wasn't hungry anyway but she supposed she ought to eat something.

She made baloney sandwiches for both of them and another pot of coffee. After she finished her first sandwich she made another one. This one had two thick slabs of cheese slid between the baloney slices.

As Ted slurped more coffee from his saucer, he watched in amazement as Maribel ate the second sandwich, spooned out the last of the tapioca from a large green bowl, munched on a pile of potato chips, had another hefty chunk of cheese and then polished off the final wedge of a store-bought blueberry pie.

"For someone who ain't hungry," Ted said sardonically, "you sure eat a lot."

Maribel sniffed imperiously. "I'm just following the diet the doctor gave me."

Ted snorted. "You're supposed to eat *one* thing from each bunch of foods, not *everything* in each bunch. Bethy told you that a hundred times."

Maribel shrugged and sniffed again. "Bethy doesn't know what she's talking about. And neither do you."

At three-forty-five, Maribel could hear the throaty rumble of the unseen school bus as it paused at the bottom of the hill. Then she watched as her two grandsons trudged into view. When they neared the mobile home they both looked over and saw Maribel at the window. They waved and grinned.

She glanced at the silent phone and hoped the boys would not stop in to see her today. The thought immediately made her feel guilty so she went to the door, opened it, and called to them. "Aren't you coming in?"

The two boys looked at each other for an instant and then raced toward the mobile home. Neck and neck, they two-at-a-timed-it up the steps, clumped across the porch and ran through the out-flung door.

"I got an A in my history report," fourteen-year-old Karl said excitedly as he bolted into the mobile home, followed by his brother.

"That's nothing," twelve-year-old Elliot said with a superior air. "I got an A in math and Mr. Planch is a whole lot harder marker than your old Mrs. Wiggins."

While the two boys wrangled about whose teacher was a harder marker, Maribel told both of them to sit at the table while she found a box of gingersnaps. "You're grandpa loves these," she said to the boys, as she always said whenever she brought out the bright yellow box with the red print. "But he likes to dunk them in water."

She shook a few of the wafers out of the box and onto a small plate. She pushed the plate toward the boys. Reluctantly, they each took one wafer and nibbled at it as they continued to jabber on about tests, gym class, the cafeteria hot dogs, and a girl who was sent to the principal's office for cursing her homeroom teacher.

Maribel, sitting across the table from the boys, wore a sweet smile as she barely listened to the back-and-forth chatter. Her stomach felt tight with buried impatience whenever she glanced at the telephone, which she did every few minutes.

A shrill jangle suddenly exploded like a razor bomb in the small kitchen. It hurled slicing darts of shrapnel-like noise everywhere. The sound of the phone shattered the boys' chatter. It also sent a balloon of hope bouncing upward through Maribel's chest. She vaulted from the chair.

"That's him!" she shouted. "That's your uncle Robbie!"

At the mention of Robbie's name, the boys forgot all about their school day. Their pleas intermingled. "I wanna talk to him, Grandma, please? No, let me. You talked to him the last time. I did not."

Maribel tried to shush her grandsons while she herded them firmly toward the door. "Robbie don't have time to talk to you two," she said, opening the door. "Not today. Now, go on home. I'll tell you about it later."

The boys complained and moaned but went out onto the porch. "Please, Gram, please?" they whined in unison. "We won't talk to him long."

"Go on, now," Maribel said firmly. "I said I'll tell you all about it later."

While she was trying to get rid of the boys she was also trying to count the number of times the phone had rung. It was either four or five but she wasn't sure.

She closed the door firmly behind her two grandsons and hurried toward the phone, banging her hip against the table. Then she pulled her hand back, turned one of the kitchen chairs around until it was facing the phone, and then sat down.

Struggling to control her excitement as the phone rang once more, Maribel tried to compose herself before she slowly lifted the receiver.

"Hello?" she said mildly.

A man's voice rushed into her ear. "Mrs. Wentzel, this is Dr. Rubin. We got your CT-scan back this morning and I'd like to see you as soon as possible. Could you stop by the office? Anytime this afternoon will be fine. We'll work you in. And bring your husband."

The balloon of hope hissed and flopped and fluttered away. Maribel could almost hear the air escaping in one long squealing whoosh as her shoulders drooped.

"Mrs. Wentzel?" the man on the phone said again. "Are you there?"

Maribel took a weary breath and shook her head. "I'm not Mrs. Wentzel," she said, disheartened. "I'm Mrs. Zeiss."

"Are you sure?" Dr. Rubin said foolishly. "Isn't this 734-4409?"

"No," Maribel said. "It's 743-4409."

"Oh," the doctor said. He apologized and then hung up abruptly.

Maribel stared at the receiver that was still clutched in her hand. Slowly, she let it clatter back into its cradle.

Ted called out. "Who was that, Momma? Was that Robbie?"

A flare of anger lit Maribel's eyes. Her voice was louder, colored by hurt and disappointment. "I told you a hundred times. I am not your Momma."

There was no response from Ted. Then he said again, louder this time, "Momma? Is that Robbie?"

Maribel's words were still loud but the heat had suddenly gone out of them. "No. It was a wrong number," she called out wearily. "Some doctor trying to find a Mrs. Wentzel."

Ted's reply sounded hollow and far away. "Oh," was all he said.

The sky had turned to slate and a cold wind now whipped the limbs of the maple tree around as Bethy's big green Buick came crunching up the hill and into the gravel-floored carport. Bethy hugged her sweater around her tightly as she heaved herself out of the old car, her bandanna flapping against the nape of her neck. She hurried into the house without looking over at the mobile home.

Twenty minutes later Mike's beat-up old Dodge came huffing up the hill. It stopped directly behind the Buick but was out in the weather. The carport was not long enough or wide enough for two cars.

Mike got out of the Dodge and looked up. The smooth slate of the sky was now overlaid with heavy low-hanging clouds. Some of the clouds were almost black.

Mike frowned and then walked slowly toward the mobile home, his head down. The wind tugged at his dark blue mechanic's uniform, lashing the blackened grease-stained legs around his ankles. He mounted the steps, crossed the porch, and knocked on the door.

After waiting briefly he opened the door and stuck his head in. "Anybody home?" he said cheerily. He repeated the question, louder this time, trying to make himself heard above the blaring rap music coming from the small-screen television set.

Ted waved him in as Maribel came out of the hallway and into the living room. "Would you turn that down?" she shouted at Ted. "I can't hear myself think with that racket going on."

Ted was sitting on a worn green rocker, directly in front of the television set, about four feet away from it. "Hah?" he asked. He glanced at Mike, his eyes expressionless. Then he looked back at the screen again where two young black girls in black leather shorts and matching halters were rapping about hookers and drugs and dead cops.

Maribel frowned at her son and shook her head. She rolled her eyes as she stalked toward the television set. She gave the volume control knob a vicious twist, nearly turning the sound completely off. Ted gave her a dirty look but said nothing.

"I don't know why he has to watch those young Negro girls jiggling around every afternoon," Maribel said to Mike. "It just isn't decent."

Mike assumed a neutral grin and then glanced from one parent to another. "You guys okay?"

Mike had the same kind of pinched Clint Black eyes as his mother. He had the same deeply receding hairline and the same thinning brown hair as his father. He also had the same deeply-etched lines that flared from each side of his father's nose and then curved down and around his mouth. There was a faint smudge of grease on Mike's chin.

Ted, his eyes still glued to the screen, said, "Momma says Robbie's going to call today." There was no scoffing in his voice this time, no derision. His words were simply statements.

Mike glanced at his mother and then his eyes dropped. He looked embarrassed and annoyed. His sparse brown eyebrows went up slightly and his head tipped to one side, as though he didn't know what to say.

Maribel lifted her chair away from the phone and skidded it back to the kitchen table again. She sat down heavily, her eyes on her empty coffee cup.

It looked to Mike as though her spine had been an upright mold of gelatin that was now slowly collapsing in on itself. Her eyes were tired and forlorn.

In an instant, a burst of anger, almost rage, surged through every cavity in Mike's body. It jetted upward into his throat like hot bile. The rage was directed not at his mother, or his father. It was directed at his brother.

Dammit! he thought.

While he and Bethy watched over his mom and dad for years, day and night, summer and winter, Robbie didn't call them, seldom wrote, never sent them any money, never even sent them birthday cards.

To put it bluntly, Mike thought, Robbie didn't do shit for Mom, or for Dad. And yet here they were—here *she* was—still holding Robbie up like some kind of god-dam holy-man movie star

Christ, Mike thought, if Robbie walked into the trailer right now I'd like to grab him by the throat. I'd like to choke the living piss out of him.

Mike relented immediately, feeling guilty and sad and depleted, all at the same time. He knew he wasn't being fair. It wasn't Robbie's fault that their mom had built her whole life around him. Robbie didn't even know she had done that. And if he had known, Mike thought, he probably would have felt guilty about it, too. Guilty and empty. It was all so painful and sad.

With a great deal of effort, Mike gathered his feelings and stomped them down. He would tell Bethy about it later, maybe, after the boys had gone to bed.

He tipped his head toward the window. "Blowing up a storm out there," he said.

No one seemed to be listening but to cover his discomfort, Mike rambled on. "Radio said they expect two, maybe three inches of rain by tomorrow afternoon. Could be more." He laughed cheerlessly. "Cars on the lift'll be dripping muddy water all over me tomorrow. I hate that. I'll be soaked by noon. Probably die of pneumonia."

He laughed again, but the sound was stiff, frozen. It hung in the air like a chilly slab of beef.

Ted was still staring blankly at the screen. Maribel was looking down at her hands, positioned on the tabletop. Mike's eyes followed his mother's eyes.

Her hands were folded into loose fists. The fingers moved slowly, restlessly.

Mike had to look away to keep the rage from coming back. "Well," he said with a jerk of his head toward the door, "I guess I better get over there." His grin was thin and forced. "Bethy hates it when she has supper on the table and I turn up late."

He went to the door and then looked back, his hand on the doorknob. "Call if you need anything," he said, as he said every other evening for the past five years. "Okay?"

Maribel's smile was also faint, almost painful. "We will," she said quietly.

Mike hesitated at the door and then pushed it open. A gust of chilly wind swept into the trailer. It swirled around the small kitchen and found a calendar that was hanging above the sink. The wind concentrated on the small white pages with the small bold numbers. It fluttered the pages briefly. A moment later the door closed, the wind died, and the pages were still again.

By midnight the gusts were nudging the trailer like a curious elephant, snuffling, pushing, bumping. The trailer's thin aluminum-skin panels wobbled slightly with the wind, making quiet buckling sounds. It rolled over the aluminum roof panels creating a dull and gentle thunder. It also pulled at the ill-fitting windows. It drew out breathy moans that rose and fell in wailing waves. The rain came down like nails on glass.

Ted, looking frail and unsteady in his oversized pajamas, padded slowly across the living room and into the kitchen. He winced when his pale bony feet touched the cold linoleum but he said nothing.

He hobbled around the table to where Maribel was hunched over, her forehead on her folded arms. There was another empty cup in the center of the table. The film of coffee at the bottom of the cup had long since dried to a thin brown stain.

For a long silent moment, Ted stood looking down at the top of his wife's head. Her white scalp was visible through the thinning grey hair.

"Probably just got too busy," he said slowly. His voice was steeped in melancholy. "Meetings, people coming and going ..." His voice trailed off.

Clumsily, almost fearfully, Ted placed an awkward but gentle hand on his wife's shoulder. There was a feeling of strangeness as the dry skin of his hand touched the coarse fabric of her white high-necked blouse. He could feel the heat of her skin through the thin material. It filled him with pity.

When she didn't move, Ted sighed and lifted his hand away. With a slow resignation, the hand descended to his side. His thin lips pursed tightly, holding something in.

"Well, Momma," he finally said softly, "we better get to bed. It's late."

Maribel's slumped shoulders rose and fell and then began to shudder rhythmically, soundlessly. Hidden tears welled up silently and then spilled over, wetting her fore-arms.

Ted lifted his hand once more and once more moved it tentatively toward his wife's shoulder. But just before he touched her blouse a second time, Maribel suddenly gave her shoulder a twisting jerk. It was as though she had felt his hand getting nearer, as though she had wanted to slough his hand off before it got there, like a dry papery snakeskin. Ted yanked his hand back quickly but his voice remained unchanged. After a long cough-free breath, his words were slow and filled with kindness.

"That's okay, Mari," he finally said, gently. "Maybe he'll call tomorrow."

Magic

(The magical qualities and amazing technologies that we take for granted in our everyday lives could be snuffed out and changed forever in a few short hours. It has happened countless times in other "less fortunate" countries. Who is to say it won't happen here?—rh)

After cautiously probing the shadows and dust, the dying sun finally gained access through the butter-knife scrapes and fingernail scratches that marred the room's single black-painted window. Broken into pieces, the fading tangerine light punctured the dust with arrow shafts and tiny sparks, converting itself to a gauzy veil of floating grit.

"Are you sure you're not too tired?" the woman said, smiling down at her six-year-old daughter.

Both mother and daughter were wrapped in dark diaphanous robes that were blackened from sweat and lightly powdered with a grey airborne residue. The hood of each robe had been pushed aside and now drooped around the ghostly throats. The two dark faces—nearly identical except for the etchings left by time—were dangerously free and slick from the heat. The woman was seated on an iron-hard wooden chair, the child standing before her.

The little girl nodded her head up and down insistently and grinned. "Please, Mommy, please?" she begged.

For a furtive moment, the woman's dark eyes snapped to the blackened window. Her head tilted almost imperceptibly. Her ears strained for any sound.

But there was nothing. Even the wind—which had moaned all day—was pressured into silence by the heat.

The woman's shoulders sagged slightly with relief. Her eyes moved back to her daughter's face. She smiled again.

"Well," the woman said softly, "maybe just one or two."

The little girl clapped her thin dirty hands but her noisy squeal of delight was immediately lopped off.

"*Shhh!*" the woman hissed forcefully. Her open hand reached out quickly toward her daughter's dust-streaked face. Her fingers lightly pressed the parted lips.

"We can't let anyone hear," she warned, her whispered words harsh and quick.

The little girl's dark eyes pleaded for forgiveness, her words muffled by the woman's fingertips.

"I'm sorry," the child said. "I forgot."

"We can not forget," the woman said firmly. "I told you that before."

A sudden pain sprang to her daughter's eyes and the woman felt immediate guilt. Her fingers fell from her daughter's lips. She made her voice soft again, gentle, understanding. "Which story do you want to hear, sweetie?"

The little girl's face brightened. Quickly she said, "The one about the light. You know. About the little handles."

"But you've heard that story a thousand times," the woman said in mock disbelief.

The little girl beamed. "Just one more time," she insisted. "Please?"

The woman rolled her eyes. "Okay. One more time. And then we have to get some sleep."

The little girl quickly positioned herself cross-legged on the gritty floor in front of her mother's chair and looked up expectantly.

"Tell me again about the little handles," she said. "And how Father used to fix them. And how they made everything sparkle and shine. And how they covered the whole world with diamonds. I love stories about magic."

The woman held up one hand and shifted her weight on the ladder-backed chair. She could feel the narrow wooden rungs digging into her spine. The seat slats pressed into her thin buttocks and the backs of her stringy thighs. But her smile was warm and gentle again.

"You are right of course," she said. "It really was a kind of magic. All anyone had to do was flip one of those little handles with their fingers and the whole room would fill with light."

"And the light was everywhere, wasn't it, Mommy? In the corners, under the beds, even in the closets. It moved everywhere, into everything, just like the wind."

The woman nodded. "And usually there was a separate handle for each room."

"Father even put one of those little handles outside my closet door, didn't he?" the little girl said. "The one I used to have before we started moving around. It made my whole closet as bright as day."

"And if you didn't want your closet filled with light?" the woman asked playfully. "Then what would you do?"

The little girl squirmed with pleasure and then shrugged. "That's an easy one. You just had to push the little handle down again." Then she grinned. "But what about the lights outside, Mommy?" she said, like she had said so many times before. "All around the house. What about them?"

"Most of those lights," the woman said, "came on automatically. Which means they came on by themselves. Your father fixed them so they would."

The little girl giggled with delight and hugged herself. "Now tell me about the store," she said. "You know, the one that had piles and piles of candy and milk and bananas and everything. You and Father used to go there every week, didn't you? That's what you used to tell me."

The woman nodded again. Her words were now textured with sadness, regret. "There was so much food they had to stack it on shelves that were this high."

She lifted one hand as high as she could reach, her fingers bent at a right angle.

"And they had freezers that were filled with all kinds of berries and vegetables. They even had frozen chocolate cakes and frozen pies and boxes of ice cream, hard as bricks."

Her hand floated down again, slowly.

Saucer-eyed, the little girl shook her head in disbelief. "Ohhh," she said. The sound stretched out like silver taffy. After a moment of thought, the little girl pushed out her lower lip and frowned.

"Why can't we have a store like that now?" she pouted. "It's not fair. I never got to see one." Her eyes blazed. "I hate the store man," she said.

The woman agreed sadly. "It isn't fair. But it's not the store man's fault. The store your father and I went to is still there, just a couple blocks from here." She gestured vaguely toward the blackened window. "A lot of the other buildings are still there, too."

But there's no one to stock the shelves now, she thought. No one to pile the lettuce and make it wet. No one to carry the trays of bread. No one to pull the meat-laden carts.

"Let's go see the store tomorrow," the little girl said hopefully. "Can we?"

The woman shook her head. "You know we can't do that," she said, sorrow in her voice. "Not by ourselves. And there's no one to go with us. Not since your father was …" Her voice faltered. "You know we can't, sweetheart."

The little girl wrinkled her nose for a moment, thinking, and then her face brightened again. "I wonder what happened to all the ice cream? And the cakes? And the frozen berries?"

The woman spread her hands helplessly. "When the electricity stopped, the ice cream melted," she said. "So did the pies and cakes. Then people started breaking windows, the people who weren't hurt or dying. They started running through the stores with boxes and bags. They took everything."

"Bad people," the little girls said angrily.

The woman sighed and looked again toward the paint-blackened window.

"Some of the people were bad, it's true," she said. "But not all of them. Some of the people were just hungry. Some had babies to feed. Some had sick children. Some had grandparents to take care of."

The woman glanced down at her daughter. "You remember your grandparents, don't you?"

The little girl's narrow shoulders rose and dropped. "I guess so," she said uncertainly. She thought for a moment, her brow furrowed. Then her face lit up.

"Grandfather was real tall and he had white hair and a scratchy beard. Right?"

The woman laughed. "You remember a *picture* of your grandfather," she said. "That was the picture your grandmother took. The day your father and I were married. Most of the time he didn't have a beard."

"Oh," the little girl said.

The woman's smile broadened. "But that's okay. You were a very little girl when your grandfather died. At least you remember his picture."

"I don't remember Grandma's picture," the little girl said, sadness in her voice. "Is she dead, too?"

The woman nodded. "They both died when the bombs fell and the soldiers came, like so many, many others." Her voice sounded hollow as shadows of ghosts tried to fill up the room.

"But to tell the truth," the woman went on, "we never really had many pictures of your grandparents. Even before the soldiers came and burned them all."

"Why did they do that?" the little girl said, annoyed. "Why did they have to burn them?"

The woman shrugged. "I don't know," she said wearily. "I guess they wanted to kill the past and everything in it. Anyway, there were no pictures of your grandmother by herself. Ever."

The shards and shafts of light had vanished. The sun was down. The light in the room was almost gone.

The woman could barely make out the shape of her daughter sitting on the floor. All she could see clearly was the little girl's teeth, almost luminescent in the darkness. Her daughter was smiling again.

"Now tell me about the magic box," she said happily. "You know," she urged.

The woman laughed out loud and then, suddenly aware of the sound of her own laughter, she lowered her voice and shook her head. "Don't you ever get tired of hearing about that?"

The little girl beamed and shook her head. "I told you, Mommy," she said. "I love stories about magic."

The woman folded her hands in her lap. She closed her eyes, painting pictures, retrieving memories, tasting buried feelings.

"Well, like I said so many times before," she began. "It really *was* a magic box. Because it held all kinds of people and all kinds of things."

"Like golden temples in Japan," the little girl prompted.

"Uh-huh. And like emerald trees in Norway. And butterflies in Mexico, orange and black and quaking in the mountain air. It even held icebergs from Siberia."

The glorious but tattered images suddenly slammed into the woman's brain like slabs of heavy wood. They nearly took her breath away.

She was amazed that the shock and disbelief were still there, acid burns that wouldn't heal.

She squeezed her eyes shut.

How could the good magic evaporate so quickly, so permanently? she thought, abruptly bewildered. How could it turn from good to bad, almost overnight?

And why?

That was the worst, the most painful question of all. Why did they have to do it? It didn't make any sense!

Tiny words brought her back to the hot black room. "Ice birds?" the little girl said incredulously. "You never told me about ice birds before."

The woman tried again to push the painful questions away. She forced a smile. "Not birds, sweetie, *bergs*. Ice *bergs*," she emphasized. "I guess I didn't tell you about them because I haven't thought about them for a long, long time."

"But what *are* ice bergs?" the little girl asked. "Are they like ice cream?"

The woman shook her head and laughed quietly. "No, icebergs are nothing like ice cream. Icebergs are huge, huge blocks of ice. Some are as big as a house, bigger even. In fact, some of them are much, much bigger than houses. Some are as big as mountains. And they're cold. Freezing cold. All the time."

"Oh," the little girl whispered, truly awed by the new concept: a glittering ice tower so tall that it pierced the clouds!

"Have you ever seen one?" the little girl said, wonder in her voice. "A real ice berg?"

"I did!" the woman said happily. "I really did. It was when your father and I went to Siberia on our honeymoon. And we had to go a very long way to see them," she remembered fondly. "We went on an airplane first. Then we went on a ship. And then on a train."

The woman laughed, reliving the frigid air and the frosty burning feeling in her cheeks and nose. "We even went on a dogsled ride," she said. "Your father and I."

"Was it fun?" the little girl said.

"Oh, yes," the woman replied. "It was lots and lots of fun. Because the sleds were pulled by big strong healthy dogs. They were beautiful dogs, too, with thick fur and romping eyes. The were not like the bony, pathetic, tongue-lolling creatures that slink around here now."

And gnaw at skulls and finger bones, she thought.

Her mind immediately shoved the image aside.

"Maybe someday we could go to Siberia," the little girl said hopefully. "Just you and me, on a big white plane."

The woman shook her head. Her breath came out in a snort.

"I don't think so. Planes don't leave here anymore. They don't go to Siberia anymore, or to anywhere else. There's no one to fly them. There's no one to sail the ships either. No one to drive the trains and buses. They're all gone. Just like the ice bergs. They're all gone, too."

The woman was silent for a moment. But her mind raced on.

The gasoline was gone, too. The oil. The spare parts that the factories used to make. Now the factories are quiet, empty; the ones that are still standing. No doctors. No nurses. No hospitals, no medicine, no telephones, no banks, no money …

The little girl tugged at her mother's robe. "Tell me about the big men with funny suits who used to run around, right inside the magic box," she begged. "And tell me about the pretty ladies. And about the bears, and the parties. I love to hear about the parties."

The woman shifted her weight on the chair. She tried again to push aside the blackness in her mind. But the blackness always hurried back whenever she thought about *before*. And that was the only way to think about anything now. As *before*. And *after*.

Suddenly weary and weighted down she said, "I can't tell you about all of those things, sweetheart. Not now."

"Then just tell me about the men who used to run around."

The woman sighed and then gave in reluctantly. "Okay," she said. "But then you simply must go to sleep. We have to get up early, you know. We'll have to move again tomorrow."

The little girl groaned. "Can't we stay here? Just this once?"

The women's narrow shoulders sagged. "I wish we could, sweetheart, I really do. But we can't."

"Please, Mommy, pl—"

A sudden sound chopped off the little girl's words. Her mouth was frozen open, her eyes wide. She jerked her head around.

She and her mother both stared in the direction of the window. The painted glass, the frame, even the ambient light had disappeared completely. It was full night now, everywhere.

Nerves were suddenly taut, spines stiff, as two hearts started to race. "Shh," the woman whispered harshly. Her hand flew up in the darkness. Her index finger was poised, uselessly, before her own invisible lips.

The little girl, too, was suddenly sitting ramrod straight, her mouth still open. Unseen, her scissored legs began to bounce slightly, nervously. "Mommy?" she whispered. Her voice was ragged with fear.

"Shh," her mother said again.

The woman bent forward, reaching out blindly. Finding her daughter's shoulder, she gripped it tightly with her fingers and then squeezed hard.

The sound they had heard was far away at first and indistinct. A drone? A hum? The woman couldn't tell.

Nor could she tell from which direction the sound was actually coming.

The little girl wriggled fearfully beneath her mother's firm grasp, scooting closer to her mother's legs.

The woman could feel the frail flesh, quivering beneath her palm and fingers. "We must be very, very quiet," she whispered urgently. "Not a sound."

The little girl's head bobbed up and down mechanically as she continued to stare toward the window, toward the sound.

The humming noise gradually turned into a groaning roar that was distant at first. Then, incrementally, the roar got bigger, and louder, and closer.

Finally, the woman could hear the shrill angry voices. She had heard the voices many times before, many other nights, in many other rooms. And they always filled her mind with dread.

As the truck neared, the shrill shouts—like crooked slashing blades—cut through the engine's roar.

The sound of the words was familiar. The meaning was not. It never was. But no matter. The intent was always brutally clear.

The woman's own spine became an iron bar. Her breath was shallow and quick. "Shh," she whispered yet again. Unconsciously, she gripped her daughter's shoulder even harder.

The little girl cringed but said nothing.

The roar of the engine died. The voices got louder, more insistent, spurting like high-pitched bullets.

Banging sounds became vicious thumps. The thumps turned into splintering wood. A shattered door slammed back against a wall.

There were screams, followed by rapid mechanical gunfire. More screams. More gunfire. And then silence.

The little girl whimpered softly. Her thin body shook. Her small fingers trembled, clutching her mother's thigh.

The woman wanted desperately to soothe her daughter's fear but she could not. Her own fear was too strong, too crippling. Her paralyzed lungs screamed for air.

The voices sputtered again, still shrill, but not as loud. There was another short burst of bullets. Then one voice, firm, loud, commanding.

The engine roared to life once more. Men and guns bumped against wood and metal as everyone clambered aboard.

A moment later, the truck seemed to groan and lurch, and then it started to grumble away.

The woman felt her wrist and wished she still had a watch. But the time didn't really matter. They always came at night. They never lingered more than two minutes, usually less. And always, always, they left more people dead.

Long tense minutes passed before the woman's breath began to move in and out almost normally. Her hand, nearly numb from pressing her daughter's shoulder, slid off helplessly and hung by the side of the chair.

Silence pressed in again from all sides, filling the light-less room.

The little girl began to whimper. The whimpers turned into moans and sniffles. Her tongue struggled with the whispered words. "Are … are they … gone?"

The woman let out a breath and closed her eyes briefly. "Yes," she said softly, her mouth dry as dust. She tried to wet her parched lips. But there was no moisture left.

"I think so," she added. "But let's be quiet for a while longer, okay?"

"Okay," the little girl said. Her voice, too, was shaking, and very tiny.

Silently, carefully, the little girl unfolded her legs. She lifted the skirt of her robe and held it out of the way. Slowly she got to her feet.

Reaching out blindly, she felt her mother's breast and shoulder. Then she scampered hurriedly into her mother's lap.

The little girl hugged her mother tightly, pressing her dusty tear-wet face against the gritty cloth that covered her mother's shoulder.

The woman's hands pulled her daughter close. She could feel the bony spine, the knobby shoulders, the twig-like ribs.

A clamp of overwhelming hopelessness gripped the woman's heart as she rocked her daughter gently, crooning.

"It's okay, sweetie. They're gone now. They're gone."

But she knew they'd be back. They always came back.

And no one was left to care.

Coming Home

(This is a flash fiction about the horrors of PTSD and its—sometimes—disastrous aftereffects.—rh)

Five years in Iraq, two in Afghanistan. No wounds of any kind. Not even a broken eardrum. Somehow, he had managed to get through more than eighteen hundred days of smoke, noise, explosions, chaos, screams, and the malevolent chatter of countless guns and shrieking rockets. No one could believe how lucky he had been. *It made no sense at all.*

And through it all, the two of them had written endless emails. Often they talked of his last leave, a time of love and growing hope. Sometimes she would tell him mundane things about work, about shopping trips to the mall, about getting stuck in the snow, about her best friend Bree who named their first child after her. *It made no sense at all.*

In emails they would try out different names, names for their own babies. What name would he like for a boy? What name would she like for a girl? They would write about what kind of home they would buy, what kind of furniture they would have. *It made no sense at all.*

Sometimes, he would tell her about the sand-storms, the suffocating heat, the weight of his sweat-soaked vest and helmet. Mostly he talked of the future, their future together. He did not tell her about the night-mare that never went away. He did not tell her about his buddy, Jake, who had tried to clear a path through a mar-ketplace, who had tried to protect a pregnant Afghani woman from the jostling mob of sullen faces. *It made no sense at all.*

Nor did he tell her about the swollen belly that turned out to be a rounded explosive device that killed the Afghani woman, his buddy Jake, and twenty-two oth-er Afghanis, including three babies. *It made no sense at all.*

She didn't tell him about her own pregnancy. She wanted to surprise him. She wanted to tell him in person. Nor did she tell him about the clingy black nightgown she had bought for their first night together. *It made no sense at all.*

Nor did he tell her about the gun that was never far away, under the pillow, even here at home, where there were no explosions, no eyes seething with hatred, no walls streaked with blood and brains and bone. The war was thousands of miles away. And he was home forever now. And finally safe. *It made no sense at all.*

But the room was dark. The gown was black. The bulge was round. The nightmare horrors came rushing back. And then in an instant, in one brief flash, in one concussive roar, she and the baby were dead. And all their dreams, forever gone. *It made no sense at all.*

When a Good Man Dies

("It is always sad when a good man dies, but sadder still when his heart's not known to those who care." Thus begins the story of Stewart Reed and his brother, Mandell. They are as close as brothers can be, and yet, sometimes, there are secrets that even brothers are reluctant to share ... until it is too late.—rh)

It is always sad when a good man dies, but sadder still when his heart's not known to those who care. But death was the last thing on Manny Reed's mind when the phone rang in his office. He had just returned from his monthly planning board meeting and the nine board members had been as truculent as ever, insisting that there should be no more development east of the Tyler Ranch tract. *None.*

Manny tugged at his blue silk tie and undid the top button of his slightly damp white shirt. He slumped into the black high-backed leather chair and swung it around to face the Sarasota skyline. He pulled the phone closer and punched in his voicemail code.

The first two messages were from a developer named Hutchins. It was the Hutchins project—two hundred and fifty-seven single-family homes all crammed into the seventy-five acre Maldon tract—that had hurled the planning board over the edge. The Maldon tract was not only too small for the zoned density. It was also east of the Tyler Ranch tract.

The third message was a nudging, prodding, I-think-it's-time-to-light-a-fire-under-the-planning-director call. That one came from the county administrator, who reminded Manny that the county commission needed a firm recommendation on the Maldon tract by Tuesday morning. No postponements this time.

Manny rolled his eyes and waited for the next message. A cool formal female voice said, "Mandell? This is Lissa. I just wanted to let you know that Stewart died on Monday."

"Je-sus Christ," Manny said softly.

"He had a heart attack in Chicago," Lissa continued, "and the memorial service will be tomorrow at two, here in Beltsville. He was under some stress lately; we all have been. But the point is, I thought you'd want to know. I realize this is very short notice so don't feel you have to come. Everyone will understand. I'm sure Stewart would have, too."

Manny squeezed his forehead with his left hand. "Stewy?"

There was a pause in the message. Lissa's voice became muffled for a moment and then cleared again.

"That's all I can tell you right now. Things have been a bit hectic so I'll try to call again next week. When things return to normal. So. As I said, there's no need for you to come to the funeral. Stewart would have definitely understood. Bye, Mandell."

Manny held the phone to his ear for another moment and listened as a tiny mechanical voice told him there were no more messages. Then he took a breath and punched in ten numbers. She answered on the first ring.

"Lissa? This is Manny. What the hell happened? Why didn't you call me sooner?"

Her voice remained calm and cool. "We had to get the body shipped back to Beltsville of course. That takes time, Mandell. I called as soon as I could. And as I said, there's no need for you to be here. I just thought—"

Manny interrupted angrily. "Of course I'll be there. Stewy's my brother. He's my best friend. Why the hell wouldn't I come?"

"There's no need to shout, Mandell," she said evenly.

Manny took another long slow breath and apologized. "I'm just shocked, that's all. He called me last week, told me about the promotion. He never said anything about his health."

Lissa's voice remained flat, mechanical. "Yes, well, he never said anything to me either. Stewart was a very private person. You, of all people, should know that."

"How are the kids taking it?"

Manny could almost see Lissa's subtle shrug. "Like kids. Their world collapsed for a day or two. They're staying with friends tonight. But by now I'm sure their brains are focused once more on their cell-phones and thrones games."

Manny squinted against the harsh sunlight that bounced off a shell of blue-green glass that covered yet another anonymous bank tower. He twisted his fist to see his watch.

"Shit," he said, "it's almost one-thirty. I'll have my secretary book a flight to BWI this afternoon. I'll rent a car when I get there."

There was an edge on Lissa's voice now. "Man-dell, really. Why are you putting yourself through all this stress? Why can't you just wait a couple weeks? Till things settle down? There's nothing you can do, you know. He's gone."

The words came out quickly, automatically. "You seem to be taking this whole thing in a very civilized manner." His eyes pinched shut. He regretted his words instantly.

"What do you want me to do, Mandell? Wail and sob and pull out my hair? Would that really help?"

Manny opened his eyes and squeezed his forehead again. "What about Mom? You want me to call the nursing home?"

"I'll take care of that," Lissa said.

Manny nodded. There was nothing else to say. "Okay. I should be there tonight. If not, I'll give you a call."

* * * * * * * *

Manny drove quickly to his nearby condo and threw a few changes of clothing into an overnight bag while his secretary arranged a flight and ran off the necessary leave papers. Waiting for her call, Manny splashed some Johnny Walker into an ice-filled coffee cup and went over the last time he had talked to his brother.

Stewy had placed the call, mostly to tell Manny about his promotion to regional manager, a promotion he clearly deserved. Stewy had worked for the same consulting firm for nearly twenty years, and Ph.D. metallurgists with global experience weren't exactly a dime a dozen.

"The guy who did *not* get the job is really PO-ed," Stewy had laughed. "He probably wants to kill me."

"He'll get over it. I hope you got a raise."

"Of course. And I get to stay in Beltsville, too." Stewy had sighed. "But all is not perfect. No more frequent flyer miles."

Manny laughed. "Well, you can't have everything. At least you'll finally be able to spend more time with Lissa and the kids. I'm sure they're all happy about that."

There was a pause. Then, uncertainly: "I suppose so. But you know kids. They'll probably get tired of the old man being home every night. Cramps their style."

After another awkward pause, Stewy cleared his throat. Hesitantly, he said, "By the way, little brother, there's something I need to talk to you about."

"Sure, go ahead. It's your nickel."

Quickly Stewy said, "I don't mean now. It's … it's not something I want to get into on the phone."

"Uh-oh. Sounds serious."

"Yeah, I guess, kind of," Stewy said, drawing the words out.

"Kids okay?"

"No, no. They're fine. It's nothing like that."

"Can't be your job. You just got a big promotion. Lissa?"

"Well, like I said, it's not something I want to talk about on the phone."

"Okay," Manny had replied, thinking. "Let's see. I believe I've got a conference in D.C. in about two weeks. I'll have to check the details with Carley, my new secretary. But I could probably make a side trip to your place. Or we could meet at the airport. Can it wait till then?"

"Oh, sure. Sure. It's no big deal. Just let me know when you're coming. We'll work something out."

That's the way they had left it. And now Stewy was dead.

* * * * * * * * *

The taxi ride to the airport was long and frustrating and so were the security lines. But once strapped into his window seat, Manny was able to take a breath and think about his brother again. It still hadn't sunk in, probably wouldn't until he actually saw Stewy lying there like some waxy stranger in a black suit. All he could see now was the man who had practically raised him after their own father—who hated life jackets—had drowned when a sudden squall tossed him off his new and skittish catamaran.

Mom was still Mom then. She didn't start drifting into Alzheimer's for twenty more years. But it was Stewy who kept Manny on the narrow road through high school. It was Stewy who pushed him into and through college, at least the undergrad part. And it was Stewy who held his hand when a brunette named Staci had torn his guts out. At least that's the way it felt to Manny at the time.

But by then, Stewy had found a beautiful girl of his own—Melissa Chelton, from Chadds Ford, who already had a Masters in English Lit from the U of Penn.

The marriage quickly produced a succession of beautiful babies. The twins, Katia and Kristopher. Could they actually be fourteen already. Then Loreen, now twelve. Rounding off the set was ten-year-old Danielle: Dani to everyone. To everyone except Lissa, her mother. To her, Danielle would always be Danielle.

Beautiful home in one of the better sections of Beltsville. Beautiful wife, beautiful children, an excellent job. Stewy even had a social conscience, spending part of every Thanksgiving and Christmas for the past ten years serving meals to the homeless at the Salvation Army. Raised money for the Shriners. Served as an organizer for the Special Olympics. And whenever he was home for the weekend, Stewy and family could always be found in their own name-plated pew in the second row of Ascension Lutheran Church. Ascension's Hampton Grace, DD, had been the children's baptizer, and Stewy's confidant, ever since he married them.

Now, Stewy dead? No. It simply couldn't be.

* * * * * * * * *

It was nearly seven-thirty when Manny steered the tan Ford Taurus rental through the open gate. The elegant three-story Tudor home was visible from the road even during the summer when the maple, oak and dogwood trees were fully clothed. It was even more visible now when most of the leaves were gone. Manny always smiled ruefully whenever he saw the beige stucco, the broad, ponderous, log-like trim, and the grey slate roof. The two brothers had shared almost everything, but Stewy would never reveal to Manny how much he had paid for the Tudor.

"Too damn much, that's for sure," was Stewy's standard answer. "But Lissa loves it. And so do I of course. Except when tax time rolls around."

The long macadam driveway wound its way through a small grove of willow trees that lined both sides of a narrow stream. The Taurus bumped over the one-lane field-stone bridge, down-shifted up the grassy incline and pulled in beside Lissa's black Escalade, which was parked in front of the house next to an immaculate dark green Jaguar convertible. Manny felt a twinge in his gut when he glanced at the garage. For some reason, the door was open. Stewy's powder blue Porsche Carrera was sitting among the shadows.

Manny switched off the engine and got out of the Taurus just as a dark-haired man in a well-tailored midnight-blue suit came out of the house. He glanced at Manny but continued walking briskly toward the Jag. Manny intercepted him with an outstretched hand and fell in beside him.

"I'm Mandell Reed, Stewart's brother. Who might you be?"

The man glanced at Manny's hand but continued walking. His eyes were hard and sharp and very blue; his expression grim.

"Ah, yes. From Florida. I'm Thomas Lutzman," he said. His delayed, almost reluctant handshake, was soft and dry. "Please accept my condolences. Your brother was a fine person."

Lutzman opened the door of the Jag and slid in behind the wheel. "I'm Mrs. Reed's attorney. We were just going through some papers. You'll be here for the service?" Manny nodded again. "Good," Lutzman said. "Perhaps I'll see you there."

He closed the door, started the car and, with a curt nod, drove off. Manny stood there for a moment, wondering why Lissa had her own attorney. Or did Lutzman just mean he was her attorney now that Stewy was gone?

Manny went back to the rental, swung his overnight bag out of the trunk and went up to the house. He rang the bell.

The door swung open almost immediately. "Mandell," Lissa said. "You made it."

Five-foot ten in flats, Lissa was as thin as ever. Her face was pale and elegant, the hint of a dimple in her narrow chin, very little makeup, no jewelry, her blonde hair shoulder-length and expensively styled. She appeared almost flat-chested in the sheer pale-green top and dark well-tailored slacks.

She seemed surprised when Manny stepped in to touch his cheek to hers. She almost jerked back but caught herself. She managed a tight grim smile and glanced down at his overnight bag.

"I'm afraid you'll have to sleep in Stewart's den. His sofa turns into a bed."

"No problem," Manny said.

Lissa closed the door, looked at him for a moment and then turned away. "My mother and father are staying in our first floor guest room," she explained as Manny followed her. "My brother Malcolm and his wife are staying in the guest room on the second floor. The apartment above the garage has been taken over by my brother Miller."

She glanced back over her shoulder. Her eyes were cool and empty. "I don't believe you've met Miller."

Manny shook his head. "No, I don't think so." He reached out and touched her wrist. "Lissa?"

She stopped and turned around. Her eyebrows went up.

"Is there anything I can do?" Manny said. "Anyway I can help? People you want me to call? Errands? Whatever."

As she gestured vaguely toward an open door the words came out in a rush. "That's very sweet, I'm sure, but no thank you. My father has taken care of everything. I still have a few things to do so I hope you don't mind if I rush off. There's a bathroom attached. I believe Jonella left some linens for you on the desk. If you're hungry the kitchen is down the hall and—"

Manny interrupted the flow. "I know where the kitchen is, Lissa. I also know this must be a very difficult time for you, but try not to push me away. I want to help if I can."

Lissa's eyes were blank, as though she'd never seen Manny before. "Help?" she finally said. Her voice was stiff and icy. "How can you possibly help?"

Manny stammered. "I-I don't know. But if we could just talk for a few minutes ..." His voice faltered and then cracked. "I loved him, too, you know. He was my best friend."

Her narrow lips grew narrower. The smile was
tight and small; it had no warmth. "Best friend? Yes, I
suppose he was. So I'm sure you knew all about it.
You've probably known about it for years."

Manny stared at her. "Known about what?"

Lissa took a breath and shook her head slowly. "I
wish you hadn't come, Mandell. I really do."

She turned and walked away, her back straight.

"Lissa?" Manny called after her. "What are you
talking about? What do you think I knew about?"

Lissa kept on walking, her small head swaying
atop the long graceful neck.

"Lissa?"

* * * * * * * *

By the time Manny located the small well-stocked
liquor closet behind Stewy's desk, the house was completely still. He'd heard a brief murmur of voices, doors
closing, an engine starting, and then silence. He downed
the first Johnny Walker in one toss and then found a tray
of ice in a miniature fridge. After a second slower drink
he took a shower in the small well-equipped bathroom
that opened off the den. Padding back and forth between
the den and the bathroom in dark blue pajama bottoms,
Manny unpacked his shirts and suit and hung them on the
shower rod. He unzipped his shaving kit, brushed his
teeth, and poured another drink. He sat down at Stewy's

desk and slowly looked around. His eyes stopped on several eight by tens that were grouped around a table lamp.

Formal wedding picture. Birth of the twins. Children growing up. Radiant smiles. And every photo: the ideal family. All except the last one, the most recent one. The kids were still grinning in that one, too, but Stewy's smile looked forced and stiff. Lissa was focused on something else, something off to the left.

More family photos were lined up neatly on the dark-paneled walls. A dozen or more engraved plaques, some gold, some silver. Five laminated degrees. Several framed newspaper articles, complete with fuzzy black and white photos. A fairly large color photo of Stewy shaking hands with a man Manny couldn't place but knew he knew.

A lifetime on four walls. Bits and pieces. Shadows. Sketches. Memories. Detritus. And who could say which was which. The truth was, Manny thought as his eyes moved around the room, it hardly added up to anything, certainly not the full multi-dimensional personality that he knew as Stewart Reed, big brother, confidant, supporter, friend.

A life without Stewy would be a life with a very big hole in the middle of it.

Manny made himself another drink and turned on
Stewy's computer. A few keystrokes brought him to his
own email in-basket back in Sarasota. Nothing important, a lot of junk mail as usual. Two lines from the
county administrator reminding him of the Tuesday dead-
line. And a note from Alison. She had heard about his
loss and wished she could have gone with him.

"Call me the minute you get back," the email said.
"Day or night. And I DO mean day or night."

Manny closed the in-box and clicked his way
back to the desktop. As he tried to shut the computer
down, the mouse slipped off the pad and bumped into the
telephone. Somehow he ended up at the My Documents
folder. Without thinking he clicked on it. Another folder
popped into view. This one was labeled "XO".

Manny debated for a few moments about whether
he should be snooping around in his deceased brother's
personal files. But curiosity overcame guilt and he
clicked on that one, too.

A small box asked him to please enter his pass-
word. Manny began to feel a tightness in his throat and
gut. His right hand left the mouse anyway and moved to
the keyboard. Eight fingers tapped the keys lightly, nervously, as he thought.

His palms felt suddenly sweaty. He wiped them
on his pajama bottoms and then typed "Stewart." Then

"Stewy." "Stewball." "Stewpot." "Stewmeat." All
names he used to call his brother. None of them worked.
He tried Stewy's birth date. He tried Stewy's two middle
names, Jason and Carter, the names of both of their
grandfathers. He tried the grandfathers' names separately
and then ran them together. He tried their mother's
maiden name and then her birthday. He even typed their
father's name, his birth date, and the name of the catamaran that killed him. Nothing worked. Relieved, Manny
shut the computer down.

* * * * * * * * *

He woke up determined to ask Lissa again what
she meant, what she thought he knew about. But it never
happened. The morning quickly spun away into chaos.
The four kids were back home, rushing around, getting
dressed, eating breakfast. There was no time to even give
them a hug. But that didn't matter. At least not to them.
They acknowledged their Uncle Manny's presence but
not much more, which was very odd. Manny had always
felt a certain bond with Stewy's kids, especially the little
one, Dani. But even she seemed to be avoiding him.

Manny had met Lissa's family only once before,
at Lissa and Stewy's wedding. He really didn't know
them but at least they tried to make small talk as Manny
poured coffee. They talked about the weather, the stock
market, the price of real estate in Florida. Lissa's brother

Miller sauntered into the kitchen and made a snide-sounding comment about how pretty Manny's burgundy tie was. Mrs. Chelton shot her son a frigid glance. Miller shrugged and walked away, munching a piece of toast. Apropos of nothing, Mr. Chelton asked Manny how old he was. When Manny said thirty-five, Chelton said, "Married?"

Manny said, "No."

Chelton glanced at his wife and then back at Manny. He shrugged the same kind of shrug Lissa used whenever she thought something was ludicrously obvious.

"Well, marriage isn't for everyone, I guess," Chelton said.

Manny started to tell them about Alison but the Cheltons both turned away when Lissa entered the kitchen. She looked chillingly stunning and very tall in a black sheath, ebony heels, pearls, and a partial veil.

Many said to her, "By the way, if you haven't made the final selection yet, I'd be honored to be one of the pall bearers."

"There are no pall bearers, Mandell," Lissa said. "This is just a memorial service. His ashes will be placed in a crypt."

"Ashes?" Manny said, surprised. "His body was cremated?"

Lissa shrugged. "That's what Stewart wanted."

Manny couldn't remember ever talking to Stewy about dying or anything related to funerals but somehow he always thought of his brother as a traditionalist. He just assumed Stewy would want to be buried in a traditional sort of way, with a traditional sort of service.

* * * * * * * * *

The cemetery resembled Arlington except on a smaller, slightly more modest scale. Lots of huge trees, gazebos, fountains, and acres and acres of manicured grass. The people who started to gather in front of the marble vault appeared to divide themselves into two groups. Lissa's family and friends on the right. Stewy's friends, mostly co-workers, on the left. Manny recognized a few of the co-workers and nodded. Then he looked around quickly and thought, "Shit."

He went to Lissa who was just getting out of the black limo with the help of a uniformed driver. "What about Mom?" he said quietly, touching her elbow. "Did you call the nursing home?"

The veil was in place. Lissa's eyes were almost hidden. "What would be the point? She wouldn't have been able to come. And even if she did, she wouldn't know what was going on."

Lissa's two brothers crowded Manny aside and guided their sister toward a row of folding chairs placed in front of the vault. A few minutes later, Dr. Hampton Grace from Ascension Lutheran began the service with one of his usual eloquent prayers, deeply intoned. At Grace's elbow was a slickly-groomed, broad-shouldered, but rather nerdy-looking man with short brown hair and a tiny mustache. Manny assumed he was someone from the funeral home until Grace introduced him as a pastoral assistant who would be available for counseling after the service, "if anyone feels the need." Then Grace introduced the president of the firm Stewy worked for, a man named Dustin Trout.

Trout gave a little speech about how valuable an employee Stewart was and how much he contributed to the firm's success. Major Wendell Jervis from the Salvation Army testified about Stewart Reed's caring heart and his love for mankind.

"Stewart loved all his brothers," Jervis said enthusiastically, "no matter *what* position they held on society's many levels."

Manny saw Lissa and her father exchange glances. It was a flat, emotionless, knowing kind of exchange.

There were a couple more short testimonials from people Manny didn't recognize. Then Dr. Hamilton Grace began his summation by telling about his own personal relationship with Stewart, how close the two of them had been.

"Almost like brothers," Grace said. "Brothers who shared the happy, glorious, sunny days of life. And brothers who shared the storm-tossed nights of blackness, too."

As Grace droned on about friendship and troubled times and private pains, Manny suddenly became aware of a disturbance of some sort going on behind him. He looked around to see a slender handsome well-dressed man, possibly in his mid-thirties. His curly black hair had an odd streak of gray or silver running back from his right temple. Lissa's two brothers appeared to be shoving the man backwards, away from the group. Manny wondered who the man was. He glanced at Stewy's boss and co-workers. They'd been distracted too, but they didn't seem to recognize him either.

It was apparent that Lissa's brothers were very angry but Manny couldn't hear their words. However, he and everyone else could clearly hear the other man say, "I've got as much right to be here as any of you!"

A second later, Dr. Grace's pastoral assistant appeared in front of the Chelton sons and was talking quietly to the young man, his palm outstretched, as though holding the Cheltons back. Then he led the man toward a sun-yellow Beamer that was double-parked beside the hearse. Another man was at the wheel of the Beamer, an older man. Moments later the two of them drove off and the pastoral assistant returned to Dr. Grace's side.

As Grace brought the service to a close, Manny watched the Beamer wend its way along the cemetery's narrow road, through a collection of pine trees and up a slight grade. The car stopped again and the young man got out. He leaned against the passenger door and watched the rest of the service. But by the time Grace had brought his final prayer to a double "Amen" the Beamer had disappeared.

* * * * * * * * *

The post-memorial luncheon was held at a quiet elegant restaurant not far from Stewy's home. While everyone sampled the buffet and offered condolences to the widow, Manny discretely asked several people if they knew who the man was who caused the disturbance. Most had no idea. One thought he might be a newspaper reporter. Stewy had been featured several times in the business and science section of one of D.C.'s daily papers. Another insisted he was "probably one of those ghouls who follow fire engines, videotape motorcycle accidents, and crash other people's funerals."

Dr. Grace's long horsey face flushed slightly below the eyes when Manny boxed him in the corner. "You know who he is don't you?" Manny said. "The man at the memorial service."

Grace's eyes shifted quickly to Lissa who was standing near her four children. They were giving their final goodbyes and thank yous. Grace's eyes snapped back to Manny and narrowed intensely. They were dark and sad.

"You're brother's at peace now," the pastor pleaded. "Can't we just let it go?"

"That's just it," Manny said, his voice quiet but very firm. "I don't know what we're letting go of."

Grace's eyes leaped back to Lissa. So did Manny's. She was now looking at both of them. Her expression was bland but her eyes were not.

Dr. Grace reached out and grabbed Manny's hand. He shook it awkwardly. "Forgive me. I really must be going."

Grace immediately went to Lissa and hugged the four kids. He gave their mother a brief hug as well and quickly left. Lissa glanced once more at Manny and then herded the children out the door.

* * * * * * * * *

There was something going on at BWI when Manny got there. He saw several policemen rushing toward the escalator. Four SWAT team members in full battle gear followed them minutes later. The passengers whispered among themselves. The ticket agent politely told Manny there would be a delay but that his flight would be announced as soon as possible. She advised him not to leave the secured area or he might be faced with another delay, a longer one.

Manny dropped his carryon next to a large artificial bush, shrugged off his jacket, slid off his tie, and dropped both on top of his carryon. Then he settled into an oddly shaped but relatively comfortable vinyl seat.

He felt depleted and sad, not just about Stewy but also about Lissa. He had stopped by the house one more time for one more attempt to understand. But her father was adamant. She was lying down, emotionally drained, and couldn't be disturbed.

Manny ran through the whole day again; what he should have done, perhaps; what he should have said; how he should have felt. But it was really too late. The day was over. The time had passed. Stewy was gone forever. And there was nothing he could do about any of it.

Gradually, and with a great deal of effort, Manny finally forced his mind back to his everyday work world. He made several calls on his cell, mainly to co-workers for updates about the Maldon tract. He called Alison, told her how wiped out he felt, and promised he'd call her the next night for sure. The last call was to Carley Mace, his new secretary. He called her at home and told her he'd be back in the office at eight a.m.

"How's the widow holding up?" Carley said. "Sounds like she's taking it pretty hard."

"What do you mean?"

"I hear someone crying in the background. You still at the house?"

Manny looked around and listened. Carley was right. Someone was crying, sobbing actually. "No, I'm at the airport."

He tried to peer between the branches of the silk-leafed bush and lowered his voice. "There's someone on the other side of this bush. A man, I think. Sounds like a major problem."

Manny talked to Carley a few more minutes about the memorial service and then hung up. He listened again and parted a few more branches but still couldn't see anything. Maybe it wasn't a man, he thought. It might be a woman who had a slightly deeper voice than normal.

"Why?" The voice pleaded, harsh and broken. The anguish and pain were obvious. "Why now, for God's sake? When things were finally coming together for us?"

Another voice came through the air a moment later, a louder voice, the voice of a cool but personable robot. That voice informed the passengers that flight two zero zero would start boarding in seven minutes. Manny got to his feet, slipped on his jacket, and draped the tie around his neck. Curious, he picked up his carryon and went around the back of the bush. Assuming a neutral face, he glanced at the crying person as he walked by.

It wasn't a woman. In fact, what he saw was two men sitting together on a teal-colored sofa on the other side of the bush. One had an arm draped around the other's shoulder. They could have been father and son. Except for the lines on the older man's face, the only difference between the two was the odd, silver-grey streak in the crying man's hair.

"I know," the older man was saying, his voice weary and kind. "I know."

Déjà vu: Dallas, 2050

("History repeats itself." We've all heard that phrase at least a hundred times. Sometimes it appears to be true; sometimes not. Let us hope that one particular time period in our history will NOT repeat itself. That would be the period depicted in this flash fiction about the future. —rh)

The first person I wanted to see when I got back was my old buddy, John. His wife, Brandi, had a smile that could brighten the sun. The woman who cracked the door was not smiling.

She peered out at me, uncertain. "David?" she finally said.

"I just got back last night," I said. "I wanted to see you guys first. John here?"

Brandi unchained and opened the door slowly. Her pale complexion nearly matched the odd flowing robe. She had always been a jeans and jersey person, rosy cheeks, laughing eyes.

"He's dead," she said, her voice flat and dull. "It happened two years ago."

"Dead?" I said, shocked. She closed and locked the door behind me. We sat on a grey vinyl sofa. "What happened?"

Brandi produced a small hand remote and pointed it toward a wide screen fastened to the wall. I stared at her.

"Everything is different now," she said. She gestured toward the screen.

A high def image blossomed and I immediately recognized my old college roommate. He was walking hand in hand with Brandi; the child was beside them. Around them on the sidewalk flowed an endless stream of people.

There was no sound with the image but John was talking and waving his arms. He looked older, but why not? Five earth-years had gone by since I left. But he still had that wide toothy grin.

When the family passed beyond the view of the first sidewalk camera, it was picked up by another camera, and then another as the family continued walking.

I could see some sort of a large logo on John's jacket. It was very white and looked like an "S."

I glanced at Brandi. "What's that on his back?"

A fist to her mouth, her dark eyes wide, she shook her head. "Watch."

A man wearing some kind of green work clothes suddenly stepped out of a doorway directly in front of them. He pulled a hand weapon from his clothes and aimed it at John's face.

There was a puff of smoke. Sections of John's head blew backwards and his body collapsed like a boneless scarecrow, face down on the sidewalk. As Brandi and the child dropped to their knees, horrified, an Enforcement officer in a black uniform approached on a two-wheeled personal unit.

As he rode by, he glanced at the body and at the sobbing woman and child. He continued on without a pause. The river of people also continued to flow around the body, and around the sobbing woman and child, as though nothing had happened.

As the screen went black, Brandi struggled to her feet. "You must go now. Quickly."

"But this is crazy," I said. "Why didn't that officer stop?"

Brandi pulled me to my feet, her eyes filled with fear. "Please, don't ask any questions. They'll come after us if you do."

"What do you mean? Who'll come after you?"

She yanked the door open and pushed me out into the hallway. "You must go away. And don't come back. Please," she begged.

"Brandi, wait!" I shouted as she closed the door in my face. I could hear the lock and chain.

All night, I thought about her warning, and about what I'd seen on the screen. But I couldn't let this go. Something had to be done.

* * * * * * * * *

The bloated red-faced officer sitting behind the Enforcement desk was wearing the same kind of black uniform I'd seen on Brandi's wall screen. He looked at my clothing and then at me. He pointed to a small metallic device on his desk. "Swipe your card."

"Card? What card?"

Through narrowed eyes he looked at my clothing again. "Where you from?"

"I was born here," I explained. "Right down the street. At St. Jude. I've been on one of our government's Exploratory Missions."

The man waved a chubby hand. "Everyone has to have a card now. Come back when you have yours."

"All I want is some information," I insisted. "About a murder. It happened less than two blocks from here. You must have a file on it."

The eyes turned into marble slits. "You are mistaken. There hasn't been a murder in this city in three years. Murder is illegal."

"I know it's illegal. But this one was captured on film. The man's wife and child were with him when it happened. One of your officers was there, too, but he didn't even stop."

The voice got louder. "You are mistaken, I said. There are no murders. Not anymore."

* * * * * * * * *

The Department of Statistical Compilations was on the third floor of a gleaming new glass tower. The smiling uniformed receptionist guided me to the History section. The uniformed man behind the counter was also smiling until I told him about the murder.

His lips became a thin gash. "You are mistaken. There hasn't been a murder in years. Not since the change."

I told him about the video. "The Enforcement guy ignored the whole thing," I said angrily. "Like it didn't happen."

"I'm sure he had his reasons," the man said. "What is this person's name? The one you claim was murdered."

"Smith. His name was John Smith. You must have some kind of record. Of him and his family."

The thin gash twisted. "That's impossible. There are no records of Smiths. Because there are no Smiths."

"What are you talking about?"

His laugh was more like a snort. "You *have* been away for a long time, haven't you? So I'll say it again. There are no Smiths of any kind. Not here. Not anywhere. Not anymore. You see, they have all been neutralized since the change. After all, that's what the change was all about, wasn't it?"

He looked me up and down again. "You say there's a wife and child?"

Shiny on the Low Dam Side

(As the narrator used to say on that thrilling old radio show: "Let us return once more to those exciting days of yesteryear"—in this case, the mid-1960s when test pilots really DID "fly by the seat of their pants."—rh)

At forty-eight hundred feet, Shiny leveled off again, lit up a White Owl stub and looked around at the spring-green mountains. Except for a haze of low dark clouds moving south across the distant New York-Pennsylvania border near Wellsboro, it was a perfect day for flying. Clear air, bright sun, not much wind.

It had been a good run. A routine takeoff. The ground crew turned back to the hangar as soon as the gear went up. At thirty-five hundred feet, Shiny had banked off to the northwest, picked up Pine Creek Valley and followed its twisting course until he was well into the state game lands beyond English Center. For an hour and a half he put the PA-31 through its paces about fifty miles north of Lock Haven. Everything checked out, everything ran smoothly. Just like the other one hundred and twelve hours of testing he'd done on the 31. True, there was a funny vibration today in the pedals when he brought it out of the fourth stall but the wheel held, the gauges were steady.

A few more stalls as light as a gull; a couple steep dives; some figure eights. Not a ripple. He decided to let engineering worry about the vibration. He'd tell them about it later. Right now he just wanted to relax a bit, see the sights, enjoy a smoke.

Shiny had been with the company since it opened the factory back in the thirties and at sixty-eight he was still the best test pilot they had. The Old Man trusted him and the trust gave Shiny an ebullient cocky attitude about nearly everything. Especially when he was flying a brand new model.

The feeling was justified. Nearly twenty million dollars and three years of work had gone into the design and building of the eight-passenger Navajo, still called the 31 by Shiny and nearly everyone else who put it together. With the exception of one-half of the fuselage, some wire harnesses, a set of seats and two wings scattered around the factory, it was the only Navajo in the world. And, outside of the Fed jockeys, so far Shiny was the only one who'd taken her up. It was *his* baby.

And a damn good one. In fact, as far as Shiny was concerned it was the best plane the company had ever built. A lot of other people thought so too. The FAA passed it without a murmur. It drew record crowds at three different air shows. A new assembly line was being put together at the factory and orders were starting to pour in from short-hop commuter lines all over the country.

In the past four months since he took it up for the first time, the 31 had become a graceful extension of Shiny's own short squat body. "That baby," he liked to say over a cold glass of beer, "would make a goddam eagle turn green."

Shiny loved to fly. Better than anything. But after logging thirty-five-thousand-plus hours in thirty-five years he'd had his share of scrapes and near misses. Like the time the controls froze up when he threw a green and white Apache into a rivet-popping spin. It was the first time he ever bailed out. It would also be the last time. As he floated toward the ground, the Apache flattened itself out, roared up the valley and promptly buried itself in a barn full of string beans.

He'd never live that one down.

Long before that, soon after he picked up his first ticket, he got too close to a ragwing's prop and lost half his scalp. He was laid up for a while but it healed over, finally. He still ran a wondering hand over his smooth pate every time he thought about it.

A click against the window on the co-pilot side caught Shiny's ear. He studied the wing and the starboard engine but couldn't see anything wrong. The prop was gleaming: a silver circle in the afternoon sun.

Looping around in another flat circle, Shiny decided to nose the 31 north along Pine Creek again and look at the weather. Then, as he leveled off, another vibration hit the plane. This one—stronger and stiffer than the first—came juddering up through the seat and down his arms. The right wing dipped suddenly. Two more clicks bounced off the window.

Battling the wheel now, he throttled back and checked the gauges again. The fuel was a bit on the low side but he knew about that. He hadn't planned on staying up very long today anyway. The oil pressure was up just a hair on the starboard engine; everything else looked okay.

He glanced out at the wings and both engines and then at the gauges once more. His round red face warped into a puzzled frown. After a time, he tried to shrug it away. Nothing more serious than a loose fairing, probably.

As he continued north, the hazy line of clouds was not so hazy anymore. The rounded puffs were turning rapidly into fat lumbering towers. Shiny studied the clouds carefully and then looked at his watch. He'd been up almost two hours, a storm was brewing, fuel getting low, and the plane was acting up a bit. He radioed in that he was heading home.

He swung the plane around and was soon looking down on Pine Creek Valley again. He could see the silver snake of Pine Creek itself slithering away toward the West Branch Valley. And off to the west, at the end of the Valley, a plume of smoke marked the paper mill, the town, the factory, and the air strip. On the south side of the Valley was a collection of breast-like humps, all covered with trees and bone-white boulders.

He couldn't imagine a worse place for an airplane factory: erratic weather, snowy winters, a flooding river, a sprawling dirty town at the end of the runway, slab-sided valleys, and wooded mountains in every direction. But the town had practically given the factory to the Old Man in the late 30s just to generate some jobs in—what it was at the time—a financially depressed area.

Shiny wondered what it would be like to work out of Wichita with nothing but wheat fields and prairies all the way to the horizon. But what the hell, he thought, at least we don't have to deal with tornadoes every five minutes.

He popped open his lighter and was about to touch the flame to his dying cigar when the whole plane went into convulsions. Violent thundering vibrations sent the gauges wild and the cigar flying. A loud clank of metal ripped through the plane's skin just behind the plane's only two seats. Pieces of paint, hot aluminum, fiberglass insulation, and wire connectors showered the cabin like sparkles of fire. Some of the debris stung Shiny's neck. He slapped at it reflexively, his face gone white.

Even before he glanced at the starboard engine again he knew what had happened. One of the prop blades had broken off and whip-sawed through the fuselage; in one side and out the other.

An instant later a fiber glass fairing, shaken loose by the clattering vibrations, tore away from the butt of the right wing and bounced off the tail section, putting a small gash in one of the stabilizers. An instant after that, a line of wing rivets was starting to jiggle fuzzily.

Five minutes of this, Shiny thought, and the whole damn plane would fly apart.

A whistle of air escaped through his teeth as he fought the wheel and the vicious drag. All the twins could fly on one engine, easily. He'd done it many times. But they couldn't fly on one wing.

Mechanically, but with the taste of rust in his mouth, Shiny gripped the wheel with one hand while the other hand moved rapidly, flicking switches, pulling levers, shutting down. Just as the 31 started wobbling, veering sharply toward the mountains, the starboard engine petered away and quietly died.

Gradually the booming noise faded; the vibrations smoothed out; the plane came back into trim. The feathered broken prop now spun slowly but jerkily in the wind, one blade a full eight inches shorter than the other.

"No more of that crap," he said, his voice shaking. He thumped the wheel lightly with the heel of his hand.

He radioed in that he'd had some problems with one of the props and had to shut down one of the engines. Fumbling around on the floor with one hand, he retrieved his cigar stub and clamped it between his teeth again. He located the lighter beside his foot, cursed all prop makers, and lit up. Slowly the ruddy color returned to his face.

Puffing on the stub, he ran one hand across his bald head and then reached around to the back of the headrest. Shreds of foam rubber oozed out of the slashed leather. His fingers dug into the foam. The gash was deep, ending less than an inch from the back of his neck.

Shiny squinted his eyes and let out a cloud of acrid smoke.

The plane settled down again and ran smoothly on one engine. A short time later Pine Creek Valley opened out onto the farmland of West Branch Valley. He flew over Route 220 and its winding predecessor, the River Road. Beyond the roads and the West Branch River, Shiny carefully banked the 31 and headed up-valley toward the west, toward the air strip.

The altimeter read forty-five hundred, a bit higher than he wanted to be. But there was still plenty of distance between the McElhattan Bridge and the strip. He would have plenty of time to bring the 31 down into a landing pattern. All he had to do was ease the wheel forward and the nose would drop.

Only it didn't.

The wheel slid forward all right but nothing happened.

Shiny turned the wheel and touched the pedals, first to the right and then to the left. The wing tips dipped as they should. He pulled the wheel back and the horizon dropped away. He pushed the wheel forward again. The horizon come up to the crosshairs but it wouldn't go any farther. Straight and level was as close as he could get to a descent.

"Hell," he said, crammed the cigar into an ashtray and snapped it shut. He twisted around in his seat, trying to get a look at the starboard wing. It looked okay except for a vee-shaped dent that ran all the way to the cabin and ended at the slit behind the co-pilot seat. The skin of the wing wasn't cut through, only creased.

Shiny glanced at the two whistling gashes on each side of the cabin but didn't see much. He knew there was nothing important behind the sliced leather panels; some wiring for the cabin lights and cigarette lighters, that's about all.

He was over the Sorgen farm now and could see the airstrip drawing closer. Lips now tightened into a grim pucker, Shiny eased the wheel forward again. Nothing. He pulled it in toward his horseshoe belt buckle and the 31 nosed up. Forward again and the plane leveled off at forty-six hundred feet. After a few more thrust-forward-pull-backs, the plane had climbed to forty-nine hundred and was past the strip and well over the town. It was then he noticed a third wind-sound.

In addition to the two shrill whistles, a sucking low-pitched moan was coming up from behind the co-pilot seat. He jiggled the seat adjustment knob trying to get the back of the seat to tilt forward. It was stuck.

Shiny checked the gauges again and the horizon glass and then the feathered engine. The broken prop was still flopping around slowly. The temperature of the remaining engine had gone up but not enough to worry about.

His feet steady on the pedals, he let go of the wheel. With one hand, he yanked at the seat knob again. With the other hand he whacked the back of the co-pilot seat. It finally broke free at the waist and tipped forward.

Through a gaping cross-wise gash in the floor, Shiny could see the city, dribbling way into farmland. "Damn," he said and glared at the hole.

It appeared to be about three inches wide, maybe eight inches long. Around it, the pushed up edges of the blue carpet had been cut clean. Wedged into the ragged slash, the end of a cable stuck up like a silver finger nipped off at the first joint. Beside it, half a dozen white and red wires, cut and splayed, bobbed in the wind like spider legs.

He could see what happened. When it broke, the propeller blade split into two parts. One part drove through the cabin, the other sliced up through the belly of the plane and almost through the floor.

Shiny took a deep breath and squirmed around in his seat, facing forward again. He tentatively goosed the wheel but the horizon remained level. It was the second cut that did the job. It had screwed up the flap controls, but good.

Snatching the mike from its cradle he flicked the switch and brought it up to his mouth.

"Jack, this is Shiny. You there?" The static was interrupted by a piercing squeal and then more static. "This is PA-31 calling the tower. You hear me, Jack?"

"Yeah, Shiny. Thought it was you. Saw you going over. Go ahead."

"What's the strip like?"

"You're clear on 18."

"Uh-huh. Well look, Jack. I got kind of a problem here. Over."

"Go ahead."

"One of the props came apart. Cut through the cabin. A couple wires parted and at least one cable's cut clean through."

Shiny looked back over the headrest again. To the left of the slash he saw an ominous bulge in the floor of the plane. God only knows what was ripped up under *that*, he thought. He turned around and shook his head. He mumbled something into the mike.

"Say again."

Shiny's bald head, usually pink, took on a scarlet glow. "I said. The goddam crate doesn't want to come *down*."

From forty-nine hundred feet, the airstrip looked like a sidewalk crowded on both sides with a couple dozen toy planes. It had been a slow year. Unsold Apaches and Pawnees were lined up all over the place with barely enough room to land.

Well, he'd been in tighter spots. He'd figure something out. As long as the weather held up a while longer there really wasn't a problem. If he cut back the air speed far enough the plane would start losing altitude whether the flaps were working or not. A tricky landing, maybe, but not impossible; despite the cluttered strip. And the mechanical problems.

Might as well make another go 'round, he thought, lose some more altitude, see what happens.

He followed the usual 18 pattern; west over the town, south at the gap, east along Bald Eagle Mountain, north at the McElhattan Bridge, and then west again to the strip. An imaginary oval. He'd been around it thousands of times.

Over the town, Shiny dipped each wing slightly and looked around. He could see the river bordering the town on one side and the low flood-control dam. A handful of skiers were skimming along behind speeding boats between the dam and the Lockport bridge. Directly below was the old steel bridge that connected Lock Haven to the motley prickle of tumble-down houses and shuttered stores of Lockport.

Past the bridge to the northwest, the Valley pinched away into a narrow steep-sided canyon that carried the West Branch River into Clinton County .

Nobody wanted to fly up that way if they could avoid it. The Renovo Canyon was a gusty bastard no matter what the wind was like anywhere else.

Off to the west: rolling farmland, valleys, and low tumbling hills spread westward most of the way to State College.

Well past the town, Shiny banked off to the south, swung around to the east and throttled back sharply. The plane started to settle into the thickening air like a fat man in a tub of warm mud. If he throttled back too much the bugger would stall. He wanted to avoid that. He still didn't know how much control was left; which cables and what wires were still intact. But the plane was sinking slowly and that was good. He wanted to drop another thousand feet before he got to the McElhattan Bridge.

He followed the pattern without a hitch. The plane was flying well enough although the air was getting hellishly bumpy as he pushed north over Bald Eagle Mountain again. Swinging back toward the airstrip he saw where the bumps were coming from. Low clouds, rain, and a few barbs of lightning were rolling their way down Pine Creek Valley; they were closing fast. If the storm was as big as it looked it would pour into West Branch Valley like a thick grey molasses in half an hour, maybe less. He wanted to be on the ground by then.

Shiny knew he could complete the whole landing pattern in about fifteen minutes if everything was working the way it should—or could—considering the circumstances. Throttling back to lose altitude, however, would also slow him down.

"Hell with it," he said with a shrug. "If things get too tight I can always set 'er down in a bean field. Let the wrecking crew truck it back to the plant."

He pointed the 31 toward the airstrip and glanced at the altimeter. Under three thousand feet now and still coming down. Dropping the gear at this speed would eat up another couple hundred feet.

He hit the switch and heard the groan of the gear unfolding and locking into position. Shiny arched his back and then settled into the plush foam-filled seat. "No sweat," he said.

He casually glanced at the instrument panel and looked away. A tiny dull pin pricked at the back of his mind. He listened carefully. Everything sounded all right, considering. But there was something. He couldn't put his finger on it.

Passing over the farm houses a mile from the strip he could see a few cows standing idly beneath a large elm tree. A John Deere tractor and a muddy pickup were parked in the middle of another field. But there was a third field, newly planted, but wide and clear; it was a good half mile long. Plenty of room to come down if he had to. Telephone and electric lines, true, he thought, but he could probably slip under them.

A gust of wind bounced the 31 sideways. Shiny's eyes swept across the gauges as he gripped the wheel. When the plane straightened out again the gnawing pin prick erupted into a white hot knife.

His eyes darted back to the instrument panel. He tapped a glass with a broad stumpy finger. "Well, hell," he growled. "Either the light's not working or the freaking gear isn't down all the way."

But he heard it going down. It couldn't be that. He thought for a while and finally decided the warning light wasn't working, probably because a bulb had burned out. Wouldn't be the first time. Nor the last. But he couldn't deny it. His gut was starting to quiver.

The airstrip was coming up and he was dead on course; the nose was planted firmly on the center line. At either end of the strip he saw two fire engines pulling into position. "Bastards aren't taking any chances, are you?" he muttered. "And you'll be disappointed as hell when I set this crate down."

As he passed directly over the field at two thousand feet a crackling voice exploded from the speaker.

"Shiny? Try your gear again. There's only one wheel showing."

"Oh for chrissake," Shiny groaned, glaring at the tower.

Beneath the nose he could see the windsock, high on a pole above the hangar. On the last go 'round it was drooping like a spent rubber. Now, bulging full, the sock was lashing around from side to side. A sheaf of papers from somebody's clipboard whirled across the runway: a tiny fluttering cloud.

"Heavy gusts and one wheel," he muttered again. He pictured the 31 coming in, ripping up a dozen Apaches and a covey of crop dusters, all squatting along either side of the strip. And, in the process, scattering itself—and him—all over hell.

He jabbed at the switch and heard the gear groan up and then down again. The crystal red light refused to come on. He could also feel a tug to the left, probably from the drag of the one extended landing gear. He cursed himself for not noticing it before.

Shiny eased back on the wheel and the plane nosed up as it passed over the town again. Turning into a goddam merry-go-round, he thought. He glanced at the river, the low dam and, further east, the Lockport Bridge. The water skiers were gone and most of the boats were tied up or were being loaded onto boat trailers. The sky was turning grey and a few drops of rain splattered against the windshield.

He fumbled another White Owl out of his pocket, stripped off the cellophane and tossed it over his shoulder. He bit off the tip, *phlupt!* it onto the floor and chomped down on the unlighted cigar.

Bringing the plane around again, gingerly, he headed down the due-east straight of the landing pattern oval, parallel to the strip but beyond Bald Eagle Mountain. He could see the thick low clouds and the fog spreading out into West Branch Valley, nearly swallowing the McElhattan Bridge. He cursed all prop makers once more and shifted around in his seat, his broad shoulders hunched over the wheel.

The radio squawked, this time with more storm-brought static, but he managed to pick up a few words.

" … the tower … fire engines …we can do … please advise, over?"

"Give me a goddam minute to think for chrissake," he said to himself. His voice was a raspy grunt. Shifting the unlit cigar to the other side of his mouth, he picked up the mike and flicked the switch. "Standby, standby, standby," he said in a monotone.

He jammed the mike back on its hook and chewed the White Owl to tatters. The gas gauge was hovering on E; maybe enough for another pass but not much more. He knew he had to come up with some sort of plan and pretty damn quick.

Still in the pattern, a few hundred feet south along Bald Eagle Mountain, he could no longer see the tower or the airstrip. It was tucked in close to the slope and blocked from his view.

He had a sneaky gut feeling that even if he could see it from this angle he wouldn't be able to see it very well. The wall of fog and rain was now moving up the West Branch Valley and over the town like a runaway freight train.

If he had to, he could still set down on that flat open bean field. But with no landing gear and heavy cross-wind gusts, plus the barns, cows, tractors, telephone and electric lines running all the hell over the place, it would be a hairy maneuver, even on a clear day. In this fog …

He thought briefly of trying to outrun the weather. But to push the 31 over the mountain and nose it back toward the landing strip now would bring him in 'way too high. He'd have to keep going, at least to the McElhattan bridge, before turning back.

Shiny pulled gently on the wheel. He didn't want to climb much higher; losing another couple hundred feet would take too much time. But a glimpse of the whole freaking valley would be mighty nice.

As the plane rose slightly, Shiny leaned forward, craning his thick red neck, trying to see over the mountain. His eyes darted from the ridge to the altimeter and back again. The second he could see over it he'd level off.

The mountains that hemmed in the airstrip and humped away in all directions were not high as mountains go, most of them topped out around two thousand feet. But high or not, you couldn't see *through* them, and you sure as hell couldn't *fly* them either.

The northern slope of Bald Eagle finally slid away beneath the port wing and disappeared into the fog. He could see the Valley all right. By now it was a roiling thick mass of cotton batting, closed in on both sides by dull grey-green mounds.

He knew where he was, roughly; over the McElhattan Bridge, although he couldn't see it. He peered out over the nose of the plane toward Williamsport. Nothing in that direction either, nothing but fog.

Still turning around in his seat looking for something, anything, a clear patch of ground anywhere, Shiny snatched up the mike again and pressed the switch. He brought the mike up to his mouth and rammed it right into the end of his unlit cigar.

He cursed and spat the mangled brown cylinder onto the floor. "Jack? For chrissake what's happening down there?"

" … got a line of flares along 18," the voice said, sounding flat and thin, almost buried in the static. "And fire trucks at both ends."

Shiny's dome turned scarlet. "Je-sus Christ. I *know* about that. I'm talking about the goddam weather. Over."

"Not good," said the voice. "Visibility down to one hundred yards. Any ideas?"

"Ideas?" He snorted. "I can't see a goddam thing. The gear ain't working. I got one dead engine, the other one's heating up. And a quart of fumes in the tank. You want ideas? I'll give you one. You can cram this goddam crate right up your goddam ass. Over."

After a moment, the voice went on calmly. "If you can get your gear up, maybe you could belly in. The runway's soaked … layer of foam … hold down … fire."

The remaining engine was starting to miss as Shiny arrowed the nose into West Branch Valley again. "Damn, bitch!" he said to the plane. "You are really putting it to me today, ain't you?"

He took a deep breath and smeared some of the sweat from the side of his stubbly jaw. He laid the mike on his lap and tightened the shoulder harness a couple more notches. He checked the gauges.

The plane was dropping smoothly when the remaining engine started sputtering. It cut out, sputtered again, coughed a few times. Then it died.

Somewhere up ahead, about two miles, lay a strip of macadam. All he had to do was find it.

Shiny's face, suddenly pale, cinched up into a determined scowl. He flicked the gear switch and heard the one good wheel folding back up into the wing. Even if the strip was knee deep in foam, a gear-up landing would rip out the whole belly of the plane. As for his own butt ...

He turned that channel off.

He had come down with a dead stick before and remembered the same eerie engineless quiet that he heard now. Nothing but the thin shriek of the wind over the wings. This time, however, there were a few other sounds as well. Like the small screams coming through the slits in the cabin wall. Like the deep devilish moan coming up through the floor. Even without the holes and with the gear down he wouldn't exactly be jumping for joy. He was convinced once more that anybody who sailed around in one of the balsa wood gliders ought to be locked up in a crazy house. Floating around without an engine wasn't flying; it was bull-eyed insanity.

He picked up the mike and thumbed the switch. "I got a mile and half, two miles. Tell those smoke-eaters to hook up their goddam hoses. I'm coming in. Gear up. Standby."

An updraft bumped the plane slightly but the descent continued, smooth and steady. He was still skinning along the top of the fog when the altimeter hit five hundred feet, then four-ninety, four-eighty, four-seventy.

The swirling mist, like a wet grey shroud, sucked up and under the wings, blotting out everything. Shiny's eyes, cold and slitted, tried to pick out anything that was darker, or lighter than the fog bank. Anything that would give him some clue as to how far ahead the strip was.

A dark shape appeared off the starboard wing. He fought an impulse to veer away from it. But the shape was gone before he could identify it.

If it was the Sorgen's barn he was coming in too fast and too low. If it was the Byler's barn he was too close to the mountain.

For an instant he thought he saw River Road black-snaking its way toward the airstrip. But it, too, faded away in the fog before he could get a fix.

Shiny ran a hand quickly over his bald head and then wiped his hand across his knee. He leaned into the harness, a criss-crossed vice across his chest. His head tipped forward to get a few inches closer to the fog.

"What the hell?" he said as a pale flat band twisted away beneath the plane. For an instant he was confused. He knew it was the river but what in the holy hell was it doing *there*!

He was drifting too wide. The road he'd seen wasn't the River Road. It was Route 220.

His brain churned frantically. His eyes snapped back and forth, from the altimeter to the fog and back again. He was down to two hundred feet and still the ground was hidden. A faint line of trees emerged off to the left, coming fast. And all of a sudden he knew where he was.

"God *damn!*" he said quietly and pinched his lips tighter. Beyond the trees, he knew, was the landing strip. He was coming in wide, sure enough. A goddam half *mile* wide!

A faint pink glow well off to the left marked the flares. At this rate, he'd be splattered all over Main Street between Janet's Restaurant and the Texas Lunch.

A hard left would send him cross-wise across the field and into the factory, if he managed to miss the control tower. And if he managed to snowplow his way through a solid row of unsold planes. Fat chance of coming out of that. A hard right would send him into a wall of granite crouching above Lockport.

The plane suddenly lifted as a buffet of wind swept up and under the nose. Then, like a trapdoor falling away, a hazy gap opened in the fog. Buildings loomed everywhere: the Mohawk Motel, the jumbled trailer park, the creamery; all sliding by in a ghostly blur.

Another gust of wind shoved the plane to the right and the gap in the fog widened. He could see the river. At least part of it. A smazy blur at first and then clearer.

The wind funneling down through the gust-driven pinched-off Renovo Canyon had opened up a short patch of choppy water. Not much. But, maybe, enough.

The low dam was slipping toward him twenty feet below the plane. On both sides of the river, the corridor of fog held tight. At the end of the patch of open water—but still in the fog—was the bridge; complete with steel girders and massive concrete pilings.

"Christ," he said and flicked the switch. His voice, clipped and loud, stabbed at the mike. "I'm coming down in the river. Between the dam and the Lockport Bridge. Get your asses *over* here!"

Shiny tossed the mike aside and grasped the wheel with both hands. He was still too damn high.

He shoved the wheel all the way forward but the plane continued to drop at its own pace. The dam rushed away beneath him. Concrete and steel were shaping themselves in the gloom.

He glanced up at the phantom structures just long enough to see a small dark truck bump over the sidewalk and jolt silently into the steel in the middle of the bridge.

His eyes jerked around. A few small boats were tied up along the river bank where the fog thinned out. Two figures waved and started running toward the bridge.

An instant later with a pounding roar the belly of the 31 slammed into the water, bounced up and then slammed down again.

Shiny's head snapped back against the torn headrest and then front again as the plane leaped twice more. His breath came in gasps. He gripped the wheel tighter. The next slam sent a spray of water everywhere, drowning the windshield, blotting out the bridge, blotting out everything.

Careening wildly now on the rock-hard water, the plane clattered and thumped. Shiny's head thudded sideways against his shoulder. He fought the sharp stab of pain and blackness, cramming the wheel hard to the right.

Again he was flung forward as the plane lurched crazily, one wing catching the water. The wheel was ripped from his hands. An iron-bound X stamped itself across his chest but the harness held. Then, abruptly, with a bone-crushing wrench, the 31 jolted to a stop.

Shiny could feel the weight of his own body; he was hanging, suspended over the wheel. Straight down, beyond the nose of the plane, the water swirled.

For a horrible eternal moment he knew he was going over, upside down in the river. The 31 teetered; the port wing angled sharply into the water, the other wing pointed toward the sky, the tail almost straight up.

Then, quietly, gently, in a slow motion nightmare, the tail settled back down and the nose rose up.

With a wet *fump!* the belly of the plane slapped against the river and water started pouring in through the floor.

A new jolt of panic leaped into Shiny's throat. Jostling, bubbling, hissing; the 31 started to sink.

"Jesus Christ!" Shiny said, "I'm gonna freaking drown!" He squirmed around frantically, gulping back the sudden nausea, clawing at the harness.

Then, finally, with the water up over the wings, he felt the solid river bottom bump against the plane's belly.

The water stopped rising.

With clumsy fingers, Shiny unhooked the shoulder harness and looked around at the grey fog. The black dripping steel of the bridge was almost directly overhead. A concrete piling, a wing-length wide, stood five yards away.

He let out a lip-fluttering sigh. "Too close," he said, wagging his head and swallowing hard. "Too damn close."

For a moment, the only thing he could hear was the peaceful almost pleasant sound of water swishing over the wings. Then he heard shouts. Grinning faces were running toward him along the river bank, arms waving; car horns were blowing.

With shaking hands, Shiny fumbled around in his shirt pocket and then climbed stiffly out of his seat. His gut was still shuddering but that would pass. A couple inches of cold water splashed around his shoes as he moved unsteadily through the plane's seatless passenger area. The door was sprung and slightly twisted but a faltering kick and then a harder one, scraped it open. Someone was rowing frantically toward him in a battered brown rowboat.

Shiny touched his lighter to a long badly bent stogie and sent a cloud of blue smoke out and over the river. He felt tired, weary; his knees threatened to buckle.

"Well," he said to the plane. "You may be a waterlogged son of a bitch but you're still in one piece."

And so am I, he wanted to add.

The rowboat bumped into the side of the plane beneath the door and Jack's grinning face looked up at him through the dwindling rain. "You brought 'er down," he said with a baboon giggle. His thick glasses were spotted with raindrops. "She handle all right? I mean, how'd she handle?"

Shiny patted the aluminum skin and sent another cloud of smoke in the air. "Doesn't float worth a damn," he said. "But outside of that, not bad. Not bad at all."

Harry Fredericks and the Almighty

*(Harry Fredericks was never very good at facing reality: real reality, that is, not his own private version. But this time, real reality really **is** staring him in the face. And it will not go away. Does that mean he'll stop using the avoidance techniques that have served him so well for seventy-plus years? You've got to be kidding. They've always worked before. Why not this time?—rh)*

Considering the abuses, illnesses, and the endless series of one physical and emotional collapse after another, youthful wiry seventy-four-year-old Harry Fredericks is incredibly healthy looking. His skin is clear with the perpetual color of pale copper. His chestnut eyes are steady beneath bushy brows. His hairy arms have rope-like muscular biceps, thick forearms, heavy wrists. His hands are strong and large, the skin leathery, cracked, the nails blunt and rough-textured. His stomach is flat, his hips narrow, his legs thin, bird-like.

Though his hairline has receded somewhat and a small circle toward the back of his head is thinly covered, the rest of his light brown hair is thick and completely devoid of even the slightest trace of grey. It's the hair of a younger man, combed straight back without a part. In the summer it becomes blondish, dry, straw-like. In the winter it turns dark, becomes coarse and oily. In the fall it smells of burning leaves; in the spring of rain and earth.

Harry Fredericks has the look—and rightly so—of a man who has worked the soil, tinkered with oily engines, spaded dozens of black-earthed gardens, cut leather for shoes, operated weaving machines and fashioned hand-rolled cigars out of broad-leaved home-grown tobacco. All the while he has done these things, and especially during times of turmoil and conflict, he has read the Bible prominently and prayed silently, but with noticeably moving lips.

If you asked him point-blank, Harry probably wouldn't come right out and say he's a saved, heaven-bound Christian, even if he does firmly believe it. That would be tempting fate … and God. He would insist, however, with his broad forceful Pennsylvania Dutch accent, that he's a God-fearing man and always has been.

He is also a man who has worked as many different jobs, moved to as many different towns, joined nearly as many different churches as he's lived years. For Harry Fredericks is a runner; a runner from life, a runner from reality, a runner from himself. But unless he can change God's mind once more, his days of running are soon to end. And he knows it. Three doctors have given him the same report.

Through that youthful-looking, healthy-looking, resilient-looking body flow the malignant seeds of cancer. Legs braced, arms folded, eyes burning; just ahead stands death: the ultimate reality.

Insidiously sucking away the very life that supports it, the cancer is spreading and destroying his body piecemeal. And while the cancer is beginning to destroy his body another kind of cancer has for years been destroying his soul. It's a cancerous drain of will and strength caused by his endless running from everything. Even now, even from death, Harry's convinced there must be a way to save himself. There must be a direction to run to; and there is.

As always before in his life one exit remains. The one final maneuver, the one final 'out' is through the door marked 'God.' Toward that door Harry is moving with all possible speed; he must not allow himself to die.

****

Since the day he was born in the large cream and brown frame house in Sneidersburg, Pennsylvania, the world of Harry Fredericks has revolved around one person: Harry Fredericks. His father, Isaac, was a stern taciturn tyrant; aloof, detached except for the rage disguised as discipline that he ladled out to both Harry and Vera, Harry's mother, with generous amounts of cruelty.

When Isaac died in a hay baler accident two weeks after buying a life insurance policy, both Vera and twelve-year-old Harry heaved a huge sigh of relief. Free at last, Vera then took over the raising of her only child with the carte blanche permissiveness of an insane check writer. Everything Harry wanted, Harry got. Everything Harry didn't want, Harry quickly walked or ran away from, with Vera's blessings.

One day when he was fourteen, Harry was disciplined at school for not doing his homework. He went home that night and told his mother he wasn't going back to school anymore. And he didn't.

One day when he was eighteen, Harry saw a brand-new fire-engine-red Ford convertible in a neighbor's driveway. He told his mother he wanted one. So Vera Fredericks mortgaged the cream and brown house and bought Harry a brand-new fire-engine-red Ford convertible.

One day when he was twenty-one, Harry came running to Vera, frightened, with the news that a quiet motherly little girl named Annie McKay was pregnant, by him, and her eight ox-shouldered brothers were after his hide. He had to run away. If he didn't, he'd either have to marry Annie or get all four of his limbs broken. Vera agreed with him; the best thing to do was run away.

A few months later, Harry's mother died from a blood infection, leaving Harry in dire need of an all-forgiving surrogate mother. He returned to the now decidedly pregnant Annie McKay and married her, with the blessing of Annie's eight brothers. He also fell to his knees, asked God for forgiveness, and promised to do better in the future. By then, the pattern of his life was well set.

****

As it was with his mother, so it was with his wife, his children, his employers, his friends. All came in a poor second whenever a choice had to be made about whose feelings, needs and wants were served first. If, like an infant, he felt full, pampered and content, Harry Fredericks would then—and only then—be capable of looking beyond himself. The rest of the time he was only aware vaguely that the people around him were actually people, individuals with their own individual feelings and needs.

Even these flashes of insight were extremely short-lived. It was as if—when he became aware that there were problems and lives beyond his own—he would mentally pack up and retreat into safer, less threatening, less complicated ground: he would retreat into himself.

When those outside problems and lives forced themselves on him he would do the same thing physically. He would pack up Annie and the children, burn the bridges he couldn't cross, and retreat to another job, another town, and always another church. For church and God were the pivotal escape points around which Harry continued to revolve—if somewhat erratically—all his life.

Vera Fredericks had been a lonely doting woman with only two reasons for living: Harry and the First Reformed Lutheran Church of Sneidersburg. From the time he could be carried in a blanket, Vera had taken him there every Sunday, morning and evening, and every Wednesday night for the weekly prayer meeting.

There, amidst maudlin hymns, endless tremblyvoiced prayers, and heavy-eyed drowsiness, Harry was fed an austere dogma of superstition, hypocrisy, and self-righteousness. It was a dogma he was later to use flagrantly, whenever the occasion warranted. That meant whenever his race from reality turned Life into an especially jumbled mess, which it did countless times. When that happened, the same procedure invariably followed. He would screech to a halt, start to crumble, and then fall apart completely, unable to cope with anything.

Finally he would drop to his knees and waddle back to the fold—a new one this time—and he would be the penitent backslider seeking just one more chance. The good people of the new flock would gather around their repentant prodigal, reorganize his life for him, find him another house to rent, another job, and then send him back into the world; a contrite righteous-filled man. And wife Annie, always hopeful, would think that *this* time it was going to be different.

But the process repeated itself mechanically, almost predictably, over the years. It was a sort of slate-washing rejuvenation, but always with a new church and a new group of brethren.

His first spiritual shepherd, the Reverend Karl Hermann, pastor of the First Reformed Lutheran Church of Sneidersburg, undoubtedly had a greater, more lasting effect on Harry than the Biblical Truths he supposedly preached. For Karl Hermann was a drunkard, a gambler, and an adulterer whose single guideline of behavior off the pulpit seemed to be: Don't do as I do, do as I say.

In later years, in his own life, Harry modified this rule slightly until it went: What I *say* I'm doing is far more important than what I'm *actually* doing. This rule was applied not only to Harry's relationship with other people. It was especially applied to his ongoing, if erratic, relationship with his own particular version of God.

Though Harry's God is the undisputed ruler of the universe; though He causes everything that happens *to* happen; though He prevents everything that doesn't happen *from* happening; He can easily be deceived. At least by Harry. Because like Harry's helpful church brethren, Harry's God knows only what Harry tells Him, and hears only what Harry says aloud.

He is a God who can't read thoughts or discern the real motives behind actions. Nor can He see the contradictions between what Harry says and what Harry does. In short, then: Harry's God is a gullible fool.

And yet, for some unknown reason, this very same God has planted the seeds of cancer in Harry's body and Harry doesn't understand it. He's sure it must have been a mistake of some sort. But the cancer is there. Of that even Harry is sure. The cancer is there and it is going to kill him. Unless …

Unless he can pull off this one final maneuver. Unless he can convince God that *this* time he really means it; *this* time there will be no backsliding; *this* time he'll be a child of God like no other. If only the cancer is miraculously removed.

But Harry Fredericks is not worried. He sees no major problem here. He's sure he can persuade God one more time that he deserves another chance. After all, he's been doing just that all his life.

And this is the task of Harry Fredericks with six more months to live.

Shadow Talk

(Communication can be a very difficult—sometimes stressful—endeavor. It often results in misunderstandings, miscommunications, mistakes, confusion, emotion, and sometimes emptiness. And yet it is the only thing that can truly unite us—as much as two separate entities can be united. And so we keep on trying. The only other choice is separation—and its painful extension—isolation.—rh)

The hot wet vinyl stuck to Derek Downs' skin every time he shifted around on the creaky aluminum lounge. His midnight blue bikini briefs looked black; the skin of his naked chest, arms, legs and feet looked bone white in the pale moonlight that angled in from the cow pasture. The briefs felt sticky, too; damp. He tugged at them impatiently and then moved their contents around to a less bunched-up collection. He glanced back over his shoulder when his wife ambled through the doorway and then out onto the screened-in porch.

Trudy Hiller-Downs was carrying a tall wet glass in one hand, a damp towel in the other. She was wearing a dark silky wrapper that ended several inches above her knees. A white rope-like belt cinched the wrapper around her waist.

"You going to shower?" Trudy said.

"In a minute," Derek said.

His right hand swung lazily off the arm of the chair toward the porch floor. When it swung back up again his fingers were wrapped around a fat oversized and nearly empty shot glass. The glass made a tiny clinking noise as it brushed the nearly full bottle of Chivas Regal that was standing uncapped next to the chair's gritty aluminum legs. Derek drained the glass with one toss and then rested its smoothness on his stomach.

Trudy studied her husband for a moment. Then she approached the empty wooden swing and draped the towel over the wood-slat back. The swing bobbled slightly from its long chains. "So how did the midterms go?" she said.

Derek shrugged. "Not bad, I guess," he said. His voice sounded thin and distracted. "I think several classes this year have a slightly higher skill level than last. I've got a couple kids who write pretty well. But my eyes are going. It's all those essays, I suppose."

Trudy looked down at her glass and then eased herself onto the swing. The wooden slats creaked slightly when she leaned over to place the glass on the floor. Both hands free now, she idly blotted her long chestnut hair with the damp towel and then re-draped the towel over the swing back.

"Can't you get a grad student to read them for you?" she said. "That's what I do."

A slight curl of impatience lifted one corner of Derek's mouth but the expression was lost in the darkness. "I could," he said flatly. "But I always read essays myself. You know that."

Trudy lifted her bare left foot and placed the sole on the seat of the swing. As her knee bent, the dark wrapper fell apart revealing a small triangular patch of white panty. The dark red polish on her nails looked black and shiny as she wriggled her toes mechanically.

"You have a choice, you know," she said. "I started using grad students two years ago and it's working very well. It's also good experience for the students. I'm sure your little girlfriend would be delighted to help you out," she added with a faint ironic smile. "By the way, is she still trying to grab your crotch?"

"That's crude, Trudy," Derek said. "Keli's not that kind of a girl."

"College girls are all 'that kind of a girl'," Trudy said.

"Except Keli," Derek said again. His voice had tightened. "Anyway, Sociology is not the same thing as English Lit. I never use multiple choice questions. You never use essay questions."

"I do sometimes," Trudy said.

She glanced at her husband again and then lifted her eyes. She let them slide beyond their property line. Beneath the moon, the thick spring grass of the pasture looked pale and gray. Each cow was a patchwork of bottomless black and shimmering white. They looked like pop-up silhouettes pasted in front of a scrim.

After a long emptiness she finally said, "You want to talk about it?"

Derek's response was immediate, the words chopped off and stiff. "No," he said, "I do not want to talk about it. Again. I mean, what's the point? You end up crying. I feel like shit. And nothing's resolved."

"Okay," Trudy said. "Then we'll talk about something else."

"Why do we have to talk about anything?" Derek said. "Why can't we just sit here and look at the cows?" He took a deep breath, held it, and then slowly wagged his head. "I'm sorry, Tru," he said. "I've been edgy all week. I've been getting a lot of pressure from Shertz again."

"About the Ph.D.?" Trudy said, still looking at the cows.

Derek nodded. "That and about getting more stuff published. I'm a scholar not a writer," he complained. "I don't do fiction, long or short. I've never been any good at it. He knows that as well as I do."

"But your literary critiques are always well structured," she said. "And so are your essays."

He grunted. "Well structured," he said. "Right, and as boring as hell."

"You've had them published," Trudy reminded him.

"I've had two things published," Derek said stiffly. "The essay was five years ago. The critique was seven years ago. That's not good enough for the exalted Dr. Shertz." Derek snorted. "Why they made that jerk a department head is beyond me."

"They made him the head of the English department because he's older than dirt and, like dirt, he's been at Trinity forever. Seems to me he did his undergrad work here, too," Trudy said. "At least that's what I've heard."

"Undergrad work. *And* grad work. *And* Ph.D. work." Derek ticked them off.

When he glanced back at his wife his eyes were immediately drawn to the triangular patch of white. He felt a faint stirring in his groin and immediately looked away.

Derek picked up the oversized jigger in one hand, the bottle of Chivas Regal in the other, and splashed in a generous shot. He downed half of the smooth burning liquid before setting both the glass and the bottle back on the floor again.

"No doubt he also graduated from good old Trinity-James Consolidated High School," Derek added. "If you ask me, the guy is a perfect moron."

"No one's perfect," Trudy said.

Derek's laugh was short but genuine. "Shertz comes close," he said. After a moment of silence he went on. "Anyway, Shertz said my only hope for tenure rests solidly upon my attainment of a Ph.D. *And* publication. The latter being 'At regular intervals', was the way he put it."

Derek glanced at the white triangle again but the tingling in his groin had already faded. "I just can't seem to get myself psyched up for the long arduous and time-consuming hassle of a doctoral program. Have you ever seen the reading list for a Ph.D. in English Lit?" he said. "I'd have to spend at least a year in Britain, probably longer."

"A sabbatical might be nice," Trudy said. "We could linger over scones and tea. We could go for walks in the rain. We could sit up all night talking. Like we used to. We don't talk much anymore," she said. "Have you noticed that?"

"We talk," Derek said.

"Oh, sure," Trudy said. "We talk about *work*. We

gossip about the tight-assed airheads we have to work *with*. We complain about the never-ending distraction of work-related *meetings*. We groan about a work *load* that seems to be, no, *is* getting heavier every year." She paused. "Let's see, what else do we talk about? Oh, yes. Mortgage payments. Car payments. Property taxes. And credit card bills."

"What else is there?" Derek said.

"I don't know," Trudy said. "Maybe nothing. But it seems like we used to talk for hours. Even if we talked about nothing at all, it was still fun. Wasn't it?"

Derek sighed. "Fun?" he said. "I'm not sure I understand the meaning of the word anymore. Spontaneous lighthearted frivolity?"

"That's close enough," Trudy said.

Derek said, "So I do know what the word means. I guess I just don't know what it feels like anymore."

The chains squeaked quietly as Trudy nudged the swing back and forth with a dangling bare toe. She tried to keep her voice even but was only partially successful. "You're not getting depressed again are you? I don't think I could go through another episode like—"

His words cut her off. "I am not getting depressed," he said shortly. "I had a hard week and a difficult day. I'm tired. I'm worn out. I'm disgusted. I'm annoyed. I'm all of those things. But I'm not depressed.

Okay?"

"Okay," Trudy said. There was a hint of warning in her voice. "But if this other thing starts getting you down—"

"It's not getting me down," Derek snapped. "It's just disappointing, that's all. And sad. And it makes me feel old."

Trudy's eyes slowly, almost caressingly, surveyed her husband's slender athletic body. The thighs and calves had been hardened by many years of thrice-a-week jogs. His chest muscles were gracefully attached to slim but firm and well-rounded deltoids. The deltoids expanded downward and turned into rope-like biceps. Even in the dim light, her husband's abdominal muscles were etched sharply above the dark blue briefs.

"Forty-four is not old," Trudy said. She grinned. "And your bod definitely looks a lot younger than that."

"Some parts of it," he added dryly.

Trudy's grin faded. "Look, we've been tip-toeing around this thing for twenty minutes. Why don't we just come right out and talk about it?"

"Because," he said, drawing the word out, "talking about it won't resolve it. We've gone over this before, Trudy."

Trudy persisted. "But maybe, for once, if we were really and truly open about it, and brutally honest, well, maybe it would get resolved. Isn't it worth a try at least?"

Derek said nothing. He stared at the cows. Two of them were ambling slowly toward a Stygian blot of tree shadow some distance beyond the fence.

"After all," Trudy continued, striving for lightness and humor, "we are both college profs. That means we are both fairly well educated, reasonably intelligent, and relatively mature."

"I like your hedging modifiers," Derek said.

Trudy smiled. "Thanks. And we've also been married for what? Eighteen years? Twenty? Whatever it is, it should be long enough for us to be able to sit down and talk about things like this. Without being embarrassed. Or awkward. Or hesitant. Or whatever."

Derek grunted. "What? A wife who doesn't know how long she's been married? Who said there's nothing new under the sun?"

"I hate snappy repartee," Trudy said. "Especially when it's used as a smokescreen." She paused for a moment and then went on. "I'll tell you what. I'll go first, okay? I'll be the first brutally honest one. And the brutal honest truth is this. I'm the problem. Aren't I?"

Derek groaned. "See? That's what I mean. That's the way it always goes whenever we have discussions like this. The first thing you do is blame yourself."

He held her gaze for a moment. Then he reached down and clinked and splashed another jolt of Chivas into the short fat glass. After glancing at her, he took a large swallow and then set the glass down again. His eyes drifted out to the pasture. The two cows had melted completely into the shadowy blot.

"Despite the hard plastic shell you like to use for protection," Derek said slowly, tenting his hands beneath his chin, "you really are a very sensitive woman, Trudy."

"Don't you mean 'overly sensitive'," Trudy said, sounding slightly annoyed.

Derek shrugged. "Sometimes you see criticisms that aren't there. You feel slights that weren't meant to be slights. You take objective comments and turn them into personal attacks."

"That's bullshit, Derek," Trudy said. The annoyance had suddenly turned into anger. "And you know it."

Derek's voice remained even and flat. "It is not bullshit. It is the truth. Whether you believe it or not, whether you see it or not, it is still the truth."

Trudy abruptly swung her bent leg down from the swing seat and placed both bare feet flat on the porch floor. She shifted her weight forward as though preparing herself to bolt. The sudden movement parted her wrapper all the way up to the knotted tie around her waist. Her legs looked almost as white as the nylon triangle. She yanked at the fabric. "I don't have to listen to this," she said.

Derek moaned, exasperated. "Trudy, you're the one who wanted to talk."

Trudy glared at her husband for a long tense moment and then looked down at her pale legs. The heat in her eyes began to fade as she tugged at her wrapper. She had to shift her weight slightly before the material came together again, covering her legs.

The wooden slats creaked, the chains pinged as she inched her buttocks backward until her hips once again touched the slatted back of the swing. Her shoulders and head, however, remained in a forward tilt, as though bolting was still an option.

"What's sad . . . " Derek began, and then stopped. He thought for a moment and then started again. "No, *one* of the sad things, at least to me, is that we missed so many opportunities. There were so many times we could have and didn't. So many times we should have and didn't. So many times we were too wrapped up in busy work. And now . . ." His voice drifted away.

Trudy crossed her legs and readjusted the wrapper across her knees. One bare foot began to bob up and down impatiently.

"Every time we talk about this," Derek continued, "I feel like I'm making a mountain out of a zit. I feel like

—or at least I probably sound like—I'm some kind of teenage stud, revved up to a hyper state of hormonal overdrive. You, on the other hand, always hold the high ground. You come across as the ultimately stable, infinitely mature woman. You may be irritated by my juvenile attitude, yes, but you are stable and mature nonetheless."

Derek glanced back at her again. Trudy was staring at the empty moonlit pasture.

"I always feel like I'm the one who's being irrational," Derek said. "I feel like I'm exaggerating the importance of something that really isn't very important." He paused. "Only it is important," he said. "At least it's important to me. And I know about the pills."

"The thing you never understood," Trudy said slowly, "the thing you never accepted, is that it's different for men and women."

"I never accepted it," Derek replied, "because I don't believe it."

Trudy's eyes were as chilly as her tone of voice. "This is really about Ellen, isn't it?" she said. "You still think of her as some kind of wild sex machine while I, on the other hand, am a cold unfeeling and sexless . . . slug."

"Ellen is history," Derek said. "Very old history. Look, my relationship with her ended five years before I even *met* you."

"But you still think about her," Trudy said.

"I do not think about her," Derek replied. "I haven't thought about her in years. But the fact is, she really did want me sexually." He grunted. "Unfortunately, I also know that sex was the *only* thing she wanted from me. 'Safe' sex. And in those days, that meant sex without the chance of getting pregnant. Her husband and I were the only two men she knew who were totally 'safe'. She couldn't possibly have been impregnated by either one of us because we both had the old cords cut. At her insistence, of course."

Trudy's tone was icy. "Sounds like a bachelor's dream come true—a woman who wants only one thing from a man, unencumbered sex. That should have made you very happy."

"It did not make me happy at all," Derek said. "It made me miserable. Because sex was not the only thing I wanted from her. It was the only thing I could *get* from her."

Derek paused. "It's ironic, I guess. With Ellen, sex accounted for about ninety-eight percent of our relationship because, like I said, there wasn't anything else. And that was sad, too."

Derek's laughter was brief and humorless. "It was more than sad. It was depressing. Because it was demoralizing. It was depleting. It made me feel empty inside, hollow. Painfully hollow."

Trudy was staring at him intently. Her brow was furrowed, her eyes confused.

Derek glanced at her, saw her confusion, and felt a twinge of pain. But he pushed ahead.

"I guess that's the saddest most depressing part of this whole thing—that we're always separated, that we're always separate beings. And I'm not talking about you and me," he added hurriedly. "I'm not even talking about men being separated from women. I'm talking about each person being separate from every other person on earth."

He glanced back at her again, his eyes searching for recognition, for comprehension. He saw neither and looked away immediately. He made himself continue anyway.

Almost to himself now he said, "Maybe that's why intercourse—sexual intercourse—is so important to human beings. And to other creatures too, I suppose. Maybe it's because … for one relatively brief moment in time, one person enters another. One person receives another. And the two become one. As much as is possible anyway. Which is not really very much. But it's all we have." He stopped and took a deep breath and then let it out slowly, shaking his head. "And now we don't even have that anymore."

Fearfully, he glanced back at his wife once more. Trudy was staring at the floor now. He couldn't tell what her expression was. Her face was encased again in clear plastic resin.

Then, after a long silence, Derek thought he saw the glisten of a tear. Then he saw a droplet. It seemed to squeeze itself out of her left eye. Slowly, it made its way down her cheek. "I'm sorry," she said.

Derek's own face tightened. His wife was crying. He felt like shit. And nothing was resolved. Again.

Norman Poder: Famous Writer

(This story was written mostly for my own enjoyment. It was fun to do and I still get a few laughs every time I go over it again. I hope it will give some of my readers a chuckle or two.)

Norman Poder wrote children's books. His life was quiet, peaceful, uncluttered. He was not interested in fame or million-dollar advances. The thought of buying a gleaming yacht never entered his mind. And the Best Seller list was something he rarely glanced at. Until he met Clarissa.

She was the new girl in the secretarial pool at Morton-Smith-Skideaux when Norman arrived one grey October morning with a neat error-free manuscript tucked inside his beige vinyl briefcase. Clarissa was impressed. Not with Norman. He seemed rather dull and lifeless in his brown time-shiny suit and owlish glasses. What impressed her was the fact that he was a writer, the first 'real writer' she'd ever met. She was even more impressed when she learned he was a bachelor.

She was *not* impressed with the books he wrote. Talking squirrels, grandmotherly bunnies, and trips to Uncle John's farm were all very nice. But they did not fit her image of what a 'writer' should write. Never mind about that, she thought. With a little guidance he would see the light.

Norman Poder did not have much experience with women. So it is not surprising that he found Clarissa completely overwhelming. She was taller than he was, heavier. Not a bad figure; perhaps a little too generous in the bust and hips. A lot of eye makeup. A cloud of very sweet perfume. What overwhelmed him most, however, was the way she talked. Which was all the time.

An hour later, after concluding his business with Henry Skideaux, Norman had found himself being towed —rather forcefully—out of the office, down the hall, and into the elevator. Clarissa had declared a coffee break. "We simply *must* have a celebration," she bubbled. "After all, it isn't every day that a writer signs a book contract!" Her unnaturally long eye lashes fluttered like butterfly wings in a high gale.

Twenty minutes later, Norman was still listening stoically as Clarissa's endless chatter bounced around the yellow walls of the almost empty cafeteria. Finally, after another breathless twenty minutes dragged by, Henry Skideaux stalked into the cafeteria and looked around pointedly. When he zeroed in on Clarissa his high pale forehead furrowed deeply. Clarissa's eyes snapped to her watch. She blushed, grimaced apologetically at Norman, and heaved herself out of her chair.

"Gotta go," she said with a bright smile. "Henry needs me."

As she hurried away, buttocks jiggling, she waggled the fingers of one hand over her shoulder and trilled, "See you sooooo-ooon."

Norman blinked at his empty coffee cup. He would not deliver another manuscript for at least six months. Maybe longer. She should be gone by then, working somewhere else. Surely Henry Skideaux would not accept *that* kind of aggravation every day.

Much to Norman's chagrin, Clarissa appeared at the door of his small second-floor walk-up on the outskirts of Philadelphia one week later to the day.

"Norman Poder! How lovely to see you again!"

She threw her arms around him and smothered him with a bosomy hug right there in the hallway. Then she thrust him away abruptly and held him at arms' length, beaming.

"I was in the neighborhood anyway doing an errand for Henry and I thought to myself, you simply *must* stop in to see Norman. You don't mind if I call you Norman, do you? Mister and Ms and all that business seems stuffy, don't you think? I'm a Ms myself, Ms Tillburg, although divorced of course but I would *much* rather you call me Clarissa, or Clare, that's what Walter always called me, my ex-husband. The rascal just up and left me one day. Never did find out why. Another woman I suppose, someone slinky and eighteen with long blonde hair no doubt. May I come in?"

Bewildered, Norman was shouldered aside as Clarissa burst into the room and settled herself on his tiny crushed-rose sofa. She patted the cushion beside her and Norman sat down obediently.

"Your being a writer must be *very* exciting," she said, her eyes darting around the small living room with both interest and disapproval. "I mean, what with big cars and yachts and cocktail parties and jetting back and forth to Europe. I know how you writers are, oh yes I do, I've met quite a few at the office, you know, and I've read all your books, too. How many are there? Seven I think and all very cute. I'm sure the kiddies just *love* them." Her eyes latched onto his. "But frankly, Norman, if I may be so bold, I think you are wasting your time on children's books. You should be writing best sellers."

She jabbed her finger into his chest repeatedly, emphasizing each example. "Adventure, mayhem, sex, demons, political scandals, Mafia lawyers, things like that. *That's* where the money is."

Norman was at a total loss to explain, even to himself, how it happened, but within two weeks Clarissa had taken over his apartment. Four weeks later she quit her job and married him. Six weeks after that she moved him—them—into a plush high-rise condo that over-looked the Philadelphia Museum of Art. And by the first of the year Norman was hard at work on a new 'realistic' novel.

"Now we're getting somewhere," Clarissa said firmly.

The next two years slid by in a swirl of work. Be-sides stories for Jack & Jill, Golden Press, and Morton-Smith-Skideaux, Norman worked on three different nov-els. Actually, it was a collaborative effort. Clarissa sup-plied the ideas. Norman did the writing.

First there was a book about four sisters—identical quadruplets—who opened a massage parlor in Las Vegas and secretly practiced witchcraft on the Mafia moguls who owned most of the gambling casinos. The next was about an ex-airline pilot who bought a rambling adobe castle in Arizona and turned it into a sex therapy dude ranch for Hollywood starlets and big-name actors. And then he wrote a suspenseful epic concerning a Playboy Bunny who joined the CIA, became the lover of an Ara-bian sheik, and single-handedly smashed OPEC.

They were disasters. Each in its own way.

After countless submissions by his agent, *Underground Bunny* was finally accepted by a small paperback publisher in Newark who used it for a tax write-off. Nationwide, it sold one hundred and three copies and got one review. The Rabbit Breeders Monthly of Crockett, Kentucky, called it a "filthy, filthy book."

Norman was disappointed by the failures but not surprised. Clarissa was not surprised either. She was outraged.

"It's your publisher, Norman," she said, stamping her chubby foot. "He simply does *not* know how to handle your talent. No hype. No gossip column blurbs. No late-night TV talk shows. I can't find a copy of the book anywhere, not even on Amazon." She wagged a finger and winked an eye. "A different publisher, Norman. Simple as that."

If the first two years of their marriage were busy, the third year was frantic. Clarissa became even more determined to turn Norman into a 'real writer' once and for all.

And Norman tried. He really did. For twelve, fourteen hours a day he made notes, planned chapters, ripped up pages, and started all over again. On a diet of Maalox and ink-black coffee he aged ten years and lost twenty-seven pounds.

Clarissa never looked better. She beamed and hovered and urged him on until another manuscript was finished. "This is the one, Norman," she said, her teeth clamped together tightly. "I can just *feel* it. Can't you?"

Another suspense yarn, *The Great Trolley Hijack* did slightly better than *Underground Bunny,* but only slightly. One reviewer called the novel 'flat.' Another called it 'uninspired.' And the third reviewer suggested Norman 'try his hand at children's books.'

Confused by yet another setback, Clarissa became hostile, then petulant, then moody. While Norman went doggedly back to his desk to try once more, she sat in the kitchen, hour after hour, unnervingly quiet. After three weeks, she suddenly snapped her pudgy fingers one afternoon and then slammed out the door. When she got home six hours later she promptly went to bed. The next morning the silence ended; the plan was ready.

She rushed a bleary-eyed Norman Poder into the kitchen and sat him down to a well-spread table and started in, green eyes blazing.

"You know how I feel about book reviewers, Norman, I think they're all crazy. They don't know what they're talking about. Any of them. But ... well, I may be wrong. Not about all reviewers of course. I still think 99% of them should be laying bricks or plumbing toilets. But one was right, one out of a thousand, maybe, but we must give credit where credit is due."

Banging pots, dropping forks, spilling salt, Clarissa hurried one. "Remember the one in that bus magazine? Called you uninspired? That's hard to take; believe me, I know. But I've thought about it, all this time, and you know what? He was right."

She paused for a breath, fussed with a pan of soft-boiled eggs and then went on. "It's the city," she announced. The egg shells exploded under her knife. Hot egg yolks geyser-ed into the air. "There's no vitality here, no real life, just dirt and noise and crowded streets. Here, eat. I know what I'm talking about, Norman. I've done some reading and I've done some checking, too. Use more salt. It helps the digestion. Do you know where the real writers go? To live, to work, to play, to get inspired. Not Greenwich Village, not New England, not Paris, not even California. Not any longer. No sir. For your information—I was reading all about it at the library—they go to Florida. That's right! By the droves they're going. And do you know where in Florida? Do you know where the hot spot is? The real center of creativity? The writing capital of the whole state?"

Norman paused, the yellow dripping spoon before his mouth.

"Sarasota," she said firmly. "That's where John D. MacDonald lived. So did Borden Deal. MacKinlay Kantor, Evan Hunter." She ticked them off one by one.

"They're all dead of course but that's beside the point. They were all on the best seller list. James Patterson lives somewhere around there, too. Anyway, that's where *we're* going to live, Norman. Because the only thing you need is some inspiration and that's exactly what Sarasota has. Palm trees, sunshine, the Gulf of Mexico, beaches, yachts, everything. It'll open up a whole new world, Norman, I know it will."

Clarisa breathed a deep satisfied sigh. She looked over Norman's head, out the window, past City Hall, and into the smoggy Philadelphia air. "We're moving to Sarasota," she said dreamily, her eyes half closed.

Norman stared at his large wife for a full thirty seconds but said nothing. When the mascara-ed green eyes came back into focus he said, "Eat, Norman, your eggs are getting cold."

* * * * * * * * *

Since Clarissa married him, Norman had earned very little money. The talking squirrel stories were getting buried beneath reams of sex and blood that didn't sell. So when they got to Sarasota they had to settle for a modest two bedroom rental near a noisy shopping center. It wasn't Bird Key. It wasn't even Siesta Key, but they *were* in Sarasota. The tennis courts, Lamborghini, and Excalibur boat would come later, as soon as Norman wrote a best seller.

While Norman was wracking his brain for an idea, Clarissa began sniffing out the addresses of every writer in the area, famous or not. Then she checked every chain bookstore, as well as every paperback rack in every drugstore, grocery store, bus terminal and airport within a hundred miles. Three weeks after they arrived, Clarissa rushed into Norman's cluttered little study with the results of her survey. She demanded an answer. "Do you know how many James Patterson books are on sale right this minute?"

Norman gulped down some gin and shook his head.

"Of course I don't know the *exact* number," she rushed on, "but it averages out to something like a dozen, dozen and a half, under his name alone and nine or ten collaborations! On each and every book rack from here to Tarpon Springs. Believe it or not, Billy's News Agency right here in town has thirty-seven different Patterson novels spread out on one rack. Thirty-seven! Bringing in God knows how much money every day. Every single day, Norman. Every. Single. Day! And you should see the house he lives in. It's gorgeous. I saw it in a magazine."

She stopped to catch her breath, gave her husband a long thoughtful look and then pinched his pale cheek.

"Thriller suspense stories, Norman. That's where the money is."

A year later, Norman's first suspense thriller was released: *Rocky Gibraltar, Hired Assassin.*"

It was not a best seller but the sales and reviews were not bad. And Norman was pleased.

Clarissa was not.

"One book," she said sadly, shaking her head. "In a year's time? Sean Flannery does a book every month, and he lives right on the beach." With a sisterly pat, Clarissa told Norman to get to work.

This time, however, Norman could *not* get to work. Try as he might, the second Gibraltar novel refused to hatch. No setting, no victim, no plot. The more he struggled and thought, the less he came up with. The strain was beginning to show.

He started sitting around all day in his baggy red boxer shorts, drinking gin. He started wandering around the house all night. Several times Clarissa found Norman in the back yard, staring up at the stars. He wouldn't shave for days on end. He started getting grumpy, short-tempered, angry at *her*, of all people, and she couldn't see why.

It couldn't have been her hints. Although heaven knows they certainly deserved a swimming pool much more than the Doones who lived next door and were retired and not wealthy and certainly not artistic, and yet *they* were going to build a pool! And anyway, she hadn't been talking *that* much about buying a house with a pool for themselves. She just mentioned it every now and then, as an incentive, to spur Norman on to greater heights.

But the more hints she dropped about having a fancy Gulf-front home of their own with their own swimming pool and tennis court, the less Norman appeared to care one way or another. Sometimes Clarissa thought he wasn't even *listening* to her. Finally she decided it was time to take off the white gloves. It was time for an ultimatum.

"If you don't write another book and buy me a house with a pool, Norman, I'll have to leave you. It's as simple as that."

Her eyes were like emerald chisels, chipping away at his soul. "I'll fly back to Philadelphia, get my old job back with Henry Skideaux, and start all over again. Find myself a *real* writer!" She snorted. "And you know what will happen then? Your so-called career will come to a shrieking halt. It'll be finished. Over. Kaput." She shrugged omnipotently. "It's your choice, Norman. Fame and fortune with me? Or a dead end street alone."

* * * * * * * * *

Norman didn't respond at all to the ultimatum but it seemed to Clarissa that things started to improve, especially when the men from Sunny Day Pools started pounding stakes in the Doone's back yard. It wasn't like Norman to be hobnobbing with construction workers, Clarissa thought, but at least he was doing something. He called it research. She called it loafing. But after a while she began to relax. After all, he had stopped growling at her. And after all his chit-chat with the construction workers, she was absolutely certain he had decided to buy a home of their own. A home with a pool. As an added bonus, she also knew he was making notes for a new novel.

Next door, sitting beneath a tangerine tree, the Doones, too, were glad to see Norman out again, walking around his own back yard, a clipboard in his hands. They didn't know him very well although the three of them had shared a six pack when Clarissa wasn't home.

"Nice sort of chap," Scotty said to his wife, his accent clipped, lilting. "Quiet, mild mannered."

"Too bad we can't say the same for her," his wife Jan said, pursing her lips. Many times she had watched as Clarissa followed Norman in and out of the house, chattering ceaselessly, shaking her index finger at him. "No wonder he looks so pale and thin all the time," Jan said to her husband.

The day the backhoe came to dig up the Doones' back yard, Scotty and Jan went away on vacation. They thought it would be fun to leave for a while and then come back when the pool was finished.

When they returned a week later they found Norman standing on their diving board, fully dressed. After raving about the crystal blue clarity of the water, the new flagstone patio, and the drooping new banana plants, Jan casually asked about Clarissa. Norman told them she was off on a house-hunting trip to Miami. He wasn't sure when she'd be back. She wanted to check out Key West, too, Norman said. And maybe the Fort Lauderdale area.

"I see," Jan said. "Well, we'll hate to see you leave, but everyone wants a place of their own."

As summer passed, the Doones swam in their pool nearly every day. Occasionally, in the afternoon, they would see Norman stretched out in the sun or reading under a tree. Bachelorhood, even the temporary kind, was obviously agreeing with him. Each time they saw him he looked more fit and tanned than ever before. And by the sound of the typing late at night they were sure his writing was going well.

Leaning over the low chain-link fence one Sunday morning, Jan and Scotty asked Norman what his new book was about. Norman smiled mysteriously and told them they would have to wait and see. And how, he asked, did they like their new pool?

"Very much," Scotty said, rolling his rrrs. "Had some trouble the first few weeks during the rains. Drain pump backed up or something. Stained the water." Scotty shrugged. "Whatever it was, it went away."

By September, Norman's new book was finally finished. Jan cheered and Scotty clapped him on the back. To celebrate, they split another six pack while Norman explained the politics of publishing. Later, Scotty suggested they all go for a swim but Norman declined, regretfully, and left. He still had a few phone calls to make, he said, to his agent and publisher.

Much to the Doones' amazement—and Norman's as well—when the book was released it shot to the top of the best seller list. Five magazines were battling for serialization rights. Three book clubs sued each other over it. And Norman was invited to every cocktail party and charity ball in Sarasota.

Soon after that, Norman Poder moved away. Months later, the gossip columns had him living in France on a sleek new yacht. Scotty and Jan couldn't imagine that, not the Norman they knew. But they were happy for him, wherever he was, and they wished him well. They seldom thought about Clarissa. "I suppose they got a divorce," said Jan. "Maybe so," said Scotty. And that was that.

Though not much of a novel reader himself, from time to time Scotty would glance at a book review. When he did, he thought of his old neighbor. One evening, while thumbing through a tattered copy of Newsweek after Jan had gone to bed, Scotty was surprised to find a familiar face peering out at him.

The beard was new, the hair longer, the face fuller, but it was definitely Norman. The picture accompanied a review of his first breakout novel.

Dated two weeks after the story had been sold to the movies, it was the most glowing review of all. Scotty, grinning with pride, skimmed from line to line.

"Great new talent ... grippingly suspenseful ... incredible authenticity ... a crowning achievement."

Then, as Scotty read on, the burgeoning pride he felt for his ex-neighbor suddenly drained away. In its place, an icy chill ran down his spine.

"With his latest Rocky Gibraltar masterpiece, *The Deep Blue Pool*," the reviewer had written, "Norman Poder has finally established himself as a master of the thriller-suspense genre. It is a good thing he has chosen writing as his profession instead of murder. Our law enforcement officials would have their hands full indeed. Who but Poder could devise such an original method of disposing of a corpse. Beneath a swimming pool, no less. Under eight feet of water and two of cement …"

Scotty did not read the rest. His hands felt cold as he entered the garage. After stuffing the old magazine deep into a trash can he went back inside and crawled into bed.

It was a year before Scotty went swimming again.

Snow

(This is another flash fiction. It's about the cruelty that children sometimes display. It can be a trait, unfortunately, that is often carried over into adulthood. Especially when the mindset continues to be "us" versus "them."—rh).

The hatless boy was hunched alone against the hard brick wall. His jacket too thin, too tight, and too tattered for the cold snowy day. His large belly pushed through several button-less gaps. He pretended not to be aware of the two snow-fort walls ten yards away. But he *was* aware of the girl called Jackie. He had been watching her all week.

"Hey, Malcolm. Come on over," Jackie called out from one walled fort. An enormous smile lit up her long narrow face.

The fat boy stared at her through thick glasses, dumfounded. "Me?"

Jackie tossed back the fuzzy hood of her bright red coat. Blonde hair tumbled out in rolling waves. Her smile got even brighter as she beckoned with a green snowy mitten. "Yeah, you. We need you on our side."

Then a girl called out from the other walled fort. "Don't listen to her, Malcolm. We want you on *our* side."

Then the kids behind both snow walls were all grinning, calling his name, over and over. "Mal-colm. Mal-colm. We want. Mal-colm."

Malcolm could not believe his ears. Since his mother enrolled him last week, this was the first time anyone at school had used his real name—anyone except his teachers. The names the kids *did* call him multiplied every horrible day.

Fatty. Tubby. Lard Ass. One kid had called him Tub-A-Guts and poked him in the stomach.

"You got a baby in there?" he had said, grinning. All the other kids had laughed.

Another kid had elbowed his buddy when Malcolm was in the boy's room. "Get a load of the new kid's face, Jake. Looks like a fruitcake that blowed up in the oven."

The other kid had snickered, peering at Malcolm's pimply forehead. "What are all those ugly green things?" he said. "Chunks of snot?"

Scalding tears had burned Malcolm's eyes. It didn't matter where he went. It was like someone always hung a sign on his back, a sign that said, "Ugly Stupid New Kid"

The girl called Jackie had been different. She had never laughed at him. She hadn't looked at him either, but at least she hadn't laughed at him. And now, here she was, calling him. And using his real name!

Her voice got more insistent. "Come on, Malcolm. Lunch'll soon be over. I'll give you some of my snow-balls."

Hesitantly, Malcolm started moving forward. "You … you really want me on your side?"

"I said it, didn't I?" Jackie said. "Now hurry *up!*"

Malcolm stared at her for another moment. Then his head swiveled to take in the kids who were lined up behind each separate snow wall. Faces grinned behind both walls; snow-crusted mittens motioned him closer.

"What're you waitin' for, Mal-colm?" some girl yelled. "Fourth of July?"

As Malcolm neared the open area between the two walls of snow, the girl from the other team called out again.

"If you come to our side I'll give you a big kiss. How would you like that, Mal-com?" Her wet kissy sound made Malcolm's groin tingle.

For a moment he was torn between the two snow armies, and also between the two girls. He still could not believe any of this was happening.

He glanced at the kissy girl once more. But then he started jogging heavily toward Jackie. He couldn't remember ever being so happy.

Wait'll I tell Mom about this! he thought.

His own tentative grin was just starting to blossom into a broad smile when the first icy snowball caught him in the throat. An instant later, another snowball slammed into the back of his neck. Another hit the side of his face, knocking his glasses off.

Malcolm lurched to a stop, stunned, confused. He tried to look around but the snowballs were now flying at him from every blurry direction. The voices were different now, too—mean, sharp, and stained with obscenities.

"Gettim!" somebody yelled.

"Blast the fat turd!"

"Go back where you came from, Tub-A-Guts. Nobody wants you here."

And then a girl's voice. Jackie's? "Look everybody! The baby's crying." Her laughter, too, was shrill and cruel. "What's the matter, Fatty? Doncha like the taste of snow?"

Suddenly, obscenities were pouring out of Malcolm's own throat, choked and wet and mixed with sobs. Clumsy and awkward, the foul words sputtered off his tongue, like chunks of filth that had never been hurled before.

Several times Malcolm staggered blindly around in a circle as the snowballs continued to pummel his body from all directions. His breath was coming in ragged gasps. Mucus and tears and icy snow slid into his eyes, blinding him completely.

He was trying desperately to smear the slimy moisture away with the sleeve of his thin jacket when something slammed into the back of his head. It was much harder than a snowball.

Malcolm was jolted forward by the blow. His breath exploded from his throat as the world turned grey. Streaks of lightning seared his neck and shot down his spine. He sagged to his knees for a moment, his shoulders jerking. And then he toppled slowly forward.

He could barely feel the grainy snow push up his nose and into his mouth as the whole white world turned black before his open eyes.

A bell was ringing, far away. The jeers began to fade. And then he heard nothing at all.

The Best Goddam Vacation Ever

(The word "vacation" has a different meaning for different people. For some, it means a cruise through the Mediterranean; mountain climbing in the Andes; skiing in British Columbia; a photo safari through the Veldt; or hunting moose in Alaska. For a profane blue collar guy like Tec-Con's janitor, Barry, "vacation" conjures up a whole different set of possibilities, and they all revolve around the phrase: "get'er done." In Barry's words, "When a guy's got a goal, he's got to keep his eye on it. He's got to study it, work on it, set things up, and then he's got to get'er done." And he ain't about to waste the first six, eight hours of his vacation time sleeping his ass off either. Nooo-way. He's gonna jump right in with all four feet. Because this is his first real paid vacation ever; and there ain't nobody gonna screw it up.

This novette is also based on a guy I used to work with. And he really was quite proud that his first paid vacation ever turned out just the way he planned it.—rh.)

Barry dumped the last of the powdery cleanser into the rust-stained toilet bowl, glanced at his Timex, and then started swishing the stiff-bristled brush. He was whistling through the broken-off corner of one of his front teeth and knew he was grinning like a fuckin' baboon but who the hell cared. He sure didn't, because he had to be the luckiest goddamn fucker in town right now. Last job of the day and only eight more minutes to go. Then: pick up the check and punch the hell out. After that, a whole goddamn week was spread out before him like a whore in hell, greased up, hot and ready to go. All he had to do on the way home was stop at Marty's Ready Cash. With the overtime he got last week, his check should be close to six hundred dollars. Not that he'd need it. He'd been stacking his stash in the closet for the past three months—a case here, a case there—so he wouldn't have to buy anything except a couple bags of chips, some pretzels, Slim Jim's.

He hadn't let anybody into his place either; not in three months, not even Daniella. That meant no screwing, no card games, no late movies, no bullshit sessions. Nothing. Because he wasn't about to let anyone screw up his vacation—his first real paid vacation ever!

Before he hired on with Tec-Con Plastics, Barry had worked mostly for Day Labor Inc., doing grunt construction work, demolition cleanup, lawn mowing, window cleaning, or anything else that paid him a daily wage. He liked the freedom of day jobs. He'd done it for years, ever since he rolled into Florida. He liked it

because, well, if a guy didn't feel like showing up at the
hiring hall that day he just said fucket and didn't. Next
day nobody said a word. But when that same guy starts
pushing forty, forty-five he's got to start thinking about
his future. And that meant thinking about bennies; like a
free membership to Sam's Club, time-and-a-half for anything over forty hours, a Christmas bonus every year, and
a paid vacation.

But it was the paid vacation, more than anything
else, that finally turned Barry into a Tec-Con wage slave.
And now, payoff time. After six months probation and a
full year of plunging toilets and mopping floors he was
finally getting his week off. And he wasn't gonna let nobody fuck it up for him. Nooo-body.

Barry flushed the toilet and waited for the tank to
fill. It took too long again so he lifted the ceramic tank
lid and balanced it across the scarred toilet seat. You
couldn't see shit in the tank because all four sides were
covered with about an inch of rusty crud and the water
usually looked rusty, too. So he had to slide his long
hairy arm into the reddish water and feel around the
slime at the bottom of the tank. Once again, the little
chain had come loose from the flush handle and got itself
tangled under the flapper. When that happened, the flapper didn't seal right, which meant water kept running and
running and running.

His blunt fingers felt the chain and slipped it out from under the flapper. He pinched the chain between thumb and forefinger, lifted it out of the water, and then wiggled the slimy little hook back into the small corroded hole in the flush-handle rod. With the flapper back in place and the water gushing in, the tank started to fill up quickly. He watched for a few seconds and then carefully slid the ceramic lid back in place.

Barry wondered who the hell would fix the goddam thing when he wasn't there next week? He shrugged: no skin off my grapes, he thought.

He glanced at his own image in the cracked mirror that hung above the sink. Like a stiff and greasy halo, his mop of scraggly red hair stuck out around the sides and back of his Devil Rays baseball cap. Some of the oily red coils were damp with sweat and pasted themselves like grimy ringlets against his neck. A matching scruffy beard started just below his watery brown eyes, covered most of the acne scars and spider veins on his cheeks and chin, and then bristled downward to the frayed collar of his faded blue Tec-Con tee shirt. He grinned at the mirror image for a moment, winked, and then turned back to the toilet bowl.

After shaking out the last of the cleanser, he tossed the yellow plastic container into the empty trashcan, jammed the bristle brush back into its cone-shaped plastic container and said, "Fucket."

Five minutes later he was slouched against the wall at the end of the time clock line, waiting like everyone else for that balloon-boobed little Sarah Raney to hand out the checks. By the time she had worked her way down the line to Barry, Sarah had stopped saying, "Have a good weekend," and "Don't spend it all in one place." Instead, she patiently reminded him that this was his check for *last* week, including overtime, but his actual forty-hour *vacation* check would be given to him the week he came back to work. Did he understand that? she asked in her squeaky little pussy voice.

He wanted to say, I understand a helluva lot more than you think I do, you stupid cunt. Instead, he slid the check into his back pocket and said, "Yes, ma'am. And I sure do appreciate it."

LeeRoy Clemson, Barry's foreman and the acting manager for the night crew, was waiting at the corrugated slide-down exit door that opened on what used to be a loading dock. LeeRoy's round face, short brown hair, and Hitler mustache made Barry think of that old Ollie What'sis Name, the fat guy with the derby in that old-time movie he saw the other night, the one with the skinny sidekick.

LeeRoy was grinning his usual know-it-all shit-faced grin. "Well, Barry, you all set for a big vacation? Old John-Boy back in molding said you're flying off to fuckin' Paris. Or is it Rome? You gonna see the fuckin' pope while you're over there?"

Barry stretched his chin forward and grinned back. "Hell, no. He only screws redneck cunts like you, Lee-Roy."

LeeRoy's face reddened. "Yeah? Well just what the hell *are* you gonna do? Bike over to Lido Beach every day? Try to pick up some rich old broad who likes to slum with scumbags?"

Barry punched his time card and stuck it back into its slot, still grinning. He patted LeeRoy's beer-rounded gut. "Don't you worry about it dude. 'Cause I'm gonna have me the best goddam vacation ever. And you can nail that to the wall."

Barry's Goodwill brogans clanked their way down the rusty steel steps and splashed through an oily mud puddle to where his bicycle was chained to an oak tree. He unlocked the thin chain, jammed the lock into his pocket, draped the chain around his neck, and shoved off.

"Don't do anything I wouldn't do," LeeRoy called after him. Barry gave LeeRoy the finger and rode off into the night.

* * * * * * * * *

After cashing his check, Barry thought, what the hell, he'd bike down 301, maybe to Main or Ringling, see what was happening downtown. LeeRoy could be a real pain in the ass sometimes but that rich old broad idea wasn't too bad. Not that he expected to lay one, but he'd never forget that old bag who gave him the twenty dollar bill.

She must have been eighty, all bent over, but dressed like a goddam queen. She had just come out of the opera house and was probably waiting for some dude in a uniform to pick her up. Barry just happened to be sitting on the curb in front of the opera house eating a taco when she walked by and then stopped. Barry could still smell that perfume in his head.

She looked down at him like he was some kind of run-over dog. Then she wagged her head, made a tsk-ing sound with her tongue and clicked open her pearly little bag. She pulled out the twenty and held it in front of his nose between her two gloved fingers.

"You can have this," she said sternly, her voice kinda croaky, "but only if you promise to spend it on some real food. Not that fast food junk. And no alcohol either. You promise?"

Barry hadn't seen a twenty in three or four days. "Yes, ma'am," he had said, sweeping the baseball hat off his head with his right hand while he tried to hide the taco in his left.

"I'll go to Publix first thing tomorrow morning, ma'am. Yes, ma'am, I surely will. Get me some real good meat. Potatoes. Beans. Everything. Yes, ma'am."

But by the time Publix had opened the next morning Barry was already drunk as a skunk. But it was a good drunk, done with some good beer. None of that cheap shit, thanks to the old broad's twenty.

This time, however, there weren't any old broads on Main Street. No old men either; but Barry didn't care about that. He never met a rich old fucker-man who didn't look at him like he was a pile of dog shit. So fuck the rich old dudes. He'd take the rich old broads any day of the week.

He decided to bike on down Main Street, real slow and easy, no cause to rush tonight. When he got to Orange he'd circle around to Ringling and then back to 301 again. But it turned out to be a waste of time. Two drunks and a hooker. That's all he'd seen. No rich old codgers anywhere, dudes or broads. Ten minutes later he was peddling north again on 301.

As he peddled he wondered if he ought to try the causeway again, maybe see something at one of those condos. Like the night after work when he saw that woman standing on a fourth floor balcony, not a stitch

on. She gave Barry a wave and a big smile, boobs wobbling, and then this dude comes up behind her, starts feeling her up. Next thing you know the guy's banging her
right there on the balcony, her leaning over the railing,
still smiling, still waving.

Barry debated whether he should turn around and
take a ride on down there again, but decided he was too
thirsty and tired. What he needed was a drink. It had
been a long day and a long week. So he hung a right,
peddled another ten minutes and ended up at his place
just off Nineteenth Street.

He pushed his bike around the back, bounced it up
the steps and onto the porch and chained it to the railing.
He could hear Lassie scratching at the door and whimpering like crazy, all excited, happy to see Barry and happy
to take a couple good healthy leaks in the backyard,
which is exactly what she did after leaping up and down
in front of him like a goddam yo-yo.

"Settle down, girl," he whispered. "You wake up
that moron Prez and he'll up the rent just for the hell of
it. The bastard."

While Lassie made her rounds of the fenced-in
patch of dirt that used to be a back yard, Barry unlocked
his own private entrance and went inside. Flicking the
light on in the kitchen sent three or four cockroaches
scurrying. One went under the gas stove that had stopped

working three weeks after Barry moved into the place. One went under the second-hand fridge that Prez had bought at Goodwill. The other roaches just disappeared.

Three more roaches skittered out of sight when he flicked on the ceiling light in his tiny bedroom. The battered red windup clock on the window sill said three-fifteen but Barry was in no hurry to go to bed. He wasn't about to waste the first six, eight hours of his vacation time sleeping his ass off. Too much to do. When a guy's got a goal, he's got to keep his eye on it. That was his motto. He's got to study it, work on it, set things up, and then he's got to get'er done, like that dude on TV says. Get'er done.

Barry went to a door beside his bed, fished a jangly keyring out of his pocket, selected the key that came with the new Slaymaker he bought at Ace Hardware three weeks ago. After he got the closet door unlocked and open, he grabbed the overhead pull chain and yanked. The bare bulb not only lit up the little closet, it also lit up the two stacks of cardboard cartons. Three cases on one stack, four on the other.

He glanced back over his shoulder to the bedroom's only window and was relieved to see the blind was still pulled down to the sill. Then he slipped his fingers into the two side holes and slid one of the cases out of the closet. He carried it to the kitchen table, pushed aside a smeary pizza box, two used TV dinner trays, a crusted toaster oven, and five mostly-empty Pepsi cans. One of the cans toppled over, rolled off the table and fell to the floor, dribbling brown liquid.

Barry rummaged around in his pants pocket and dumped everything he found onto the table, including a box cutter, some loose change, his stained nylon wallet, an unwrapped stick of gum, and the cash from his paycheck. He stuck half the cash in his wallet and carried the other half back into the bedroom, along with the box cutter. He glanced at the window again and then knelt by the head of the bed. After sliding out the blade of his box cutter, he wiggled it along the edges of an electrical wall outlet. The plate popped off, revealing a small rectangular empty space. He wadded up the cash and stuck it in, then snapped the plate back in place.

By the time he got back to the kitchen, Lassie was scratching and whining again, this time to get in. Barry opened the door, filled her water bowl, and dumped some dry dog food into another bowl. Grinning, he pulled out a blue-labeled can and popped it open. Barry tipped the can toward Lassie and grinned.

"Here's to you, old girl, and to our first real honest-to-God vacation. Je-sus Christ."

* * * * * * * * *

He had been dreaming about a giant black-headed woodpecker that had clamped its claws onto a telephone pole and was pounding hell out of it with this long golden bill. The telephone pole suddenly turned into Barry's head and the pounding got louder and louder. He thought his whole skull was going to crack open. That's when he woke up and heard his name.

"Barry? You in there? I know you are so get your ass outta bed, you hear me? You got a phone call. Says it's long distance. Barry?"

Barry swung his legs off the bed and felt the room sway for a few seconds. "God damn it, Prez," he grumbled. "I'm coming, all right? Who the hell is it anyway? You sure it's for me. Goddam middle of the night."

"Said he wants to talk to Barry. That's you ain't it. And it's not the middle of the night. It's two-thirty. In the afternoon."

Barry squinted at the window. Even though the blind was still pulled down, a thin razor of light sliced through his eyes, right to the back of his skull. With a grunt and a belch he heaved himself to his feet and lurched toward the kitchen.

Several empty beer bottles clanked and careened across the floor, bounced against the door jamb and skittered under the kitchen table. He wondered why he seemed to be leaning to one side. Then the sock-covered toes of his left foot bumped into his left shoe, kicking it under the table. His right shoe was still on his right foot.

Lassie crowded around his legs as he swung the door open but she didn't go out into the hallway until Barry did. Prezton March was already closing the door to his own apartment. The phone was hanging from the wall just outside Prez's apartment, right below the "Manager" sign.

"Lo?" Barry said, grabbing the phone as Lassie wriggled around his feet.

"Jesus Christ, Barry, where you been? This phone call's costing me a goddam fortune."

"Who the fuck is this?"

Barry leaned unsteadily and pushed firmly on Lassie's flanks until she sat down. She looked up at him expectantly, her tail thumping.

"It's your goddam brother. Who the fuck d'ya think it is?"

"Larry?" Barry said. He blinked his eyes and pinched the end of his nose. "That really you?"

"'Course it's me for Christ's sake."

"You ain't called me in what? Three four years? How'm I supposed to know what your goddam voice sounds like? So what d'ya want?"

"Whaddya mean, what do I want? You think the only time I call is when I want something?"

"That *is* the only time you call me, Larry. You know that and so do I."

Larry cleared his throat. "Yeah, well, okay. Maybe I do. But you don't have to be so goddam snotty about it."

"I ain't got no money, Larry. I'm flat-assed broke. Busted. Zippo. I'll be eating dog food before the weekend's over."

"I ain't stupid, you know. You just got paid last night. Probably got a couple thou wrapped up in some hooker's panties in the closet somewhere. You been working steady for more'n a year now."

"How'd you figure that?"

Larry snorted. "Like I said, I ain't stupid. I talked to your goddam landlord yesterday. He told me where you're working, so I called them. Told'em I was verifying your employment record. Told'em you were gonna buy a house and I was your banker." Larry laughed. "Fucker believed me, too."

"I got no money, Larry. I'm running on empty."

"Look, all I need's a couple thousand."

"A couple what? Jesus Christ, Larry, what for?"

"Well," Larry said hesitantly, "it's kinda hard to explain. I got myself in kindova situation. And I'd be a lot better off if I could, you know, go somewhere else for a little while. I thought maybe I'd take the old Grey Dog out to California. Maybe Oregon."

"Where you living now?"

"Pittsburgh."

"Pittsburgh! A bus ticket from Pittsburgh to LA costs maybe a couple hundred. What you gonna do with the rest of the money. If I had it. Which I don't."

"I thought I'd set myself up in a little business of some sort, you know? Hell, you could even go in on it with me. You wire me the money. I go out there and set things up. Couple weeks, you come out and we run it together. Brothers, right? Partners." Larry laughed. "Remember all the shit we used to do together when we was little? Had a helluva good time, you and me. It could be like that again, you know." He paused. "So. What d'ya say, little brother?"

Barry laughed. "Whadda I say? I say you're as crazy as a fuckin' loon, Larry. But I'm not. So fuck off."

Barry slammed down the receiver and shook his head. He looked down at Lassie who was still looking up at him, waiting. "Ain't that something, girl? Fuckin' guy is fuckin' in-sane. Couple thousand bucks," he grumbled.

He reached down and scratched the dog behind its ears. Lassie wriggled her hind quarters and flopped her tail up and down even harder. Barry smiled. "Vacation time is here, girl. What d'ya say to that?"

* * * * * * * *

By five o'clock he had a nice buzz on and Lassie was asleep in the other room on top of the bed, her head on Barry's pillow. Barry opened the fridge and looked in. His stomach was starting to grumble. A quart of milk had turned sour, a slab of cheese had something growing on it, so did a bowl of noodles. He wedged all three items into the freezer next to a pile of frosted stuff that he couldn't even remember putting there. Then he filled the fridge with Bud Light cans.

Five minutes later he was walking up Bermuda Street toward the 7-Eleven. A dingy red convertible slowed down and a horn blew. There was a woman at the wheel: blonde, too much makeup, bright-red low-cut sweater.

"Hey, Barry," she called out. "How you doing, sweetie? Why ain't you at work?"

"Vacation, baby. Whole fuckin' week off."

"My-oh-my, ain't that sweet. Well, you gonna need a little company, I can see that right now. I'll come by later, okay?"

The car continued down the street. A hand waved out the window. Barry kept on walking. By the time he got to the 7-Eleven, sweat was running down the side of his face and into his bristly red beard. It tickled a bit and he knuckled the wiry hair as the thick glass door whooshed open, hurling a gush of cold air at him.

"Hey, Barry," the fat grey-haired man behind the counter said. "No work tonight?"

"Vacation, Slu. All damn week."

"That don't suck. Need some beer?"

Barry shook his head. "Been stocking up. Got enough to see me through, I think. If I don't, I'll come back. All I need now is some food."

"Got some subs. Left over from yesterday but still fresh. Half price."

Barry shook his head. "Naw, nothing like that. Just some snacks. Chips, pepperoni sticks, pretzels, you know."

"Sure," Slu said, pointing. "Still right over there, aisle two, as always. Having a party?"

Barry went to the aisle and started crinkling bags off the shelves. "Yeah, just me and my girl."

"Hey, man, you got a girl? That's great. What's her name?"

"I just call her Lassie," Barry said.

"Lassie," Slu laughed. "Chrissake, sounds like a dog."

"Oooh, yeah," Barry said with a wink. "She's a bitch all right."

* * * * * * * *

He woke up when Lassie began to paw at his leg. She was sitting in front of him, looking up with that I-gotta-go-out-now look. When Barry leaned forward to scratch her ears something slid off his chest and into his lap. He blinked at it for a moment, trying to focus his eyes. When he realized what it was he picked it up and held it out toward Lassie. He belched and said, "You like pepperoni?"

Lassie sniffed at it, licked it tentatively and then sneezed. She got to her feet and pranced toward the back door. Barry stuck the pepperoni stick into his mouth like a cigar. Then he heaved himself out of the maroon vinyl recliner that was parked in front of a small television set. A handful of pretzels fell from his lap to the floor. Barry ignored them. The volume was muted but there was a very serious-looking man with a short white beard on the screen. He seemed to be staring right at Barry, intensely, his lips moving rapidly.

Barry teetered toward the back door and opened it. Lassie dashed outside and disappeared. The only light in the yard was the slightly warped and elongated square that fell outward from his back door. He could see his bicycle still chained to the porch railing but not much else. He closed the door and found a nearly empty can in the sink. He downed the dregs in two gulps. It was warm but what the hell, there was still a couple of cold ones left in the fridge and many more to make cold.

He pulled another can from the fridge, popped the tab, took some swallows, and went into the bedroom. After lugging another case back to the kitchen he clanked it onto the table. He took another couple big swallows and started looking for his box cutter.

He looked everywhere: drawers, cupboard, fridge. He even looked in the freezer. But the only thing he could find was a bent paring knife with a black handle. He downed some more of the beer and slit the carton open. He squinted at his left hand for a good thirty seconds before he realized he was bleeding.

"What the hell ...?" he muttered.

He brought his hand closer to his face and then looked around the kitchen, not sure what he was looking for. He tried to pick up the beer can again but it slipped out of his hand and fell to its side on the floor. Some of the beer *glugged* itself out onto the brown linoleum. Barry stared at the spreading puddle for a while and then went to the kitchen sink. He held his hand under the running faucet and watched the red stream curl itself into the drain.

* * * * * * * *

"You okay, man?" someone was saying. The voice sounded familiar but he wasn't sure. Barry tried to open his eyes. They seemed to be glued together. The right one finally cracked open a bit but immediately clamped shut again, seared by the bright light. Barry groaned.

"Hey, wait a minute, man," the voice said hurriedly. "I'll pull down the blind."

Barry could sense the slight darkening and tried again. He had to squint but he finally got them open. He looked at one face and then the other. "What the fuck's going on?" he muttered. "Fuckin' Shriners' convention?"

The younger guy made a face. "Your dog's been barking for an hour, Barry. Morrie and I thought you mighta died in here."

The older guy nodded vehemently. His sparse grey hair was rumpled and stiff. "Jonny's right. Thought you mighta checked out in here. Prez gave us a pass key. Said he didn't want to know what was going on. Call 911 if you must, he said, but don't get him involved."

"I fell asleep is all," Barry grumbled. "Always make a big fuckin' deal outta everything."

"Well excuse me," the young man said haughtily. "Next time we'll let you die in your own puke. Come on, Morrie. Try to do the guy a favor, maybe save his life, and that's the thanks you get. A freakin' cave-dweller is all he is. A drunken freakin' cave-dweller."

Morrie looked back from the doorway. "Pot of strong black coffee. That'll do it." He gave another short nod and then grinned and closed the door quietly.

* * * * * * * * *

Barry flipped through the channels looking for re-runs of Bevis and Butthead. He had called the cable company about three months ago, told them to cancel his service because he couldn't afford it anymore, since they upped their rates again. They stopped sending him bills but they never turned off the cable. This hour of the night all he could get was a couple taped basketball games, black and white westerns, two old Charlie Chan movies, and a slick-looking dude demonstrating meat grinders. He pressed the mute button and went down the hall to the toilet. He missed the bowl a couple times but what the hell. Give old Prez something to scream about.

* * * * * * * * *

Barry pushed the door open and held his hand in front of his face, shielding his puffy eyes. The sun sat like a tomato on top of the smoke stack. A few pink clouds were drifting toward the Gulf. And Lassie was barking her head off.

"What's the matter, girl? Think you see a rabbit? One of those tree rats, more like it." He slapped his thigh and barely felt the sting. "Come on, girl, settle down."

Lassie looked over at him. Then her long nose dropped to the ground and she ran back and forth along the chain-link fence. She stopped and looked back at Barry again. "Give it up, girl. Whatever it was it's gone. So forget about it, okay?"

Barry shaded his eyes again. Christ, he thought. Sun going down already. Where the hell'd the day go?

He was about to head back inside when his eyes jerked to a stop on the porch railing. He frowned at it, licked his lower lip for a moment and then his mouth dropped.

"Oh for Chrissake," he said disgustedly. Both hands went up in dismay.

His bike was gone. Again. This time they took the chain, too. One of the links was still on the porch steps, clipped off clean.

* * * * * * * * *

The perfume was so strong he could barely breathe. Well, it wasn't just the perfume. His nose was wedged so deep between Daniella's double Ds that he thought he had died and gone to heaven. "Come on, baby, don't be like that," he whined.

He could feel Daniella's hand fumbling with his pants. "It ain't me, Barry. You're the one who ain't in the mood. What's the matter? Doncha like me anymore?"

"'Course I like you, Dani. I love you. You know that. You and me gonna get married. Soon as I get a few bucks set aside."

Daniella took her hand out of his pants and pulled away from him. She pushed herself upright and stretched her legs out in front of her. Stuffing a pillow behind her shoulders, she leaned back against the wall. She wiggled her hips and tugged her skirt, pulling it down as far as it would go, which wasn't very far. After buttoning two of the buttons on her tight black blouse she ran a hand through her stiff blonde hair.

"I think you got the hots for that faggot upstairs," she said. "That's what I think. Girls ain't good enough for you anymore. Especially me."

"What the hell you talking about, Dani?" Barry said. "You're the only one that revs my motor."

She looked at his pants. "Yeah, right," she said. "That's not the way it looks from here. You got any cigarettes?"

Barry patted his shirt pocket and then jammed his hands into his pants pocket. He yanked them out and felt a sharp stab in the middle of his forehead. "What the hell you talking about? I don't even smoke. You know that."

"Oh, yeah," Daniella said. "I forgot. Got any beer?"

Barry waggled his eyebrows up and down. "Now you're talking." He swung his legs off the bed and pushed himself upright. He wavered for a second and then sat right down again, heavily. "Jesus," he said, touching his forehead.

Daniella leaned against him. He could feel the double Ds against his back. "You all right, sweetie?" she said. "A little tipsy? Want Momma to hold your little hand or whatever?"

"I need a beer is all," Barry said. "Then we'll see who's ready or not." He pushed himself up again, wavered a bit and then walked gingerly around the foot of the bed. He went to the closet and opened the door proudly. "This is my private stock," he said. "Been saving up."

Daniella twisted around. "Yeah, I can see that. Got any more cold ones?"

"Should be a whole shitload in the fridge."

He moved toward the doorway and wobbled going through. He glanced back over his shoulder and grinned. "Don't go away."

* * * * * * * *

Jesus Christ, he thought, suddenly panicked. I must be fuckin' blind!

His hands shot out and waved around wildly but he couldn't see anything. His head was splitting. His gut was full of slimy rocks. He felt like his mouth had been jammed with mud balls.

"Dani!" he shrieked. "You still here?" His voice seemed to bounce around the room, hurting his ears. Then he heard a movement of some sort, out in the kitchen, a kind of clicking sound. "Daniiiii!"

He tried moving his feet but something was holding them down. Ojesusjesusjesus, he thought, what the hell is going on?

His hands reached out again, lower this time, and he felt the sheets, the mattress. He fumbled under the sheets, feeling his bare chest, bare stomach. Christ, he didn't even have any shorts on. He shifted his weight to one ham, trying to get up. That's when he felt a sudden warmth spreading wetly between his legs, under his legs.

"Shit," he muttered.

Lassie began to bark and whine, scratching fiercely at the door. "I'm in here, girl. You all right?"

He swung his head to the left and felt an enormous amount of relief. He could finally see the faint outline of light that edged the window blind. He wondered if it was day or night.

* * * * * * * * *

Barry hadn't seen the creep for weeks. One guy at 7-Eleven said he got busted. Another guy said some dude cut his throat. But there he was, bigger than shit.

Same camo tee-shirt, same torn jeans, same rundown loafers.

"Barry, my man. How's the old dangle hanging?" The grin was as empty as the eyes.

Barry tried to brush by him. "Fuck off, Chick. You and me got no business."

Chick fell in beside him, still looking at him, still grinning. "Hey, man, that's no way to talk to an old friend. Way I hear it, you been on vacation couple days. That right?"

"None of your business I am or not.

"'Course it is, man. 'Course it is."

He laid his hand on Barry's arm. Wedged between his index and middle finger was a little plastic packet. "The thing is, I got some stuff that'll make it a real vacation, dude. Top of the line and cheap, too. Just came in last night."

Barry shrugged the hand away. "Told you once, told you a thousand times. I might drink a little beer every now and then but I ain't now scum-sucking gutter-crawler like you. Never will be, neither. Cause I don't do that shit. And I never fuckin' will."

"Come on, man, don't be talking like that. I'll even give this to you for free. 'Cause we're buddies, you and me. Known each other for years."

Barry lurched to a stop and shoved the guy with both hands. Then he took a sudden wild swing at the guy's head. But his fist missed by more than a foot. The momentum spun Barry half way around and he nearly fell to the sidewalk. Somehow he managed to keep his balance while the dealer leaped back lightly and chuckled.

"Oo-wee. We got us a new Mike Tyson on our hands. A honky Mike Tyson, in the flesh." He held up his hand. "But that's okay, Mikey, I still love you. And when you need me—and you will need me one of these days, Barry, my man—I'll be right here waitin'."

* * * * * * * *

It took three tries before Barry got the door open. His hand kept slipping off the knob. He found the chain, yanked on it, and the bulb and its cord swung crazily, throwing warped shadows up and down and all around. It felt like the whole closet was rolling sideways.

Barry grabbed the jamb with both hands. He held on tightly until his guts stopped churning. When he finally looked down he could not believe his eyes.

"Wot the fuh?" he said.

How could somebody steal his beer? He kept the closet door locked. All the time. Three cases? Where did the other four go?

* * * * * * * *

It was the shivering that woke him up, that and the cold air. He tried to open his eyes but only one of them seemed to work and all he could see was a cold circle of light. Then he saw a face, half covered with a mask. A green mask. He couldn't see the mouth but it looked like the eyes were smiling.

"Welcome back, Barry," a woman's voice said. "We thought you were going to sleep all day. It is Barry, isn't it?"

His face hurt, his chest hurt, his right shoulder hurt. He nodded. "Where am I?" he managed thickly. His mouth hurt, too.

"The ER at Memorial. A deputy found you near Twenty-third Street. Do you remember what happened?"

Barry tried to think, but all he could come up with was bits and pieces. "There was a car. Ugly green. Couple kids. Red light. A lotta yelling. I don't know, somebody started pounding on me. Things got all screwed up."

"The deputy found your wallet about a block away but there was no money in it. No credit cards. No driver's license."

"Don't have none of those," Barry mumbled. Christ his mouth hurt.

The woman took off the mask. She looked very young, pretty blue eyes, bright smile, like some high school cheerleader. "You don't have a driver's license?" she said.

He shook his head. His neck hurt, too. "Got in an accident couple years ago. Lost it."

"I see. And no credit cards either," the woman said. It was a statement. Barry shook his head again. "Well, at least your insurance card was still in your wallet so you won't have to worry about that. You still working for … what is it? Tec-Con Plastics?" Barry nodded. "Good," she said. "Think you can get up?"

Barry tried to lift his head but everything started to spin. He let it drop on the pillow again.

"Okay," the woman said, patting his shoulder. "Just rest for now. I'll come back in a little while. We'll see how you're doing then."

* * * * * * * * *

Barry gingerly touched the large lumpy bandage that covered most of his left cheek. There was another bandage on the back of his neck, a third on his forehead. The pain was starting to crowd back in so he slid the last pill from the little amber tube and sloshed it down with part of a beer. The ER girl had told him not to drink alcohol while he was taking the pills but what the hell. It wasn't like he was drinking grain alcohol, or even whiskey. Just a fuckin' beer.

He stared at the television screen for a while, barely aware of the chubby man in the business suit. Pulpit
of some sort, big cross, colored windows. Barry rummaged around beside both his hips and then at his crotch.
When he finally found it, he aimed the remote at the
screen and slowly flipped through all the channels.
Nothing but preachers and panels of newsmen, all looking slick and very intense, like the world was about to
fall on its ass.

Barry reached down with his left hand and felt
around the carton. He pulled the tab of the last can and
took a few swallows. With that and the pill and a little
luck he just might get some sleep.

He looked at his wrist but the Timex was gone. He
couldn't remember when he had last seen it. Did that
pretty nurse swipe it when he was knocked out? Who
knows?

He leaned sideways in his chair and tilted his head
until his neck started to pinch again. But it wasn't
enough. He could see his bed but he still couldn't see the
lamp stand and he couldn't see the clock. But it didn't
matter. He wasn't going anywhere. Not till tomorrow.

Lassie came up beside the chair and nuzzled at his
leg. Barry reached down and scratched his ears. He took
a deep breath and sighed. He felt good, contented, peaceful.

"Seven cases in seven days," he grinned, ignoring the pain of his cracked lip. "We got'er done, girl. We got'er done."

Time to Go

(Another flash fiction, this time the subject is facing—or not facing—eternity.—rh)

His silvery hair, neatly trimmed only a few weeks ago, was falling out in clumps. His scalp, usually pink, now had a slight greenish cast to it. His right wrist was raw and enflamed from the silver handcuff that encircled it. The other end of the handcuff was connected to the frame of the bed. It jangled with every yank.

"I'll sue, you know," he shouted again, yanking the chain. His voice was thin and hoarse from hours of yelling. His midnight blue pajamas were made of silk and edged with white. The name 'Jake,' also in white, was comprised of elongated letters in a diamond pattern. Old English Script; elegant but very hard to read.

"And I've got the best attorney in the state. Never lost a case. Never," Jake shouted. "And he won't lose this one either. I'll see to that."

The constant thrashing had loosened even the fitted sheet. The top sheet had twisted itself into rope-like coils that hung from the bed. One crumpled pillow was still stuffed behind the man's neck. The other pillow still lay in the far corner of the room where it had been hurled that morning.

"I'm not sick!" Jake bellowed. "Get a doctor in here. He'll tell you."

Jake's loud voice was just one among many that clashed with the moans and the cries and the ceaseless pleas that were coming from nearly every room, from the hallways of Jake's wing, and from every other hallway in the building. Each hallway was now crowded with beds and IV poles. There was barely enough room for the nurses to scurry, sometimes sideways, from one room to another, from one bed to another, from one body to another.

The removers had an even harder time. They not only had to sidle themselves through the narrow openings between the beds. They also had to maneuver the collapsed empty stretchers *in*, and then the body-filled and sagging stretchers *out* through those same narrow openings. And always the hands of the patients; reaching out, clutching whatever they could reach; scrubs, sheets, pajamas, hospital gowns, even the IV poles with their dangling tubes and empty bags.

"It's a mistake, I tell you!" Jake shouted again. Then he glanced at the man in the other bed, a bed that had somehow been shoe-horned into the tiny room.

There was barely enough space between the two beds for a nurse to squeeze through. If a nurse ever came.

"It's a mistake!" Jake shouted again. His eyes took in the other man's torn and dirty jeans, the dingy undershirt that was plastered to the boney chest, the shoes that were scuffed and lace-less. There were no sox. The other man's ankle skin looked paper thin and very pale, except for the greenish cast.

"You belong here," Jake said to the man. "Anyone can see that. But I don't." He grunted and looked away. "And why the hell they put me in here with someone like you I don't know. But sure as hell, I'm going to find out. And I'm going to *get* out. Out of *here!* "

He pressed the call button again and then flopped back on the bed. The movement yanked the silver cuff around his wrist and brought another grunt, this one of pain. He glared at his roommate again. "And why the hell do I have one of these and you don't?" He rattled the handcuff chain and gave it another yank. Pain seared up his arm.

The roommate raised his boney shoulders. "Don't need one, I guess. I ain't going nowhere."

"That's the trouble with people like you," Jake grumbled. "You're nothing but a bunch of goddam sheep. Not me. Nobody leads me around by the nose."

"Somebody musta led you here," the other man said. His giggle turned into a gut-wrenching cough.

"Like hell they did," Jake said. "Somebody drugged me, that's what they did. Knocked me out. That's the only way they could have gotten me in here. And when I find out who did it, I'll sue the hell out of them."

"We're all in the same boat, my friend," the other man said. "Might as well accept it."

"I will *not* accept it," Jake said. "Because it's a mistake. There's nothing wrong with me. *Nothing!*" He raked his fingers impatiently through his silvery hair. Another clump came loose in his hand.

The Gun

(This is a a short story about Time. Sometimes it's like a fluid, Time is. It flows effortlessly, seamlessly; smoothing out bumps, filling in gaps, easing through cracks. At other times, Time is like a solid: motionless, permanent, immutable. And yet, Time can also appear to be a gas; visible at first, like a thick and heavy fog, and then—sometimes in an instant—it evaporates, disappearing completely, as though it was never there. For fast-food worker LaVar Davis, Time is all of these things, especially now: when the barrel of a venomous black handgun is pressed against his forehead.—rh)

The stale odor of congealed fat, seared beef patties, and burnt tomato permeated the chilly air that was gushing from the ceiling vents. But LaVar Davis was conscious of neither the cold air nor the rancid smells. His whole being was fixed on the blurry shape towering over him, and on the arm that was angled downward toward his face.

The shoulder was very fuzzy and out of focus. So was the grungy tee-shirt sleeve and the stringy black bicep. The thin muscular forearm was slightly in focus. The corded wrist and the scuffed and gnarly fist were

more in focus still. Sharply in focus, with an almost sur-
real edge, was a large black hole—a perfect O. It was
bobbing wildly, less than a foot from the center of
LaVar's forehead.

LaVar knew, deep in his gut, that any second now,
out of that hole would come a round lead slug, nearly the
thickness of his thumb. He knew logically that the incredible speed of the slug would make its short flight impossible to see. And yet his mind could picture the explosion of flame and smoke quite clearly.

The slug, rounded at the front end to a dull fat
point, would erupt from the black hole. It would look
shiny and smooth, as though fresh from a mercury broth.
The distance between the bottomless black hole and
LaVar's flat sweat-shiny forehead was a gap of inches.
But in his mind, it took at least ten seconds for the slug to
cross that gap.

LaVar could visualize the slug with an almost
supernatural clarity. It was coming straight toward him,
slowly, inexorably, like the image in a super slo-mo film.
After a seemingly endless transit, the chunk of searing
lead would slowly slam into his forehead, punching a
hole through the bone.

His brain would sense a blinding scarlet flash. The
slug would flatten slightly as it burst through the bone. It
would then explode like a grenade deep inside his skull.

And LaVar would cease to exist.

But before the explosion could happen there had to be an enormously loud metallic click as the gunman cocked the hammer back.

The focus of LaVar's shiny black eyes leaped upward in an instant. From the black hole, his visual focus snapped directly to the face beyond the enormous handgun.

LaVar's tongue flicked around his parched lips. "Come on, bro," he pleaded, his eyes like twin black moons. "I got a wife and two kids. I know how to keep my mouth shut."

The gunman chuckled coldly. His teeth glowed like wet fresh bone. "I know how to keep your mouth shut, too, dude," he said, grinning.

LaVar waggled his head frantically. "Naw, man," he begged. "You don't have to play this out. Cut me some slack, bro. That's all you got to do."

The gunman's grin suddenly dissolved and his words were ejected like frozen spittle. "I'm tired of this shit. You are dead—"

The words were suddenly lopped off as the gunman jammed the frigid metallic hole against LaVar's forehead and pulled the trigger.

Like grapeshot from a musket, the enormously loud click bounced off the walls and plate glass windows.

It echoed among the stacked chairs and streaky mauve tabletops. Then it slammed back into LaVar's ears as his body convulsed with terror. His heart nearly burst through his ribs.

But nothing happened. No flames. No smoke. No shiny screaming slug.

For an instant, a grunt of surprise was the only sound that hung in the cold greasy air. Then—his fierce eyes wide with shock, his forehead creased with confusion—the gunman twisted the gun sideways. He stared at the barrel like it was some kind of black steel viper.

To LaVar, the gunman's grunt was an oral switch thrown deep inside his brain. In a shattered second, the frozen terror that had crippled both his mind and his body was suddenly gone. And before the thought had formed in his brain, LaVar's body slammed into motion.

Like a sleek-muscled stallion, he hurled himself forward, his shoulder plowing into the gunman's gut, his hands shoving the weapon aside. The hunk of heavy steel flew out of the bony fist and clattered across the floor, careening off chipped table legs.

Running wildly toward the exit, LaVar recalled with delight that the heavy glass door was still unlocked. True, had he locked it, as he usually did every night after closing time, the gunman would not have gotten in. But it was also true that had he locked it, LaVar himself could not get out, not without fumbling for keys.

As soon as his feet hit the ridged rubber trip mat the thick glass door began to move outward, but much too slowly. A high-pitched animal grunt erupted from LaVar's throat as he slammed his shoulder into the thick glass. Something crunched inside his neck as he shoved the door aside. He ignored the pain and spurted outward onto the sidewalk.

Like bent rainbows, neon lights glowed in all directions. A sliver of moon was crouched on a roof across the street. Stars sprinkled a midnight sky. And another man was just outside.

LaVar's stomach pitched. This guy was standing on a piece of shadow-darkened sidewalk, just beyond the heavy glass door. He was looking down the street. At the whooshing sound of the opening door his head jerked around.

For a moment, LaVar lurched to a stop, stunned. It had never occurred to him that the gunman inside might have an accomplice outside.

The accomplice was clearly surprised, too, by LaVar's sudden appearance. He let out an indecipherable yelp, stumbled, and then flew backwards as LaVar slammed into him. The man's chest took the full force of LaVar's shoulder. An instant later the man was sprawled on the sidewalk, cursing and sputtering. A gun skittered out of his hand.

LaVar leaped over the man, raced across the small empty parking lot and plunged into the equally empty street. He knew that his very life depended on how fast he could run. And he was enormously thankful that he had thrown away the Marlboros, lost twenty pounds, and started jogging more than a year ago.

LaVar wished he was wearing his new blue and white running shoes. His shiny black loafers had stiff leather soles. At every step, they slapped painfully against the iron cement of the sidewalk.

As he ran, LaVar clawed at his yellow tie. He ripped at the crisp white fabric of his shirt. Buttons popped off and shot away like spinning ivory flares. The tie flicked into the gutter.

He glanced back over his shoulder. Both men were now in the parking lot. Both were on their feet. And each had a gun in his hand.

LaVar was running flat out. He couldn't see the orange spurt of fire that erupted from the two black holes behind him. But he could hear the tight muffled popping sounds. He could also hear the piercing whines, the shrieking ricochets as searing chunks of lead splattered off concrete and crashed through storefront windows

Less than a yard behind him, shards of glass collapsed to the sidewalk. An instant later, an errant slug triggered a rust-encrusted burglar alarm. Hysterical up-and-down wailings began to slice through the night, screeching at silent buildings.

LaVar ran faster, bent forward in an awkward humpy crouch. He tried to reduce himself to the smallest possible target. His breath was coming in steady bursts. His heart was thumping strongly, confidently. Only his feet and ankles hurt. He would have given his right thumb for the comforting spring of his running shoes.

More jets of fire erupted behind him, more husky popping sounds. More whistling slugs zipped past his head and hips.

The two men behind him were running now, too. Their gait was clumsy and laborious—a sharp contrast to the smooth flow of LaVar's pumping legs and the rhythmic stroke of his bent arms.

Above his own surging breaths, LaVar could hear the panting curses and the heavy thumping footsteps of the men. He knew he could outrun them easily. But he also knew he could *not* outrun the heavy globs of burning lead.

With ridiculous ease, any one of the slugs could sear away the fragile cotton of his shirt. It could also plough easily through flesh and bone. His only hope was to keep running low and frantically pray for a miracle.

LaVar's head rotated jerkily as he ran. His eyes

swept the street in every direction. "Where are the cops?" his mind screamed in anger. "Where are the freaking cops?"

He glanced to the right and then to the left as he raced out into an intersection. The yellow light of a traffic signal was blinking slowly overhead. Each blink was paired with a tiny metallic click. Each pulse of light scattered the street with faint sprays the color of mustard.

The yellow light bounced off storefront windows. Ineffectively, it probed inky alleys, shadowy doorways. The only thing that actually held and then tossed back the yellow sheen was a glass-fronted sign which stood tall on black pipe legs. The legs were rooted in dirt, directly in front of the gothic bulk of Pierce Cathedral.

Nearing the sign, LaVar glanced at the flagstone steps that angled steeply upward from the sidewalk. He was certain the huge stone building would be a perfect haven, an effective buffer from searching slugs.

But he was also certain the enormous wooden doors would be stoutly locked and hung from hinges as large as a giant's fist. The arch-shaped oak was likewise toughened with criss-cross straps of decorative iron. Nothing less than an overloaded cement truck could rupture the wood and splinter the peace.

He swung away from the church and left the street, springing lightly onto the sidewalk. Ten yards later, a cracked and jutting piece of concrete caught the toe of LaVar's right loafer. The sidewalk that had been flowing smoothly beneath his feet suddenly jerked sideways and then tilted steeply. The concrete came rushing upward toward his face.

As he lost his balance, LaVar's hands automatically shot forward, trying to stop the inevitable.

But the instant reaction didn't help. His landing was hard and jarring. His palms skidded painfully across the sidewalk. The rough cement peeled back layers of skin and bunched it into rumpled rows.

The rock-hard cement also slammed into his knees and chest. His chin bounced off the coarse gray surface. He felt more skin peel away, this time from his chin, as a mass of stars burst inside his eyeballs.

Skidding forward, LaVar was vaguely aware that the little finger on his right hand had been shoved outward at an unnatural angle. He could feel a streak of pain split the side of his wrist and forearm as the small bone in his finger snapped like a dry twig.

Seconds later he was aware of another searing pain, this one in his left knee. When he tried to push himself to his feet, a third stab of pain streaked upward through the bones of his right arm and settled in his shoulder.

He wondered briefly if one of the slugs had finally

found his flesh. Or had the fall crookedly wrenched a ligament in his arm or shoulder. He couldn't really tell. His neck was hurting, too.

For the first time, LaVar knew he would not be able to outrun the two men. Despite his superior physical condition, the sudden painful injuries were quickly tipping the balance in their direction.

LaVar heaved himself painfully onto one knee, the knee that didn't hurt. He wiped his palms, wet with blood, across the front of his open ghost-white shirt.

The stains look black under the high greenish light of the street lamps. He tried to smooth the rumpled skin on his palms. The ragged edges of tissue were now oozing blackness freely.

Another shrieking chunk of lead screamed by his right temple. He could almost feel its heat and its maniacal speed as it hurtled by. Instantly, the slug created another avalanche of shattered glass.

LaVar tried to remember how many shots the men had already fired. It seemed like hundreds, surely dozens. But that wasn't possible. No pistol, no revolver, no handgun he ever heard of could hold dozens of bullets.

And yet he couldn't remember a time when the popping sounds had stopped completely. Nor could he remember the men pausing long enough to reload their guns. And yet the flames kept spitting out, the whining shrieks kept ripping the fetid air, over and over again.

It doesn't make any sense, LaVar thought.

Ignoring the crosshatch of pains, LaVar shoved himself upright. He tottered for a moment, wavering, light headed. Then he lumbered forward again, his gait crouched and limping.

With the two men less than twenty yards behind him now, LaVar's own breath was coming in panting gasps. Surely the gunmen must be breathless, too, he thought. And yet their vile shouts were still incredibly loud. The gunmen didn't sound breathless at all. Or even tired.

That didn't make any sense either.

All of a sudden LaVar saw a police car in the middle of the empty street. It was cruising very slowly, soundlessly, its headlight beams protruding like cones of ivory.

LaVar was stunned. The police car had seemed to materialize right before his eyes.

One second the street was completely empty and silent except for the hostile yells and the pounding feet behind him. A second later a full-size car—with two full-size men in uniforms—was right there, in the middle of the street, not fifteen feet away.

LaVar shrieked with delight, unable to believe his

own eyes. He started stumbling toward the car, yelling hysterically, frantically waving his bloody hands.

He could see the two policemen quite clearly. They looked like cardboard cutouts. The detail of their faces had been drawn with a needle-tipped pen.

One man, the driver, had a tiny razor cut just below his nose. Small stiff hairs jutted from his right ear.

The other man had thick bushy eyebrows. There was a small waxy lump near his left temple.

The interior of the car was lit by an odd lavender glow that formed black shadow-patches above the policemen's chins and around their deep-set eyes. The light also cast a faint purplish blush across the two stern faces.

LaVar's shouts grew louder and more frantic as he raced toward the cruiser. But no matter how hard LaVar shouted or how wildly he waved his arms, the two officers continued to stare straight ahead.

LaVar was running alongside the cruiser now, next to the driver-side window, screaming for help. His eyes were wide and shiny; his face was slick with sweat. Slaver, spewed by his desperate shouts, splattered across the window glass.

But there was no reaction at all from the policemen. They sat like statues, like rigid manikins, their motionless eyes focused on infinity. Suddenly frustrated and furious, LaVar thumped his bloody palms against the window glass as he stumbled along beside the slowly moving vehicle. Crumpling his hands into bloody fists, he began to pound on the roof of the police cruiser, five, six, seven times.

But there was still no reaction from the two policemen. There was no acknowledgement at all that he was less than a foot away, walled off by a thin skin of shatterproof glass.

LaVar ran beside the police car for nearly a block, pounding and screaming. Black smudgy bloodprints quickly stained the glass and the roof of the car. But the policemen continued to stare wordlessly ahead.

Gradually then, LaVar felt himself slipping backwards. At first his fists pounded the cold metal directly above the cop's head. Then his fists were pounding above the rear door, then the trunk lid. And then his fists were flailing the air.

He didn't know whether the police car had picked up speed or whether his own exhaustion had started dragging him backwards.

Shock and disbelief hurled his brain into an iron wall. His exhausted body stumbled to a teetering, shoulder-sagging stop.

Bent over and panting painfully, he couldn't believe what had just happened. It wasn't possible that the policemen didn't know he was there. With all of his pounding and shouting and screaming? It simply wasn't possible.

And it wasn't like they were ignoring him either. It was like he didn't even exist, like none of this was really happening.

Gasping for breath, LaVar wobbled around in a circle as the police car pulled inexorably away. As it moved on down the street it gradually got smaller, and smaller, and smaller.

LaVar's body was twisted and heaving. His face, drenched with sweat, was tilted upward toward the black sky. His arms, bent slightly at the elbows, stretched outward from his shoulders. His bloodied palms were turned toward the black sky in supplication.

"They knew I was there," he gasped painfully, as if trying to explain the strange phenomenon to a stupid child. "I *know* they knew I was there. But they wouldn't stop!"

Hopelessness squeezed his brain. Time—an engorged tar ball plunged into ice—had stiffly congealed. It had turned into a rimy lump of granite, unmoving, unfeeling, dead.

The police car had disappeared completely now. He hadn't seen it turn a corner. He hadn't seen it pull into an alleyway. It had simply disappeared. Only the two gunmen were still there, maddeningly, in the street behind him.

They were still running. They were still shrieking obscenities.

But somehow the distance between LaVar and his two pursuers had lengthened. It was as though the street behind him was being stretched slowly and steadily away from him, like a black rubber sheet. LaVar was at one end of the sheet. The two men with guns were at the other end.

Although the feet of the pursuers were still thumping forward their bodies appeared to be drifting backward, getting smaller and smaller, just like the police car.

The eruptions of ruby pistol flame had grown smaller, too. The spurts tightened into small red blips that appeared and disappeared, motes in a gargoyle's eye. Slowly the blips faded, dimmed. And then they, too, winked out.

When LaVar's head swung forward again he gasped. Just beyond the dark towering buildings he could now see a sprinkling of trees. A moment later the sparse scattering of bony trunks and blurry leaves thickened, expanded, and turned into a forest.

As swiftly as he could, LaVar raced toward the misty mass of safety. Once among the oaks and tangled vines he felt a thrilling surge of strength, a tidal wave of hope.

His calf muscles, on fire from the endless running, now felt suddenly fresh and strong. His lungs, cramped and straining before, now felt loose, clean. His brain was enriched by scarlet blood.

LaVar was now convinced that he could run forever. But he also knew that he no longer *had* to run forever. In fact, he knew he did not have to run at all, not anymore. The crisis was over.

The lumbering dash quickly slowed to an effortless trot. The trot became a comforting stroll.

His life was his own again. All he had to do now was wend his way easily through the wooded parkland that lay between the city and his home.

He pushed a tiny button on his watch. The calm blue-lit face said dawn was near. The pale but rising sun would soon turn black leaves into gray, then navy, then turquoise. Finally the leaves would take on the deep rich green of an Irish hillside.

LaVar could not remember the last time he had felt so liberated, so joy-filled, so certain of everything. The incident with the guns and the two robbers began to feel like a vague blurry nightmare. It had been a frightening nightmare, terrifying even. But it was still only a nightmare. And nightmares fade like lavender smoke.

In its place, his mind could see his freshly painted

home, less than a block away. His mind could also see his wife, Tisha. It could see the wide dark eyes of his daughters, Rose and Amber.

LaVar wondered if Tisha would still be up, waiting for him, like she was every other Friday night.

Despite the damp, musty, leaf-cluttered woods that surrounded him, LaVar could almost smell the faint sweetness that always seemed to surround his wife.

Even when the two of them worked outdoors in the summer heat—painting, planting, mowing—even then the sweetness clung to her, exuded from her.

LaVar pictured Tisha's outline as she slept on her side. He could visualize her quite clearly.

Beneath the pink sheet her hip stood out rounded, sensual, like an ancient mountain smoothed and caressed by eons of soft rain. The mound dropped away quickly toward her valley-like waist. And then the surface began to climb again, following the smooth line of her back, following the slope of her graceful neck. The memory of those undulating lines that rose and fell so gently filled LaVar's chest with a warm lightness.

In a few minutes, there would be no need for mental images. He would be seeing the porch, the front door, the hallway. He would be seeing the stairs that led to their bedroom. He would be seeing his wife. And all of those things would be real, solid, touchable.

As LaVar's gait increased, a balloon of joy inflated in his chest. A moment later he burst from the park, free of the trees. He flew across the empty pre-dawn street.

The instant his feet touched the creaking floor of the porch, he yanked the screen door outward. It clumped and twanged against his shoulder. His right hand gripped the cold smooth doorknob. He gave it a twist and a shove. The door flew open, banging against the living room wall.

Startled and immeasurably pleased, LaVar immediately saw his wife standing in the hallway. A light from behind pierced her nightgown. It outlined her shoulders, her waist, her hips. It haloed the smooth descent of her thighs.

Her hands were reaching out. Her arms were open, accepting. Her lips were forming a perfect O.

LaVar's joy was unspeakable. His body was poised in the open doorway, ready to plunge once more into lasting peace.

But suddenly something was horribly wrong.

In an instant, he felt the nerves and muscles of his face snap tight. They twisted his mouth, warped his cheeks. His face became a hideous mummified mask.

Instead of his wife's eternal sweetness, the odor that suddenly filled his nose was burnt and oily. It was the smell of congealed grease. It was the smell of seared beef patties and slices of burnt tomatoes. Erratically tumbling the rancid smells, a torrent of chilled air was still gushing from a ceiling vent, washing over his sweaty horrified face.

The perfect O of his wife's mouth was once again a circle of steel. The face above the O was not his wife's face at all, had never been his wife's face. It was the same slithery skin of the gunman. The eyes were still blazing, the teeth were still wet-bone shiny. And the voice was continuing, ragged and shrill.

"—meat," the gunman concluded, slowly, forcefully. "Dead fuckin' meat."

The impossibly loud metallic click split the air like an axe. In the same instant, the O finally exploded as a shriek of red horror punched a hole through the bony plate of LaVar's forehead. It splattered its way through the jellied brain and out the other side.

And the darkness came down forever.

I Saw A Man Walking

(This story is based on an actual event I witnessed while I was studying for a psychology degree many years ago at Temple University in Philadelphia. It was such a poignant sight that it has remained with me—hauntingly—all these years.—rh)

I saw a man walking up and down the steps. He couldn't seem to stop. The day was cold, grey. The steps were made of concrete; so was the sidewalk. The tall building, too, was made of huge blocks of icy stone. The man was made of frosted wood. Or so it seemed.

Rigid back, frozen face, wind-stiff hair. A long grey coat. A long grey scarf. I wondered. What was under that long grey coat? Bark, dry leaves, and a sturdy trunk? All covered with searing frost?

Or maybe a suit and a scarlet tie that was made of Chinese silk? A starched shirt, crackling and white? Yes, likely that. Because the overcoat was very nice, with a handsome tailored cut; his shoes were shiny, too. But he couldn't seem to stop.

The man would trudge up the steps, his face empty. He would pause for a moment on the broad blocky stoop. His hand would reach out to the brassy door, inches away from a copper push-plate, worn by countless palms and blurring years. After a moment of almost-touching, the hand pulled back and sagged to his side. Another moment. Another beat. Then: like a new recruit in robot mode, the man would pivot, eyes straight ahead, and walk back down the steps again.

On the sidewalk he would pause, straight and still, for a very long beat, looking neither left nor right. Passers-by would veer around him where he stood. They looked uneasy, frightened. They walked faster. Some glanced back. Most did not. But it mattered not what they did. For him, they were not even there.

The honking traffic, the dirty ridges of curb-side snow, the parked and salt-stained cars, the grey faceless buildings across the street; he didn't see any of them either.

I wondered. Should someone be told? Someone inside the building made of icy stone? There were doctors in there. Ph.Ds. Psychologists. Professors. All of them spent their days and many nights, thinking: about behaviors, about abnormalities, about experiments, textbooks, theories, students. And about tenure. Their brains were full of knowledge, full of facts, full of multi-syllabic words. But would they know what to do with this man? This man who couldn't stop?

A bus whooshed up to a cross-street curb. Some got off, some got on. A few by the windows looked again and then they looked away. A cop car paused for a changing light; the driver glanced up at the walking man. He poked his partner. Both men laughed and wagged their heads before the cop car followed the bus, as both of them drove away.

Up the steps. Down the steps. Up and down again. Again. And through it all the endless question continued to churn and churn. Why did no one come and help? The man who could not stop.

Cinder Girl

*(Internet dating and chat rooms have become popular
pastimes, if not obsessions, for just about every teenage
girl in this country, as well as throughout most of the civilized world. Dangerous? Only in the minds of old
codgers past the age of 30. To teens and young adults,
the internet's social media is the be-all and end-all of existence. It's "where it's at!" It's "Awesome!" It's
"Life!" With a capital L. But signing onto a chat room
can also lead to unexpected surprises. Unless, that is,
you have a plan.—rh)*

The tabloid was spread open on the kitchen table between a sticky brown jug of syrup and a stack of sagging
waffles. Cindy's mother read the screaming headline
aloud.

"ANOTHER GIRL RAPED BY WEB CREEP"

She raised an eyebrow and looked at her daughter.
"Did you see this?"

Cindy avoided her mother's eyes and idly stabbed a
wedge of syrup-soaked waffle with her fork. Impatiently
she said, "There are creeps everywhere, Mom, not just on
the net. And nobody does a thing about it."

She forked a wedge of waffle into her mouth and chewed for a moment, her eyes dark, her brow furrowed. The lines smoothed out when she glanced at her mother again.

"Besides," she added casually, "I don't have time to surf the net. In case you've forgotten, I've got the girl's weightlifting team three afternoons a week. Trinity Youth Group every Tuesday. Chemistry club. Candy Striper work at Hope Memorial. The anatomy course I'm taking at night. Plus all the extra credit stuff I have to do for my Honors English class. I barely have time to brush my teeth."

"Good," her mother said firmly. "It's the idle kids who get into trouble."

Cindy got to her feet. "By the way," she said between munches, "was there any mail for me yesterday? I ordered some stuff from a place called Science Warehouse. For chem club."

Cindy's mother turned away from the cluttered breakfast table and was rummaging noisily through the drawer next to the sink. The clatter of silverware echoed harshly against the kitchen's yellow plaster walls. "It must be here somewhere," she muttered. "How can it just disappear? It's got a red and white handle."

"Mo-om," Cindy said again in a sing-songy way. "You're not listening."

"Of course I am," her mother said, still clattering forks and spoons. "A package from Science Warehouse." She gestured vaguely toward the doorway. "It's on the hall table, I think. Where I always leave your father's mail."

Cindy grabbed her schoolbooks and gave her mother a one-arm fly-by hug. "Catch you later," she said. For a second, her eyes darted toward the drawer her mother was searching. And then they darted away.

Cindy trotted into the hallway and whirled an anorak off the coat rack. She slipped first one and then the other arm into the pink wooly garment, shifting her books from hand to hand. She found the small cardboard box on the hall table and slid it into the anorak's slash pocket.

As she rushed out the front door she could hear her mother's questioning voice, apparently aimed at her father now. "Well, somebody must have seen it. A knife with a bright red handle couldn't just walk away."

Forty minutes later, Cindy and her friend, Terrianne, were being jostled by a mob of other students who had also gotten off the school bus. A dark-eyed boy with greasy pink hair and a crooked sneer sidled up beside them. He bumped Cindy's hip with his own and grinned.

"So what d'ya think, Cind?" he said. "Want me to teach you the facts of life?"

"I already know the facts of life, creep," Cindy said, her eyes cool and challenging. "Maybe I could teach *you* a few things."

The guy guffawed. "Sure. And the Pope's a Muslim. You think I was born yesterday?"

"Could be," Cindy said airily. "You're always acting like a two-year-old brat who doesn't know his you-know-what from a broomstick."

Terrianne and the boy both lurched to a stop and gawked at Cindy. Terrianne grinned. "Guess she put you back in your playpen."

The boy's face turned red when both girls burst out laughing. He stalked away muttering obscenities.

"You're terrible, you know that?" Terrianne said, still laughing. They entered the noisy echoing hallway. "Does your mother know you talk like that?"

"Like what?" Cindy said innocently. "There's nothing dirty about a broomstick. Besides, what Mom doesn't know won't hurt her." She glanced at her friend. "And Gregg is a total zero."

Terrianne wagged her head. "Some girls would kill to get a date with that guy. He happens to be the school's hotshot quarterback, you know."

"Jock or not, he's still a zero," Cindy said. "Anyway, they all look alike with their pants off."

"Cin-deeee!" Terrianne said, scandalized.

That night in her room, Cindy climbed into her faded green cotton pajamas and opened the small cardboard box from Science Warehouse. The miniature blue bottle had been wedged inside a thick bubble-wrap envelope which in turn had been surrounded by a squeaky mound of styrofoam peanuts.

Using a square-handled magnifying glass, she studied the tiny print on the bottle's scarlet warning label. Then she smiled.

"That ought to do it," she said softly.

She shook the bottle, heard the quiet chuckle of liquid, and looked at the label again. Satisfied, she wrapped the bottle carefully using the only pair of black nylon panties she owned. Then she pushed the silky wad all the way to the back of her sweater drawer, next to a battered half-empty pack of Marlboros. She rearranged the sweaters to cover both items. Then she sat down at the computer and logged on.

As she waited for the quiet hum of the start-up, she wondered how it all started; when had she made the decision? She couldn't remember that part exactly. It was more like an idea that just popped into her head one day. Then, like a germinating seed, it slowly started growing. All by itself.

The chat room part was something else. She distinctly remembered logging on for the first time about a month ago. It had been so easy. And she hadn't been nervous at all. The hardest part had been the preliminary search and then choosing which particular get-acquainted chat room she wanted to sign on to. There were hundreds of them. Thousands. But after a week of skipping around from room to room and observing a lot of the chatter she found what she was looking for.

She selected a room called Silk'n Steel and keyed in her first message.

"Hello? Anybody out there? This is Cinder Girl. And I'm looking for someone to light my fire."

The response to that very first message had been overwhelming. Twenty-three guys had keyed in during the first thirty minutes and they all sounded promising. She finally focused on one who called himself "Best Beaux" and quickly cajoled his instant messenger address. From there it was all down hill on an icy slope.

When the boot-up ended this time, Cindy signed on again with Best Beaux and a message immediately popped onto the screen. "Where you been, Cinder Girl? I've been trying to reach you for two freakin' hours."

"Sorry, Beaux," Cindy typed back. "Went to a youth meeting at the church. We discussed perverts on the web. You know any?" She posted two smiley faces that had halo rings over each head.

"Cut the crap, Cind. I gotta talk to u."

"OK," Cindy typed. "Shoot."

Beaux wrote, "We've screwing around with this instant messaging shit for weeks. I think it's time for a hookup. In the flesh. Whaddya say?"

"Your place or mine?" Cindy typed back.

"Yes!!!" Beaux typed in bold twenty-four point type. "Now you're talking! How about neutral ground? A hotel? I'll pop for the room."

"Whoa, Trigger," Cinder typed. "Not so GD fast. How do I know you're not some kind of pre-vert yourself just looking for an easy lay? Or maybe you're a cereal rapist."

"That's s-e-r-i-a-l, dimbo."

"Whatever. A girl's got to be careful, got to protect herself, right? So convince me again that you're not some kind of unregistered sex offender."

Best Beaux typed, "Groannnnn. How many times do I have to tell you this stuff?" But he rambled on for several paragraphs anyway, describing himself once again as a soon-to-be rock star guitar player, six foot tall, two-ten-all-muscle, thirty-ish, and **"well-endowed."**

"If you know what I mean," he added with a couple smiley faces of his own. "B & B," he added.

"Yeah, yeah," Cindy typed back. "That's what they all say. Big and Bad."

"Only this time it's true," Beaux wrote. "I **AM** B & B. Anyway, since we're playing tell-and-tell, tell me again about your goodies. And tell me what you're wearing now, right this minute."

Cindy looked down at her rumpled green pajamas and flat chest. She gave her statistics as 39D-23-38, long blonde hair, green eyes, one-fifteen.

"And loose and free at twenty-three," she typed. "What am I wearing? A black see-through teddy with scarlet puff-balls on the tie strings. But I usually sleep in the raw."

Cindy giggled as she typed the words. She had never owned a teddy in her life, or even a sexy little baby doll. But so what? Beaux was probably short, fat, and fifty-five. The whole thing was just a come-on anyway, right? A means to an end.

In the school cafeteria the next afternoon, Cindy clattered her metal tray on the table. "Touchy-Feely Freedman was at it again this morning," she said to Terrianne who was scowling at her pale stringy meatloaf and pale stringy beans.

As Cindy sat down across from her, Terrianne grunted and pushed a faded bean around with bent-tined fork.

"So what did he do?" Terrianne said, "grope you again?"

"Not me," Cindy said. "The girl named Meesha Something. He told her to stay after class. You know, the redhead with the sagging saddlebags?"

Terrianne looked up, her brown eyes wide. "You're kidding," she said. "That tub of wobbly lard? Freedy the Freak must be getting desperate."

Cindy grinned. "He probably got thrown out of his porny-horny chat room."

Terrianne gave up on her lunch and placed the fork back on its tissue-like paper napkin. One tine pointed toward the ceiling. "You really think Freedman is into porn?" she said. "He teaches math for God's sake."

Without waiting for an answer Terrianne went on. "You know what? I'd like to check out one of those porn sites myself. Just for the hell of it, right? Probably a real LOL."

Cindy shook her head. "Don't do it, Ter," she warned. "Once they have your email address you'll get snowed under with porno junk. How to go from a 34A to a 44D with just a dab of magic cream. How to tighten the old love slot. Crap like that. Besides, there's no telling who you might run into. Perverts. Child molesters. Rapists. Maybe even a murderer." She grinned. "At least that's what my mother says."

Terrianne laughed. "Your mother's probably right." She glanced around the cafeteria and then lowered her voice. "But haven't you ever wondered what it would be like to be with a man? You know, a real hunk. That tall dark stranger. Someone who knows what he's doing."

Cindy laughed. "I think you're turning into a pervert yourself, Ter."

Terrianne winked. "I'm working on it." She looked at Cindy for a moment. "Seriously though," she said slowly, "have you ever gone to one of those porn sites yourself?"

Cindy shook her head. "Too dangerous."

At eleven-thirty that night, Cindy increased the volume slightly on her MP3 player, just enough to cover the sounds of the computer's startup. Thirty seconds later Best Beaux's words marched across the screen.

"Name the day and the time, Cinder Girl. I got a hotel all picked out. The Lincoln Tower West. You know it? It's in your town. We'll have ourselves a blast. Whaddaya say?"

Cindy paused for a long time, her fingers hovering above the keyboard. Was this really the right one? she wondered. The best one to start with?

Finally, she closed her eyes, took a deep breath, and let her fingers fly. "OK dude. UR on. Friday nite. Seven-thirty. Lincoln lobby. How will I know you?"

"Yow-weeee!" Beaux typed. "I'll be the one wearing a Seattle Mariners baseball hat. And if the desk clerk gets nosy just tell him you're there to meet your brother, Frank Morgan. That's the name I'll use to get a room. Tell'em our Mom and Dad will be along later. Family reunion. Got it?"

"Got it," she typed.

Early Friday morning while she was helping her mother fold the wash Cindy said, "By the way, I won't be home for supper tonight. A girl named Mary transferred from Garfield High last week. She wants me and a couple other girls to meet her for pizza at the mall. We'll probably chill there till it closes. Maybe take in a movie."

"Oh," Cindy's mother said. "Well, that's okay I guess. Your father and I have to go to one of those dreadful retirement functions. They always drag on till midnight." She glanced at Cindy. "How will you get there and back?"

Cindy stacked the folded clothes into the laundry basket. "To the mall?" she said. "Mary's dad'll take us and pick us up. I probably won't be home till after eleven. That's when the mall closes on Friday nights. Do we have of those plastic baggies?" she added. "The zipper kind?"

Her mother picked up the laundry basket and headed toward the doorway. She nodded toward the sink.

"Down below. Next to that green window cleaner. What do you need a baggie for?"

Cindy pulled the cabinet door open, found the blue and green box and pulled out a single plastic bag. "Got some stuff I want to take to chem club this afternoon. Don't want it to leak. Stain my clothes."

Cindy went to her room, locked the door and pulled one of her father's neatly folded handkerchiefs from her pocket. Then she retrieved the black nylon panty wad from her sweater drawer. After unwrapping the small blue bottle she popped it into the baggie. She also stuffed in the handkerchief and then zipped the bag shut.

The bulky brown winter coat kept out the icy wind late that afternoon as she walked the three blocks from the purple-walled Let's Party! store to the sad old Lincoln Tower West Hotel on 101 South Ridgeway. The thick coat also concealed her flat chest, and its deep pockets provided a safe place for the new blonde wig, the plastic baggie and everything else.

Before reaching the hotel, Cindy ducked into the entryway of a closed but still-lit pawnshop. Her back against the wind, she fished the blonde wig out of the coat pocket and shook it vigorously. After pinning her own brown hair into a sloppy flat bun, she pulled the wig on over top of it. After checking her image in the pawnshop window she stuffed a few final brown wisps out of sight. Satisfied, she walked the rest of the way to the Lincoln.

Except for the unshaven clerk who was hunched over the front desk reading a tabloid newspaper, the hot stale-smelling lobby was empty. The clerk fingered the frayed collar of his dingy white shirt and then looked up. He studied Cindy through narrowed suspicious eyes.

"C'n hep ya?" he said sullenly.

"Is it okay if I wait here for my brother, Frankie?" Cindy said with a sweet smile. "He should be along any minute. My folks, too. He said he phoned in a reservation a couple days ago. Frank Morgan?"

The clerk glanced at his log book, nodded, and then turned back to his paper. Cindy shrugged off the heavy coat and sat down on a hard straight-backed sofa. She laid the folded coat next to her on the worn gold fabric and patted the lumpy pockets.

Every few minutes she looked at her watch and every few minutes the clerk glanced at her. Finally, a half hour later, a gust of chilly air rushed into the lobby as a middle-aged fat man came through the front door. He was wearing a Seattle Mariners baseball cap.

Cindy's mouth dropped open. God, she thought. That's Best Beaux?

He was at least forty-five, maybe fifty. He was also short, his skin sallow, and his raincoat looked as shabby as his faded baseball cap. His dark pig-like eyes leaped from Cindy to the desk clerk and back to Cindy again. The clerk was now eyeing him suspiciously.

"Hi, Sis," the man called out loudly. "Sorry I'm late. Folks'll be here later. Their plane was delayed by the weather."

Cindy got to her feet tentatively as the man approached, his arms outstretched. She could feel the desk clerk's eyes boring into her back. "Hi, bro," she said, allowing a chaste hug. She held him at arm's length. "You look weary. Old, even. Bad trip?" she grinned.

The man ignored the smirky grin. "My plane got snowed in, too," he said, "just like Mom and Dad's. I ended up on a Greyhound. What do you say we wait for the folks in my room? Sure hope their plane gets through."

While Cindy lingered near the elevator, Beaux talked jovially to the desk clerk, slipped him some cash and then got the room key. A few minutes later Beaux joined Cindy in the small stuffy lift and poked a round lighted button. The door bumbled shut.

As the two of them rose alone, Cindy said coldly, "If you're in your thirties, I'm in my terrible twos."

Beaux glanced down at her flat chest. "You're no thirty-eight D either. And what's with the wig? It looks like a Goodwill reject."

"It's called a disguise," Cindy said sarcastically. She pulled the wig off, raked a hand through her own dark hair.

Despite the cynical tone of voice, Cindy felt her stomach starting to quiver. The man was shorter than she was and that was good. But he was also a lot heavier than she was. She decided he must weigh two hundred pounds, most of it fat. So the placement would have to be just right. It would all depend on balance.

The quiver in her gut got worse. She was beginning to wonder if she could actually go through with it.

A light binged "Nine" and the two of them got off the elevator, Cindy first. She could feel Beaux's eyes fastened to her backside as she ambled down the musty dead-air hallway.

"See anything you like?" she said over her shoulder.

Beaux chuckled. "View looks good from here."

When they got to room nine-o-eight, Beaux jingled the key and grinned. "You sure you're over twenty-one?"

"You sure you're under eighty?" Cindy replied.

Beaux laughed. "A man is as young as he feels," he said. He grabbed his crotch. "And I feel as young as a Tennessee stallion."

"We'll see," Cindy said.

Once inside the room, Cindy secured the dead bolt and leaned her back against the door. The heavy coat was still draped over her arms as she looked around the room and then at Best Beaux.

"Might as well get started," she said, her voice flat, bored. "I'll need the money first of course. Business is business."

Beaux gawked at Cindy for a moment and then his face turned red. "Money?" he said angrily. "Who said anything about money?"

"You don't think I do this for free," Cindy said.

"You're a hooker?" Beaux replied, stunned. "I thought …" His voice faded away.

Cindy's hands began to perspire. She took a breath and kept her voice cold and calm. "Just what *did* you think, Mr. B and B?"

Beaux's flabby face sagged with disappointment. "I dunno," he muttered, looking suddenly lost. "I just thought you were, you know, out to have some fun. Like me."

He hesitated. "I guess … well, I guess I didn't think about hookers using chat rooms, you know?" His grin was embarrassed. "This is the first time I ever tried any-thing like this."

"Oh, sure," Cindy said, her voice sarcastic. "It's my first time, too. I'm a virgin."

Beaux insisted. "No, I'm serious. I just got this new laptop about a month ago. You were the first person I ever talked to in a chat room."

"Well, well, well," Cindy said. "Beginner's luck." She glanced at her watch. "What do you say we get on with it? I haven't got all night. Other fish to fry, so to speak."

"You have other customers?" Beaux said, clearly disappointed.

"Of course," Cindy said.

Beaux wagged his head, still staring at Cindy. "I can't believe this," he said, clearly crestfallen.

Cindy held out her hand. She rubbed her thumb against the tips of her fingers. "The money, please."

Beaux fumbled with his back pocket and then pulled out a warped and bulging wallet. "I didn't bring much extra cash," he said. "I didn't think I'd need it. You take credit cards?"

Cindy laughed unpleasantly. "Do I look like I'm wired with a swipe slot? Don't answer that."

Beaux grimaced. "How much you want?"

"How much do you have?"

Beaux thumbed through a sheaf of twenties. "I'll need some money for cab fare," he said, glancing up at her. "To get back to the airport. Is a hundred okay?"

Cindy appeared to think for a moment and then shrugged. "Yeah, I guess so. Since it's your first time. My usual rate is one-fifty so my pimp'll probably beat he shit out of me."

"Jesus," the man said. "I don't want that to happen." He counted out six twenties and handed them to her.

Cindy took the bills and stuffed them into her coat pocket. She could hear a tiny muffled clink of glass against steel. "So," she said, "why don't you take your clothes off while I use the john."

Beaux nodded stiffly. He sloughed off the raincoat and started tugging at his tie. "Everything?"

"Whatever turns you on," Cindy replied. She winked and patted the winter coat that was still draped over her arm. "I got that sexy little teddy in my pocket. Remember? The black one with the little red pom-poms?"

Beaux stood there for a moment, uncertain, and then he grinned. "Oh well. Might as well make the best of it. That's what I always say." He snickered and winked. "Hey, I wore my special shorts, too. They have this stuff printed all over them. You know, sexy porn stuff."

"Cool," Cindy said, sounding bored as she crossed the room.

She went into the bathroom and closed and locked the door. Standing before the sink, she rummaged in one of the coat pockets—the one with the blonde wig—and pulled out the plastic baggie. She slipped something else out of the same pocket and quickly moved it around to her back. There was a momentary glimpse of red as she carefully slid the thing between her slacks and her tucked-in blouse.

After retrieving a battered half-empty Marlboro box from the other pocket, she dropped the coat into the tub. She fingered a bent cigarette and an orange lighter out of the half-crushed box and lit up. She turned on the overhead exhaust fan and then sat down on the closed lid of the toilet, watching the smoke being sucked swirlingly up toward the chrome ceiling grill.

When the Marlboro was half gone she took a final drag and then stuck the stub under the faucet. She soaked it with water and then wrapped the sogginess in a long strip of toilet paper. She got to her feet, lifted the toilet lid, threw in the wad of paper and flushed.

"You ready?" she called out.

"Uh, yeah," Beaux called back hesitantly. "You want me on the bed or what?"

"Wait a minute," Cindy said, undoing the lock.

She opened the door a crack and peered out. Beaux was standing at the foot of the bed. His sagging white flesh protruded obscenely over the white boxer shorts.

She could see a series of sexually explicit screen-printed drawings in fluorescent pink across the white material.

"Now then," she said seductively. "I want you to turn around, sweetie, away from me. And then I want you to close your eyes."

Obediently, Beaux turned his back to the bathroom door and then pinched his eyes shut.

"Now I want you to stay that way," Cindy said. "Until I tell you to turn around again. Okay? It's a game I like to play. Men enjoy it, too."

"But what do I do?" Beaux said.

"That's the beauty of it," Cindy said. "All you have to do is stand there. And think about all those wild and sexy things you've been dreaming about. You know, the things we'll be doing together, you and me. Can you handle that?"

Beaux chuckled eagerly. "Sure I can. I already thought of a couple things." He wagged his head. "Man, this is really gonna be something. But it better be worth a hundred and twenty bucks," he warned.

"Oh, it will be, sweetie," she said. "Don't worry about that."

Cindy pushed the bathroom door open a little wider. "But remember," she said. "Don't turn around. And keep your eyes shut. Tight."

"Okay," Beaux chuckled. "I'm a-thinking. And it's a-growing."

Cindy moved quickly now, her heart pounding. She took the little blue bottle and the handkerchief out of the plastic baggie. She placed the handkerchief on the broad edge of the tub and unscrewed the bottle cap. She set the cap on the sink counter and then dropped the empty baggie into the tub on top of her coat.

Her heart was thundering behind her eyeballs and she took several deep breaths to calm her nerves. She held the final breath for a moment and then let it out slowly.

You can do this, she told herself. You can. Do this.

Taking the folded handkerchief in one hand, the blue bottle in the other, she slowly poured the clear liquid onto the snowy white cloth. She poured with her arms awkwardly stretched out in front of her, careful to keep her face as far away as possible from the handkerchief.

The bottle made tiny gurgling sounds as she emptied the contents onto the cloth. With shaking fingers she quickly stuffed the wet cloth back into the baggie and zipped it shut. A sickly sweet odor hung in the air for a moment before being sucked upward by the ceiling fan.

"Eyes closed?" she called out. She tightly screwed the cap back onto the empty bottle and set it on the counter again.

"Eyes closed," Beaux laughed, the sound husky and strained. "But everything else is wide open. Up and Adam, that's what I always say."

Cindy came out of the bathroom slowly. "Good," she said soothingly. "That's the way I like it, too."

A sickening disgust crept into her throat as she looked at Beaux's sagging backside, flabby shoulders, and skinny hairy legs. But she was glad to see his thick-heeled shoes positioned neatly by the bed. In his droopy black sox, Beaux was definitely shorter than she was. And that would give her all the leverage she'd need.

Cindy planned her moves carefully as she inched closer to the flabby back, unzipping the baggie. Lifting the wet cloth out brought another swirling whiff of over-powering sweetness. Cindy leaned her head back, turned her face to the side and took several deep breaths. She was less than a foot away now.

"Can't say I like your perfume," Beaux started to say. "If you asked me, it's a tad on the strong—"

His words were abruptly cut off by one smooth movement. Cindy jammed her left knee into the small of Beaux's back as her left hand snaked around his head. The palm of her left hand strapped itself firmly across Beaux's forehead and pulled backward viciously. She could feel several vertebrate crunch as her right hand clamped the ethyl oxide-drenched cloth tightly over Beaux's nose and mouth.

Hands flailing wildly, Beaux struggled with all his strength. He tried to twist away from the two muscular hands and the choking stench. But it was too late. Cindy simply pulled back harder with both hands, bending his neck even further back, nearly lifting Beaux off his feet. His croak turned into a muffled grunt.

Within seconds, the struggles weakened, the arms drooped. There were several more shudders and kicks, all futile. Beaux grunted once more and then his flabby body sagged. The cloth remained tightly pressed across his nose and mouth.

With her head still twisted to the side, away from the cloud of ether, Cindy's lungs were starting to plead for air. Her head was beginning to feel light and woozy, too. But she held her breath a moment longer as she slowly eased the heavy body to the floor.

She kept the handkerchief plastered across Beaux's face until her lungs began to scream. Then she pushed herself quickly to her feet and rushed away from the body. Air rushed into her lungs with several panting gasps. The dizziness faded as she squeezed her eyes shut for a moment. When she opened them again she looked at Beaux. His chest was still rising and falling slowly.

Cindy took another deep breath. Her hands were shaking. She could feel the slippery wetness under her arms and across her back. But she had to keep going. It was almost over now.

She knelt near the body, retrieved the damp cloth and quickly shoved it into the baggie. She zipped the plastic ridges together and then waved the baggie around, trying to disburse the remaining traces of sweetness.

She studied Beaux's stretched-out body. His neck was bent backwards at an unnatural angle but he was still breathing. He appeared to be sleeping. A tiny pulse was throbbing below his ear but the beats were uneven.

He might die on his own, she thought, from the broken neck. But on the other hand, maybe he wouldn't. She couldn't take that chance. Even paralyzed he could still identify her.

She took another deep resigned breath and shook her head slowly, sadly. "Sorry it had to be you, Best Beaux," she said softly. "But a girl's got to start somewhere."

Her right hand slid slowly around to her lower back, to the waistband of her slacks. When her fingers touched the red and white handle they gripped it tightly. She pulled out the long slim-bladed fillet knife and held it above the rising chest. Its glittering blade bobbed lightly in her shaking right hand.

Her left hand moved across Beaux's rib cage and then stopped. She placed the point of the blade directly below the breastbone and angled it upward.

With one swift shove, the blade passed through the skin. It made only the tiniest slit before it plunged into the suddenly stuttering heart. Breathing deeply, Cindy leaned her own chest down hard against the handle of the knife. After a while the stuttering heart stopped completely. The pulse in the throat was gone.

An hour later, Cindy was back in her own bedroom. While she waited for her computer to boot up she picked up the straight pin she'd retrieved from her mom's sewing box. She scraped a tiny single hash mark along the side of the monitor. When the Silk'n Steel chat room appeared on the screen her fingers began to move lightly across the keys.

"Hello!" she typed. "Anybody out there? This is Cinder Girl. And I'm looking for someone to light my fire."

The House

This is a flash fiction about houses that sometimes devel-op a personality all their own as Warmth and Darkness come and go.—rh)

A chilled wind blew through the empty house. It crept down hallways, hissed past shards, poured through splintered wood.

It snuffled among the closets and rooms, scattering dust, clattering blinds, and nudging doors that squeaked and groaned.

Late at night, when the wind went away, there was no sound at all. Only a deep pervasive pause, like a breath held tight, and waiting …

Then one day, change arrived, unannounced—three in a car with silver wheels.

One unlatched the sturdy door and the three walked in, trailed by a new and gentler wind, a wind that carried the warm brown scent of new-turned earth and sun-warmed rocks.

Footsteps echoed through all of the rooms, attic to basement, front to back. Voices floated upon the breeze and gamboled along the dusty halls.

The voices lightly fingered the walls, coaxing them all to an upright stance, a hopeful and stalwart position.

When the three went away to seal the pact they did not take the wind along. Nor did they take the echoing sounds, quieter now but warm and full.

And with hesitant fear, the house began to assemble once more the delicate tendrils of hope.

The following weeks turned to hectic months, all of them flowing with promise and dreams. All of them filled with the pungent odors of colorful paints, the gentle swirl of thick new drapes, the thudding and rasping of hammers and saws.

The once-dark cave was slowly transformed to a shining castle of light. And the light let loose an infusion of joy, sequestered for much too long.

From dusty rafters to basement floors the house felt full at last. It was certain now it could absorb no more of life, nor love, nor gentle warmth. Any more of *anything* would surely be too much.

Yet more of everything *did* gush in as a bundled gift with muscular lungs and whirling fists.

New additional sounds flowed in, filling the house both day and night, sounds that no longer allowed the walls to doze in the sun and creak at the moon. But the house did not regret the loss for it knew the sounds from other times.

It also knew the day had come for the unwanted ghost, the icy shadow, the empty Dark to once and finally for all be gone.

But even then, time moved on and 'finally for all' was not to be.

Before, the wails had been lusty and loud and they never continued for very long, quickly muffled by warmth and sleep.

Now, however, the wails went on. And on. And on. And on.

Sometimes the hours trudged endlessly by with cries now different as cotton from steel. Bottomless nights would drag themselves up to a searing dawn; but even then the wails went on.

No matter how long the bundle was held and walked and jostled and hugged, the cries would never give way to peace. Until one night they finally did.

During that night came one more change as the Dark seeped up again.

Stilling the sound and chilling the warmth it darkened each corner of every room, filling the tiny bedroom first. Then room followed room as each filled up from floor to ceiling and wall to wall.

But with every bend and stair step up, the house fought back, trying to stop the rising Dark. It tried with the strength of its will alone to save the light and hoard the warmth. But the last of its strength was finally gone and the Dark had won again.

In time, all warmth was sucked away, replaced by stillness and cold. Then stillness, too, gave way at first to the sounds of blame and pain. Then to the sounds of anger and pain. Then to the sounds of pain alone. And then …

A chilled wind blew through the empty house. It crept down hallways, hissed past shards, and poured through splintered wood. Late at night, when the wind went away, there was no sound at all. Only a deep pervasive pause, like a breath held tight, and waiting …

Patty's Day

*(This short story is adapted and expanded from a charac-
ter that played a real and a poignant if secondary role in
my first Jesse Eichenlaub novel, "Crosshairs." It seemed
to me then and still does now that she deserves a story all
her own. Here it is, still poignant, still real.—rh)*

Patty Simcox got out of bed a little before dawn as
she usually did, her brain sharp and clear, her mind and
body eager to start another day. She flicked on a small
bedside lamp that she herself had fashioned out of wood
and leather. It had been one of her very first craft
projects and it was still her favorite. The base was
shaped like a stagecoach, its parchment shade trimmed
with rawhide strips. The lamp complemented the vaguely western motif of her tiny bedroom

Slipping into a pair of run-down beaded moccasins, she padded toward her bedroom's single dormer
window. The moccasins made a hushed whispery sound
as they crossed the faux fur deerskin throw rug. She
pushed the tan wagon-wheel curtains aside and, with
some difficulty, wiggled the warped and sticking sash a

few inches upward. She bent over to sniff the clean chilly air that swirled in over the sill.

There was one thing she missed more than anything else during her winter circuit of arts and crafts festivals up and down Florida's east and west coasts. She missed the chilled early-morning air that smelled of rocks and leaves and earth and wood smoke. Winter mornings in Florida were sometimes cool but they rarely smelled of earth and wood smoke. Fish often, salty air sometimes, wet sand maybe. But no, she thought, Florida mornings could never replace the mornings of north-central Pennsylvania, especially in the fall, even when snap-shooting deer hunters descended on the area like mosquitoes on a bleeding hog, blasting away at anything that moved.

As Patty took another long breath she could feel and taste the cold air at the back of her throat. Finally, reluctantly, she straightened up, arching her aching back. She could hear the vertebrates snap.

The sky beyond the pane was still dark except for a band of grayness outlining the wooded hills that rose steeply beyond the hidden burbling of Pine Creek. She could visualize a small cluster of deer bedding down for the day in the midst of a well-secluded thicket. She could almost hear the sleepy scolding of grey squirrels as they peered out of their tree trunk holes for the first time since sunset. She imagined a black bear scrabbling around for a few shriveled berries, deep in a blackberry bramble.

She felt good, alive, hopeful. A wellspring of contentment ballooned in her chest. It was going to be a good winter season. She could feel it in her bones.

Patty called out to the grey-muzzled Springer Spaniel who was still snoozing on her bed, on top of his favorite thick red blanket. "Up and at 'em, Buck, old boy," she said with a smile. "We've got miles to go before we sleep."

Buck—named after a long-ago country singer, Buck Owens—uncurled himself with a leisurely yawn, stretched, pushed himself slowly, painfully to his feet and then waited for Patty. Wobbling slightly on the soft mattress, his soulful brown eyes followed her as she came over to the bed. His short tail bobbed hopefully.

"Old Arthur giving your joints hell too this morning?" she said. She cradled both of her arms under the old dog's chest and abdomen and lifted him gently, lowering him to the floor. Buck's feathered stubby tail waggled. "Believe me," she said, "I know how you feel. These old knees of mine are getting creakier every year."

Patty tossed her faded blue nightgown onto the bed and pulled on her favorite traveling clothes: an ancient colorless pair of stretch jeans and a washed-out western-style white flannel shirt that had black piping and arrowhead pockets. The shirt had once belonged to her favorite uncle. She would wear it until it fell apart.

After stripping the bed and pillow, Patty carried the nightgown and linens to the small utility room off the kitchen. She could hear Buck's toenails clicking behind her as he padded from room to room, following wherever she went. Finally tiring, Buck flopped under the kitchen table, contented now to follow Patty's movements with his eyes alone.

Patty flicked on a small brown plastic radio in the kitchen. "This is the last time the old washer will feel water and soap until next April," she told Buck as she stuffed in the sheets and nightgown. She carefully measured and then poured in the soap and softener. The drive from the Pine Creek Valley to Jacksonville should take three days at the most. She used to do it in two but not anymore. Joints and bladder wouldn't stand for that now.

But, no rush. She had packed plenty of clean underwear in her overnight bag, plus several extra shirts and jeans and her dark blue windbreaker. No laundering needed for at least a week, she figured.

As the washer sloshed quietly, Patty made the final runs between her craft room and the refitted 1999 Blue Bird school bus that she had dubbed The Orange Crate. The last items she carried out of the kitchen were her blue overnight bag with the Nittany Lions logo and a battered but still serviceable red and white cooler. The cooler was filled with three cheese and peanut butter sandwiches, a pair of Golden Delicious apples, and two cups of non-fat blueberry yogurt that she'd packed the night before.

Squatting in the middle of The Orange Crate with Buck at her knees, she emptied the cooler and stacked her sparse food supply into a small propane-powered refrigerator. A red bungee cord secured the cooler beneath a handmade workbench. The bulging overnight bag was crammed between the driver's seat and a scuffed and dented kick panel.

Buck's ears perked up when they both heard the sound of gunfire echoing across the Valley. "It's okay, Buck," she said, gently stroking the old dog's head. "It's just some hot-shot Dan'l Boone sighting-in his rifle." She glanced at her wristwatch. Deer season opened in less than an hour. "Could be a damn poacher, too," she told Buck, annoyed by the thought, "getting an early start."

She hated deer hunting season. She hated bear hunting season, too. She could never figure out why anyone got a thrill from blasting the life out of some soft-eye deer.

"But, to each his own. Right, Buck?" Buck's stubby tail bobbed briefly.

Back in the kitchen, Patty stopped for a moment when she heard the voice of George Jones. It was coming from the brown plastic radio. Years ago, Jones had started recording many of the songs written by Willie Roy Bryant. In fact, back in the 70s and 80s when country music was still king, Willie Roy's songs had been recorded by nearly every big name in country music, both male and female. George Jones had probably turned more of Willie Roy's songs into hits than any other country singer. So Patty always had a soft spot in her heart for Ole Possum Jones. She still choked up when she remembered the massive crowd of mourners that paid their last respects in Nashville.

She had an even softer spot in her heart for her uncle Willie Roy. She could hardly believe her ears when Judge Kurtson had read the will in '98 when Willie Roy died. Willie had no wife, no children, no living brothers or sisters. So he had signed over to Patty all the royalty money and, more importantly, the copyright ownership of nearly two hundred of his songs.

If it wasn't for Willie Roy, Patty would still be trying to cram art and music into the rowdy-headed kids at Winston Davis Klink Elementary School in Glen Haven.

"What a drag *that* was," she said, smiling down at Buck who was now sprawled in the middle of the worn, chilly, linoleum-covered floor. With his head resting on the remains of a shapeless dirty blue sneaker, Buck watched Patty's every move.

The royalty income didn't amount to much, not anymore; especially since Jones died. But she still got a check every six months. And it was those checks that covered the shortfalls when the craft business took a nosedive, which it seemed to do on a regular basis.

By seven-thirty, the sheets had been washed, ironed, and stored in the linen closet. The sink in the bathroom and kitchen had both been scrubbed one last time, along with the bathtub and toilet bowl. The pipeline from the well to the house had been turned off and the water lines upstairs and down had been drained to keep the pipes from bursting during the winter freeze-up. The electric and phone companies would turn off her service tomorrow and turn it back on April 1st when she always returned.

Patty had also made her usual postal arrangements with Ed Pickens, her nearest neighbor and also the local mailman. Starting today, Ed would collect her mail daily and sort out the junk. She would call him every Wednesday night from whatever Florida campground was "home" for a few days. Every Thursday morning Ed would FedEx the important stuff to her using the campground's mailing address. She and Ed had been follow-

ing that routine for nearly ten years and she'd never yet
been late for a monthly bill.

Traci Holton, Patty's only niece, had been pester-
ing her for years. "You've got get yourself a laptop, Aunt
Patty." It was a refrain Patty had heard during nearly
every phone call and had read in nearly every one of
Traci's monthly letters. "That way you could pay all
your bills online and we could also keep in touch with
emails. No matter where you are."

Patty always said she'd think about it. But she
didn't really want any kind of computer. She had had her
fill of them when she was still teaching.

The kids were always miles ahead of her with their
technical knowledge and she never did catch up. Now
she didn't want to. Nor did she feel the need to. She preferred keeping all the craziness that was going on in the
world 'out there,' where it belonged.

Patty took another leisurely walk through the
house, checking each of the window locks one more
time. Back in the kitchen, she glanced at her watch and
decided there was enough time for one more cup of coffee. She listened to an unidentified but very familiar
male voice singing a country song about pickups, dope,
and tequila. What happened to all the songs about love
and families and kids growing up? she thought. She
turned the radio off with an impatient twist of her wrist.

She shook her head with a snort of derision. "Country singers all sound the same nowadays, Buck. Every damn one of them. Even the girls all sound the same."

She bent down and scratched Buck behind his ears. His eyes closed contentedly as he let out a heavy sigh.

"Back in the day when country was king," Patty went on softly, "nobody confused Waylon Jennings with her favorite, Buck Owens. Nor did anyone think Skeeter Davis sounded like Kitty Wells. Lefty Frizzell with Porter Wagoner? Hank Snow with Ferlin Husky? Hell no! They all had their own sound, their own style, their own fans. Now ..." She shook her head again. "You heard one you heard 'em all."

She patted Buck on the head and straightened up, laughing. "I sound like a senile old crab who thinks the world's going to hell in an egg carton don't I, Buck? Well, to tell the truth I do think that. But I'm neither senile nor old. At least I don't think sixty-seven is old. In dog years, I'm probably still a silly romping pup."

The teapot started its shrill whistle as Patty pulled her favorite Nittany Lions coffee mug out of the cupboard. She set the dark blue mug on the table next to a single packet of sweetener, a plastic spoon, and a jar of instant coffee. As soon as she flicked the knob under the burner the gas flame vanished, the shrill whistle died.

Reaching behind the small stove, she twisted a knob. The knob shut off the line to the propane tank that was sitting on cinder blocks around the side of the house.

She spooned in the instant coffee, tore off a corner of the sweetener and dribbled in the white grainy powder. After pouring in the hot water and stirring for a moment, she carried the steaming cup out onto the porch. Buck followed along behind her, toenails still clicking.

Delicately blowing on and then sipping the hot coffee, Patty ambled across the porch, down the wooden steps and out onto the gravel driveway. The sun was still hidden behind the steep hills but the sky was already as blue and as deep as the sea. There were no clouds, no breeze, only stillness.

She always hated to leave Pine Creek. She hated to leave her little cabin, too. Most of all, she hated to leave her quiet and peace-filled life.

But she always knew she'd be coming back. So that made the pain a little less edgy, a little more tolerable.

Patty tilted her chin up to look at the sky, marveling at its depth and blueness. She started to inhale another deep draught of crisp pine-scented air when a loud pop erupted from the woods. In the same instant, a heavy bullet sliced across two hundred yards of crystal air. It ripped through Patty's throat, severing her spine.

Like a life-sized Raggedy Ann, Patty immediately collapsed into an awkward unnatural heap. The Nittany Lions mug shattered on the gravel. A spray of black coffee leaped upward in a slow-motion arc, and then splashed down again, darkening some of the grey knuckle-sized stones. Patty frowned for a moment, puzzled. She wondered why the bright blue sky had suddenly turned black. And then she died.

Buck, who had been heading back toward the house, reached the bottom of the porch steps just as the shot was fired. With a yelp, he lurched forward reflexively, bumping into the weathered hickory steps. He yelped again, this time from the pain. And then he looked around, confused and frightened. The only thing he saw was a young antlered deer, bounding away at full speed.

Buck's droopy ears perked up questioningly. His forehead wrinkled as he looked over at the familiar heap in the driveway. A red stain was spreading quickly across the front of the white flannel shirt. Buck turned around, looked toward the woods once more and then walked painfully toward the body.

The smell of blood made him pull back momentarily. But there were other warmer more comforting scents still emanating from the angular mound of flesh, bone, and cloth. Those scents reassured him enough to move forward again, but slowly, cautiously.

He nuzzled the upturned hand and whimpered. When he got no response he lowered himself onto the gravel next to his dead mistress. He laid his muzzle on top of the callused palm and sighed, waiting.

He was still there, still waiting, five hours later when Ed Pickens' mail truck pulled into the driveway.

All He Had to Do Was Call

(This short piece is based on an incident that happened to another man I worked with; in a different time period. It's about something we all have to face sooner or later: dying. Or to use a much more palatable (acceptable?) term: "passing."—rh)

He wasn't crying, exactly. The tears were just seeping silently down his thin deeply-grooved cheeks. He blotted the wetness with a mashed lump of tissue.

"I never did nothing to nobody," he said. His coarse voice was quiet but intense.

"What do you mean, Cal?" I said softly.

"I never cheated on my wife for one thing. And I could have. Believe me, I had lotsa chances." He took a breath and let it out. "I never cheated on anyone else either. Never stole any money. Never spread around a bunch of shit about anybody. Hell, I never even lied very much. 'Specially not to people I know. It just don't make no sense."

Cal touched his forehead for a moment. "Funny thing is, I never prayed much either. Now I'm praying all the time."

"About what happened?" I asked.

He shook his head. "No, I never believed in that shit, praying for yourself. Didn't seem right to me. I just want an answer, that's all."

His eyes swept the room as if searching for something. His voice grew louder. "I musta done something to somebody."

His eyes came back to mine again. I held his gaze. "You didn't do anything, Cal. Shit happens, that's all. I heard you say that yourself. A hundred times."

He shook his head and looked away. "It ain't the same. This is goddam different."

His eyes were blazing now. "This is me, for chrissake. Don't you get it?"

"But it could have been me," I said quietly. "It could have been Jose. It could have been Chris himself."

"But it wasn't," Cal protested. "It wasn't any goddam one of youse. It was me." He looked down at his calloused hands. His voice was almost a whisper now. "You don't understand. Nobody does."

A puff of disgust erupted. "Fuckin' Jose never even came to see me. Can you believe that? Him and me working together every fuckin' day for the past five years? And he don't even come to see me?"

"Has anyone else been here?"

Cal shook his head. "Just you. And you and me don't even work together anymore."

Both of us were silent for a moment, lost in our own thoughts. Cal looked out the window. The sun was shining bright and hot. The sky was as blue as a turquoise ring.

"Maybe they just don't know what to say, Cal."

"They don't have to say a fuckin' thing. All they have to do is sit here for a couple fuckin' minutes. Is that too much to ask?" His eyes were glistening, demanding. "Is it?"

I shook my head. "No Cal, it isn't. I don't know why they don't come."

He dabbed at his eyes again and then dropped the wad of tissue on his lap. "They said six months, maybe less. Can you believe that? Six fuckin' months."

"Did they say anything about the shark cartilage?"

"Said it's a bunch of shit. Christ, I don't know. They're probably right. But you can't just sit here and wait. You gotta try something. Anything."

His cellphone erupted. It had been lying silent on the nightstand next to the bed. Its ring seemed maddeningly shrill but upbeat, cartoon-like.

Cal grabbed for it, nearly knocking over a glass that was also on the nightstand. Water sloshed over the rim, splashing the open Bible.

As he snatched it up, the cellphone looked tiny and fragile in Cal's large fumbling hands. It almost disappeared completely as he eagerly punched the talk button and then clamped the phone to his ear. His voice was suddenly strong.

"Hello?"

A string of small faraway words quickly drained away the hope. Cal's twisting face turned scarlet. "I don't give a shit about the state police," he yelled. "And I ain't giving no money to nobody. I'm dying for chrissake. So fuck off."

He hurled the phone across the room. It bounced off a flowered sofa and then ricocheted off two sets of stubby wooden chair legs. It disappeared under one of the chairs.

Cal's wife leaned through the doorway. "You okay, honey?"

"Goddam fuckin' phone," Cal muttered. "Everybody wants money. Give money here. Give money there. That's all they want. Goddam donations."

She studied his face for a moment and then she glanced at me. Her smile was thin and weary; apologetic. "I've got to take Cal for a treatment in a few minutes."

I got to my feet. "Of course." I reached down and patted Cal's boney knee. "I'll come back tomorrow. Okay? We'll talk some more."

Cal stared at his hands as though he hadn't heard me. "All he had to do was call," he said.

A Small Round Hole

(This is another short story adapted from my novel "Crosshairs." It's about, possibly, the most colorful character in the novel, a character that has always held a special place in my pantheon of colorful characters. I never knew his given first name but his nickname seemed to capture his persona perfectly: Mange.—rh)

It was a perfect spring day. The sky was deep and blue and crystal clear. The air had the sweet crisp tang of new growth, flower buds, and warm wet earth. Down the embankment, fifty feet below the level of the narrow two-lane roadway, the icy crystal-clear water of Pine Creek burbled and chuckled among the countless rocks and boulders that protruded upward from the Creek's bed.

Pine Creek itself was about forty feet wide and three feet deep at this time of year. Most of the snow melt had already sluiced down the V-shaped valley, joined the east-flowing West Branch and then merged with the south-flowing Susquehanna River whose ultimate destination was the Chesapeake Bay.

Mange Paulhamus didn't give a shit about the ultimate destination of anything. All he cared about was winching the crumpled remains of a blue Dodge Durango out of Pine Creek, up the fifty-foot shale-covered embankment and onto the bed of Speedy's new top-of-the-line International tow truck. And that was gonna be one helluva lot easier said than freakin' done.

In his thirteen years as Speedy Bowe's right arm, Mange had winched cars, trucks, pickups, SUVs, even a fistful of cab-over Freightliners out of all sorts of tight spots. But this job had to be the worst he'd ever done. There were boulders, tree stumps, flood-dropped logs, and layers of rotten shale everywhere, both on the embankment itself as well as in the Creek.

The shale was the worst of it—slippery crumbly shit that tore hell out of your pants and ripped up your knees. Going down the embankment you were sliding on your ass. Coming up you were sliding backwards on your palms, knees and chin. One foot forward, four freakin' feet back. Slick as a patch of greased-up ice.

Mange grinned, remembering the EMTs—one man and one woman—as they scrabbled down the shale and splashed into Pine Creek, frantically looking for survivors. But there had been only one person in the Durango and he was a freakin' mess. Mange had overheard the EMTs talking about it.

The steering wheel had broken off on impact and the steering column had punched right through the bastard's beer belly, spewing guts and everything else all the hell over the inside of the Durango. After deciding the poor bastard was deader than shit, one of the EMTs—the man—had to scrabble back up the shifting shale, fasten a rope to one of their body baskets and then lower the basket down the embankment hand over hand. Once that was accomplished the female EMT gathered up what was left of the body, stuffed it into a black plastic body bag and bungee-corded the bag to the basket. Then it was her turn to climb back up to the road, shale-slipping and shale-sliding all the way.

When she finally reached the road, the EMT stopped for a minute to catch her breath. Then, working together, the two of them muscled the body-filled basket back up the slope hand over hand. Naturally, the basket got hung up on every boulder, stump and tree limb on the way.

Mange had watched gleefully, certain the dead guy was going to pop out of the basket any second and then tumble ass-over-jawbone back down to the Creek.

It didn't happen. But both EMTs were cursing and sweating by the time they finally transferred the lumpy body bag onto a stretcher and slid the stretcher into their ambulance.

Then Mange had to stand around with his thumb up his nose for another hour waiting, while the sheriff

and his fat-assed deputy finished looking things over.
Cut and dried, the deputy had said to Mange before the
two lawmen headed back toward Glenn Haven. The
smell of beer was all over the body and all over the inside
of the Dodge. There was also a paper sack full of empty
Bud cans on the back seat.

The narrow twisty up-and-down course of Pine
Creek Road could be unforgiving. Especially when a
driver was careless. Or sleepy. Or drunk. This driver
had definitely been drinking. Nobody had any doubts
about that. He had lost control of the Durango and
smashed through the guardrail. The car cartwheeled
down the shale embankment, shattering windows, ripping
off fenders, collapsing the roof and mangling the steering
wheel as it went. The Durango ended up on its crumpled
roof in the middle of Pine Creek.

Like the man said. Cut and dried. It happened all
the time.

Only this time Mange was on call when it happened. So it was his turn to scramble down that slippin'
and slidin'-ass shale—dragging the winch cable—and
then wade into the icy snowmelt water of Pine Creek.
The water was so cold it felt to Mange like he was plunging his hands into a bucket of fire. Then he had to grub
around *in* that ice water with his bare hands and arms,
trying to feed the winch cable over and around the front

axle of the Durango and then hook the cable onto itself. Next he had to climb back up the shale, patch his bleeding hands, and then winch the crushed remains of the Durango up the embankment.

Like the EMTs' basket, the mashed-up car got caught on every stump and boulder on its way back up the slope, making the winch whine like a bitch in heat. Twice, Mange had to slip-slide further down the embankment, an eight-pound sledge in one hand, and then bang away at whatever stump or rock was tying things up. He also had to avoid smashing up the Durango any more than it was already smashed up. The sheriff had said the driver's insurance company would want to look at the car later on.

While Mange worked and sweated and cursed, he thought about the ongoing squabble he'd been having with his boss, Speedy Bowe. Mange had been telling Speedy for months that he had to have a raise and he also had to have some kind of health insurance for his wife and kids. If he didn't get both the raise and the insurance real soon, well, he'd just have to flat-ass quit.

Mange knew he could get a job in a minute making snowmobiles at the Grizzly Plant in Glenn Haven. Hell, Grizzly always hired in the spring. Early summer was when the orders started rolling in from dealers everywhere. Stockpile the bastards in August and September;

sell 'em off when the snow begins to fly. Worry about the winter layoffs next winter.

When he finally got the Durango chained down on the flatbed of the wrecker, Mange patted the chest, side and back pockets of his water-soaked and greasy coveralls. He finally found what he was looking for in a snap pocket on the outside of his left coverall leg. But the pack of Marlboros was now a mashed and soggy red and white lump with a stream of brown water oozing out of it.

Mange cursed and hurled the colorful lump out and over the shale. He turned away before the cigarette pack silently disappeared under Pine Creek's frothy fast-moving water. He found a spare pack of Marlboros on the shiny dash of the new wrecker along with a slim black lighter. After pulling a slightly bent Marlboro out of the box he tapped it gently against the lid, straightened the bend, and lit up.

Mange rehearsed his raise and insurance speech as he walked slowly around the wrecker, tugging at the chains, making sure the Durango was fastened securely to the bed. That was when he noticed for the first time a perfectly round hole through the outside of the front left tire, near the rim. It was a small hole, just big enough to squeeze in the filter of a cigarette butt.

After staring at the hole for a moment he took another drag on the Marlboro, raked his grimy fingers through his black greasy hair and shrugged. The hole was probably poked through by one of the sharp-edged river rocks when the whole shebang slammed into Pine Creek. Happens all the time.

But Mange craned his long neck and peered up and under the Durango's chassis anyway, trying to see the backside of the tire. Instead of another matching tiny hole, there was a huge gaping wound with shredded pieces of steel mesh and rubber exuding from it. It was the kind of large raggedy tear that is caused by an exiting bullet. A heavy bullet traveling at a high rate of speed.

Mange peered at the large hole for a long moment, scratched his stubbly chin, looked at his watch, climbed back into the wrecker and cranked it up. Shoving it into Drive, he said, "Fucket. Not my problem."

A Bird That Flies …
A Bird That Soars …

(This is another story about airplanes and about the pi-
lots who fly them. More importantly, it is the story of one
particular pilot; a man named Chuck who devoted all his
energy into becoming the best pilot he could be. In fact,
he never wanted to do anything else BUT fly airplanes
for a living. And with a lot of hard work, assertiveness,
and single-minded devotion, Chuck achieved his goal
quickly. He did not, however, become the pilot of one of
today's giant airliners that carry hundreds of passengers.
He became a company pilot whose "office" was one of
the small six-and-nine-passenger planes that the compa-
ny not only owned but actually built. It was Chuck's job
to fly the company's CEO and VIPs anywhere they want-
ed to go. And by the time he was thirty, Chuck was a man
who was really living his dream—until he wasn't. This
story is actually based on a pilot I knew at the time, and
about his life and career as a pilot; and as a human be-
ing.—rh.)

Chuck Cornelious has changed. When I first met
him in the upholstery department of an aircraft factory in

upstate Pennsylvania he had a little cardboard sign inside the lid of his toolbox. The sign had a drawing of a slit-eyed crafty-eyed vulture sitting on the knobby branch of a dead scraggly old tree. Beneath the vulture was a single word: *Scheme*. That was Chuck's motto. In fact, it was his whole life.

We were both working in the factory at the time, back in the mid-60s. What I was doing there is not important; what Chuck was doing there was. He had just gotten out of the service a couple months before. I don't know what he did in the Air Force but I know he wasn't a pilot although that's what he wanted to be. He wasn't an officer either; no college degree and not enough time left to go through OCS—Officer Candidate School, sometimes called Officer Training School, OTS—at least not when he caught the flying bug. I doubt he would have gone through OCS anyway; that would have been the hard way. And the hard way was definitely not Chuck's way.

When his term of enlistment was almost up he started applying for a spot in the Air Force's training school for helicopter pilots. That, of course, would have meant another four year hitch, maybe even six years; but what the hell, he wasn't married. He'd get room and board plus a clothing allowance plus pay plus a commission and also learn how to fly choppers. At the time, the

Air Force was really beating the bushes for helicopter pilots because of Viet Nam. The reenlistment officer was certain they could work something out.

Two months, dozens of phone calls, fourteen interviews, three physical exams, seven batteries of psychological and mental aptitude tests, and eight hundred and fifty miles of red tape later, Chuck said, "Shove it. Six more years of this I don't need. Not even four."

So he took his severance pay, set fire to his Airman's Handbook and grabbed the first Greyhound out of Denver where he was stationed at the time. His destination was Albuquerque. Waiting for him there was a dark-haired, addle-brained but well-constructed young woman named Priscilla. Sil, or Silly, as it later became. He never told me how they met. But he did tell me the uncle she lived with in Albuquerque had died about the time Chuck and the Air Force parted ways. As a payment for her care-giving chores, the uncle's skimpy will left Sil with a rundown twelve unit motel on the edge of town. The roof leaked; the swimming pool was empty, except for wind-blown sand and tumbleweeds; the coke machine was permanently out of order; and every mattress in the place had either broken springs or soiled covers; usually both. Chuck's experience with all of these drawbacks was first hand, from an earlier two week leave and a couple three-day passes. But Silly loved him and the motel would bring at least twenty thou, he thought. It brought thirty-two thou, which was a lot of money in the 60s.

When he wasn't keeping Silly happy, Chuck spent most of their honeymoon studying flying magazines. One classified ad caught his eye.

"Workers needed at aircraft factory in North Central, Pennsylvania. Good pay, good working conditions. Fringe benefits include flying lessons at very low rates."

Within two days, Silly had been persuaded to think that *she* was persuading *Chuck* to move back to his home state. "Your parents are getting on in years." She wagged her finger at him cutely. "You really should be near them."

Chuck scratched his curly brown hair. "Maybe you're right. But what about you? New Mexico is your home."

"You know my uncle was the only living relative I had. As far as New Mexico is concerned they can give it back to the Sioux." So much for Silly's knowledge about Indian tribes, Chuck thought.

By the end of the month, Chuck, his wife and the thirty-two thou—minus travel expenses—were driving through western Pennsylvania in a '63 Dodge station wagon. The car wasn't new but it had a lot of space for boxes, suitcases, overnight bags and whatever else they didn't want to part with.

"Have you seen this?" Silly asked Chuck while they were driving through western Pennsylvania. She was leafing through a magazine that had slid off the dash and onto her lap as they wound around a hairpin curve.

"Seen what?" Chuck studied the road ahead, pretending to look for any deer that might leap out of the wooded hillside. He had seen the magazine before of course, read it from cover to cover.

"This ad for factory workers. Must be around here someplace. Says North Central PA. Isn't that where we are?"

"Not yet, sweetheart. That's where my folks live."

"You're kidding." Silly was dumbfounded.

"No. I'm not."

"Is there an airplane factory there?" she said, staring at the side of his face.

Chuck shrugged. "Don't know."

"Well isn't that amazing? I wonder where it could be?"

She closed the magazine and tossed it over her shoulder. It landed on the back seat between a blue overnight bag and a pair of fur-lined boots. "It's almost like fate," she said. "Don't you think? Us coming here at this particular time? And an airplane factory at that? That gives flying lessons? Along with a good-paying job? It's got to be fate," she said, nodding her head firmly. "What else could it be?"

Chuck waited for almost ten minutes before answering while Priscilla fiddled with the radio. The reception in that part of the Allegheny Mountains was either nil or tub-thumping hillbilly music that faded in and out with every curve in the road. She finally snapped it off and started buffing her nails.

"It seems to me," Chuck started slowly, "there is a factory, maybe seventy-eighty miles from Clearfield."

Large brown eyes, wide and fluttery, turned toward him. "Maybe that's the one. D'ya think they make airplanes there?"

"I'm not sure," Chuck said slowly.

"Well why don't we stop on our way to Clearfield? We could find out."

Chuck explained to her that in order to get to the factory they would have to drive *through* Clearfield and then drive another seventy or eighty miles.

"Oh," she said. Lines formed on her brow as she thought and thought.

Chuck glanced at her for a moment and then studied the twisting road ahead. "I'm not sure they'd hire me anyway," he said. The tone of his voice was just about the way he wanted it.

"Of course they'd hire you," Silly exclaimed. "Why wouldn't they? You were in the Air Force. You know about planes. And you're interesting in flying. Isn't that true?"

Chuck shrugged again but said nothing.

Silly made a *tsk*-ing sound and shook her head. "Honestly, I don't know what's the matter with you. You have more ability and brains than anyone I ever met and yet you're so un*sure* of yourself."

"Do you really think I could get a job there?"

"I don't doubt it for a minute. They'll be dying to hire you, the minute they see your background. Probably make you an engineer right off."

Chuck said he still wasn't sure they'd hire him but he'd check it out. Sometime.

Their visit to his folks' little farm lasted less than a week. Chuck got along with his parents all right, especially his dad. There was no problem there. The two of them had a great time hitting all the bars in a not-too-nearby town. They picked up a couple plump turkeys on the second night, Chuck told me later, and the four of them went at it in the straw-filled bed of his dad's Ford pickup.

No, the problem wasn't with Chuck's dad. He even tried to put the make on Silly but she just giggled and didn't really know what was going on. Chuck thought it was funny also but for different reasons. Chuck's mother did *not* think it was funny. An argument erupted between the two women and Priscilla was asked to leave. Chuck could come back any time he wanted to but "not with that woman."

Priscilla and Chuck's mom later arranged a delicate truce, Chuck said. After all, his Mom had thought, she *is* making her son happy and that was something to be grateful for. Mom's eyes, however, never again left Silly when she came to visit. And Mom never let Dad out of her sight either; as long as "that woman" was in the house.

* * * * * * * * *

Chuck and Priscilla rented a used mobile home that was less than a mile from the airplane factory. To those who live in the area the name of the town is obvious; for those who don't the name is irrelevant. It was just a small, mean, blue-collar town wedged between two mountains and covered with soot. The biggest events that happen there—outside of the opening day of deer season and the opening day of trout season—were the Thursday night fights at the Texas Grill.

Even today the Texas is open twenty-four-seven every day of the year. The menu at night is mostly limited to chili dogs and greasy coffee. The menu during the day is increased to include greasy home fries, greasy eggs, greasy soup and, so help me, greasy ice cream.

During the day the clientele of the Texas was comprised of overweight shoppers in faded overalls, night workers waiting for the three-thirty whistle, and a handful of college kids who went there to dig the local color. The clientele at nights was a bit more restricted. Second shift workers on their way home; and all the belligerent drunks in Clinton County. Sometimes these two groups overlapped; at other times they confronted, and then merged. This merging usually occurred on Thursday night; especially on a payday Thursday night which came every other week for the factory workers.

As soon as Chuck hired on at the factory he and Silly bought a new single-wide mobile home of their own and were awaiting the birth of their first child. During the wait, Chuck was working the night shift and taking flying lessons during the day. He did his solo in near record time and had no trouble picking up his first ticket. He also picked up some cronies: Jeski, Jeeves and Don.

Hank Jeski was also taking flying lessons. He worked at the same factory on the same hours but in a different department. Jeeves was a factory worker at night and an education major at the local state teacher's college during the day. Jeeves was not a pilot. Nor was Don Stalling. I'm not sure what Don did during the day except smoke two or three packs of cigarettes per eight-hour shift, study Freud during breaks, and try to calculate how many days he could cut work in a two week period without getting fired. The union and management had conjured up a very complex formula concerning absenteeism and I believe Don was the only person in the factory—including the president of the company and the president of the union—who understood how it worked. At any rate, he never got fired.

The fifth member of the group on one particular night was me.

The evening started out in typical fashion. It was payday night. Phone calls circulated around the plant during the ten-thirty break. Everyone would meet at Chicken Pollard's at twelve-forty. Chicken always had enough money in the back room to cash any check that came along. I used to fantasize a tunnel running from the back room of Chicken Pollard's all the way down the block to the First National Bank. How else could he cash several dozen paychecks every other Thursday night? However he did it, Chicken never ran out of money. He never ran out of beer either, or whiskey, or vodka, or gin, or any other kind of alcohol.

A bar booth is okay for four people. Trying to squeeze five in borders on the obscene. So after a drink or two I usually went back to my own one-room efficiency above Janet's Restaurant. Sometimes Don would come along and we'd talk in the dawn and curse the first shift whistle at seven a.m. You could hear the damn thing all over the valley. But on that particular night the five of us closed Pollard's around three and managed to squeak in a few more drinks at the Town Inn which stayed open a little longer. The Town was where the college kids hung out. It was also where a sometimes sixth member of the group named Jim got cut up in a brawl with the Redhead's husband.

After the Town locked up there was only one place to go: the Texas.

By the time the five of us sat down—elbow to elbow around one of the Texas' stamp-sized tables—all the latest rumors and gripes and suspected liaisons had been rehashed a dozen times. The talk turned back to more standardized but still fruitful topics. The existence or non-existence of God was one of Jeeves' favorites. He also enjoyed talking about his new Bridgestone cycle which he preferred to call his Philosopher's Stone. Jeeves was a student of alchemy in addition to history. Don went over the pleasure/pain theory for the forty-seventh time. And Jeski's recurring blockbuster was the fact that, at that time anyway, "no one, not one single person in the recorded annals of medical history had ever recovered from hydrophobia!"

The only thing on Chuck's mind, outside of laying the Redhead himself, was flying. What would the next step be? Multi-engine license? Instrument? Or instructor? All of them of course but in what order? Which would be the *best* next ticket.

Everybody talked at the Texas, nobody listened. That was the standard operating procedure. And it didn't matter that no one was listening because everyone had heard it all before anyway. The purpose of the exercise was to drain off the final bit of blurred energy so we could all go home, slump into an anesthetized trance and forget about the asinine jobs we would have to face the next afternoon at four. Sometimes the exercise worked.

This particular night—morning now but still dark —nerves had been drawn tight. None of us had even won the check pool so everybody had to buy their own drinks all night. Rumors of another layoff had cropped up again. That generally made everyone jittery. Everyone except Chuck, who still had something like fifteen thou in the bank. At least that's what he kept telling me.

"A layoff means only one thing to me," he said coolly. "More free time for flying." He leaned back in his chair confidently. "I've decided. The next thing on my list is a twin engine license. And I just happened to know of a place in Florida where I can get one in a couple weeks."

"What about Priscilla?" somebody asked in a rare moment of silence.

Chuck shrugged. "What about her. She'll drop the kid whether I'm here or not. I just blew fifteen bucks on the annual ambulance service so let them worry about her."

"Where do you expect to get the money for all this?" Jeski asked. "With a wife and a trailer and a car to pay for and now a new kid at the door." Apparently I was the only one who knew about the motel money because everyone demanded an answer; or else they scoffed at the whole idea of Chuck spending his whole layoff time taking flying lessons.

Chuck was not one to take a scoff lightly. "I have a hundred right here," he said, pulling out a wad of tens and fives. His triangular face was lined and red. "If I'm not on a plane to Florida three days after the next layoff the money goes to anyone who wants to match it."

The mumbled protests that followed were cut short when a big beard in a Woolrich jacket and Red Ball boots tried to snatch the money out of Chuck's hand. None of us had paid any attention to the guy when he first sat down at the counter and started slurping his coffee. But we saw him now as he towered unsteadily above our table and floundered for the money.

Chuck rammed a bony elbow into the man's gut, grabbed the money again and scrambled backward, toppling the chair he'd been sitting on. The beard roared and swung at the air. Surprised curses were flung about, more scraping chairs tumbled to the floor. The Greek behind the counter—one hand on the cash register, the other hand on the phone—waited to see what would happen next. "Stay away from the goddam window," was the only thing he yelled.

The bear finally fell. He had two strong arms but ten not-so-strong arms, *en toto*, were much stronger. The Greek hooked a thumb toward the back door and we dragged the guy out, clattering him into the garbage cans.

The sky was growing lighter. It had started to snow and the ground was still white and clean. By noon it would be grey from the airborne schmuck the paper mill belched out twenty-four-seven. But by eight we would all be asleep and it wouldn't matter what color the snow was.

"The bet still goes," Chuck said as we all hunched together on the sidewalk. He was nursing a swollen lip.

"Ahh let's go home," Jeeves muttered. "My old lady's gonna kill me."

Chuck and Jeski poured themselves into Chuck's station wagon and fishtailed off. Jeeves' Bridgestone exploded to life and gingerly laid down a single track through the fresh snow. Don, in his I. Goldberg army surplus parka, humped up the hood and waddled away toward the Eagle Hotel: a penguin ghost in the twilight snow.

I crossed the street and climbed the stairs of the old opera house. It had been converted into an apartment building a few years back, complete with cardboard walls and very little heat. The jukebox in Janet's on the first floor was clearing its throat for the breakfast crowd. Through the floor of my room came Jerry Lee Lewis belting out "Great Balls of Fi-yah!" Through the thin wall beside my bed came the sexual panting of Helena and an amorous friend.

* * * * * * * * *

No one matched Chuck's one hundred dollars. And it was a good thing. Three weeks later the layoff came. Three weeks and three *days* later a postcard appeared on the mirror behind Chicken Pollard's bar. A palm tree, an orange grove, and a twin engine Cessna were triangled across the front of the card. On the back was a message, cryptic to all but four regular customers. "Fifteen bills equals twin engine ticket equals high revs and no Gs." It was signed by Chuck. Another signature below, in a flowing hand, said "Margie."

Three months later we were all back at the factory. Chuck and I were both working in the upholstery department by then, building leather seats for the 230, which was the company's latest entry into the short-hop commuter-line business. Chuck watched the Redhead sway down the aisle; she was followed by a cloud of gaudy perfume that almost blotted out the shortage of soap—almost. He slammed a leather-upholstered seat back on the work table, partly to make the leather cover slip on more snugly.

"Aren't you going to ask me?" he said, still watching the rolling hips as they moved on down the aisle.

"Ask you what?" I said.

"How I swung the Florida deal."

"Okay, how did you?"

"Nothing to it. What's love? I asked my wife. She thought for a moment and said, 'Love is when you'd do anything for a person, anything he asked you to do.' I said, like shoveling snow? 'I guess so,' she said. Would you go outside and shovel the snow off the driveway for me? I asked. 'Right now?' she said. I nodded. 'Well, sure,' she said, 'I guess it wouldn't hurt the baby.' I patted the bulge. Probably be good for it and you both, I said."

"That got you to Florida?"

"That was the warmup. When she came back inside, all pink and rosy, I pulled her into bed, gently of course. I didn't want the kid popping in the trailer."

"Of course not."

"What's love? I asked her again. She looked at me a while, thinking I was joking. When she decided I wasn't she said, 'Like I told you before. It's when you'd do anything for somebody.'"

"I said, Does that also mean *give* anything to that somebody?"

"She said, 'Yes, I suppose so.'"

"I said, Even fifteen hundred dollars?"

"Without quivering a lip she said, 'Of course.'"

Chuck squinted his eyes, slit-like and crafty. "That's all there was to it. I wired the money to a flight school north of Miami, picked up my layoff slip, signed up for unemployment, and took off."

"You had a good time?" I asked.

"You see the postcard?" I nodded. "I had a good time," he grinned. "Picked up the ticket, too," he said, flashing a twin engine license in my face. "Among other things," he winked.

"Yes," I said. "I saw the postcard."

"But you didn't see her," he said, his eyebrows waggling up and down.

* * * * * * * * *

When the baby got sick I thought—or maybe I hoped—I'd see a change. Silly was working for the company by then, too, somewhere in the office. When

Chuck wasn't flying around from one airport to another, impressing the airport waitresses, he watched the baby while Silly worked during the day. When he could get a plane, a grandmotherly lady next door kept the baby until Silly got home. Chuck was still working in the uphol-stery department at night. But there were rumors circling around the plant like buzzards around a dead dog. The rumors were different this time. No layoffs. Massive hirings.

That was in '66 and the economy was really boom-ing. At least the personal aircraft industry was booming; that was all anyone around town knew or even cared about.

The plant was upping the production schedule con-siderably. On two assembly lines the number of planes to be produced was doubled. On the other lines production also increased but not quite as much. Two primary ef-fects resulted. The first thing that happened was a tremendous increase in hiring. Men who didn't have a retirement plan or seniority considerations to worry about elsewhere were lured in from every mountain village within fifty miles. Ex-coal miners, ex-railroad brakemen, farmers, loggers, construction workers and college drop-outs engulfed the town like a mud slide.

The wives of some of the production workers were hired, too; at least the wives whose husbands were too stupid, weak, or uncaring to protest. A handful of other women had been working in the factory as welders for years, some as far back as World War II. But they were the exceptions and a breed all their own. The new women were never really accepted by the old group.

The girls, as the new women were called regardless of their age, worked almost exclusively on the second shift so they could watch the kids during the day while the husbands worked. The husbands would watch them at night.

The economy of the town skyrocketed. Sporting goods stores were calling in frantic orders for more deer rifles, fly rods, hunting bows, and nearly everything else that was dear to the locals' hearts. Chevy and Ford pickups appeared in nearly every driveway, most with piggyback camper shells. A Chris-Craft dealer set up a new business near the new flood-control dam. Bud's Cycle Shop threw up a new building just outside of town on the road to State College. And used house trailers were blocked up on both sides of the river all the way up Pine Creek Valley.

Everyone suddenly had to have a place "up crick." In summer the trailers were used for beer parties and trout fishing parties. In winter for beer parties and deer and bear hunting parties. That's what the men spent their overtime pay on. The working wives, or so it seemed, spent most of their new money either on clothes or divorces; sometimes both.

It was a definitely a time of changes—major changes.

The second effect of the production schedule increase catapulted Chuck to another rung. By then he had added an instrument license, a commercial license, and was hard at work on his instructor's ticket. At the same time he was charming the grey out of Beth Miller's hair.

Beth was in charge of the personnel department for the factory and was also a major stockholder in the company. Her most important attribute, at least from the workers' point of view, was her incredible memory. During her lunch break strolls through the plant she would call everyone she talked to by their first name, whether they had been hired six weeks, six years, or twenty-six years before. In a factory of that size—then about eighteen hundred souls—it was quite a feat. She knew Chuck's name especially well.

At least once a week he would stop by her office and shoot the breeze with Beth. He always kidded her about going up with him for a short hop to Altoona or Selinsgrove or anywhere else she wanted to go. But Beth wouldn't be caught dead in any plane, not even one of the planes the company built.

Some years before, the son of the company's president was killed in a plane crash. He had switched on the auto pilot during a flight home from Yale, fell asleep, and slammed into the side of a mountain. It was said that Beth and the son had been more than casual friends. Beth's husband denied the rumors.

In the midst of the '66 boom, Beth had an idea. Why not run another ad campaign in the flying magazines and also in a couple of the country's big newspapers: "Free flying lessons and low cost plane rental available to all aircraft workers. Call collect."

The ad worked. A second flock of college dropouts, ex-GIs, and moony-eyed flying bugs swept into Beth's office begging for flying lessons, and also a job. The minute he got it, Chuck casually displayed his new instructor's ticket to Beth. The following Monday he was out of the union and on the "staff."

To prepare for the new instructor position, Chuck went right out and bought some new threads, perfected his swagger, twisted his crooked grin just a shade more, and went to work.

It was obvious to anyone that Chuck loved flying. It was, in fact, his life. Everything else was detritus and bullshit. I used to wonder what would happen to him if, for some unknown reason, he would no longer be able to fly.

If Chuck loved flying, however, he loved being a pilot even more. He loved talking about temperature inversions, isobars, the FAA, runway eighteen, and seven niner whiskey: his single-engine classroom. It was a Cherokee, no different from the two dozen other Cherokees that crouched along the runway. But to Chuck, seven niner whiskey was heaven. Swaggering across the grass in his dark blue suit, dark sox, and black shoes, his narrow shoulders swayed, a counterpoint to his slim hips.

He reveled in the wide-eyed admiration of the fledgling pilots assigned to him. Chuck's own instructor—back in his pre-any-kind-of-ticket-days—was now his back-slapping wench-humping buddy. Back then, however, he had made things rough during Chuck's own student days. And Chuck was going to follow that tradition, right down to the letter.

Spiel off the check list from memory at least four times between the apron and the plane. Goose the flaps and rudder at least twice. Untie and retie and then undo the tie-downs once more. Unblock the wheels, check the flaps again and also the sock that billowed above the hangar. Scan the sky in both directions. And *then* climb aboard. This routine could be increased for any of the junior jocks who had a tendency to adopt Chuck's swagger much too soon. The pre-flight routine would never be decreased no matter how many hours the student went up each week.

Once strapped in, the check list was gone over several more times; the "clear" signal was called out loudly even if the field was empty. The engine was allowed to warm up at the proper RPM while tower instructions were asked for and received. As soon as the plane started clattering and bumping between the grass and the runway, Chuck would start firing questions. For the newer students, he would wait until they were safely in the air. The more experienced students, however, had to think of at least three things at the same time: the feel of the plane, the takeoff procedure, and the rapid-fire questions. Chuck was convinced, as his own instructor had been, that any pilot worth his wings must be able to operate on a minimum of three open channels at the same time; more if possible.

Chuck's teaching methods were very simple. Yelling was allowed; so was badgering; and insults were especially effective. The most minor offense, the least deviation from the rule book, was met with an abusive tirade. In Chuck's eyes, there were no minor offenses, not in flying. An un-flicked switch or a ten second daydream could kill you. Like most pilot, he was fond of telling everyone who asked, "Statistics prove it without a doubt. Flying is considerably less risky—from the

standpoint of lives lost—than driving a car. That's because pilots pay attention to what they're doing. Car
jockeys don't."

As for the plane crashes that did occur, Chuck never hedged. "It is not mechanical failures that kill most of
the people," he would say. "It is mental failures." It was
the cocky jock who didn't bother to find out the weather
conditions, not only where he was, but where he was going. The newbie who forgot to check the flaps. Or the
airhead who just generally screwed off and didn't pay attention to the 'rules of the air.' These guys—and others
like them—were the ones everyone heard about; when
they came down in someone's backyard or tried to land
in a muddy corn field after running out of fuel. These
things were not going to happen to any of Chuck's students.

A few of the young students dropped out after a
week of Chuck's harangues, or switched to another instructor. For the most part, however, the kids loved every
minute of it; for they wanted desperately to be pilots.
Chuck was undeniably a pilot; they felt that the minute
they saw him; and they would do whatever he said, no
matter how he said it.

All of the adulation and dictatorial power was not
wasted on Chuck. It did not slide off his back and disappear. He sucked it up like a dried sponge. The native

confidence and the controlled assertiveness he had been born with now blossomed into full-blown arrogance.

* * * * * * * * *

When Chuck took on the job as instructor I lost track of him. He graduated from our group into a different group; a group made up of the other flying instructors, engineers, administrators and other such factory VIPs. From time to time he would drop in to Chicken Pollard's for a drink or two but most of the time his hangout became the Tomahawk. That was were all the VIPs went Friday and Saturday night. Hank Jeski, a licensed pilot himself now—although still working in the factory—was our only link to Chuck.

Jeski and Chuck were still buddies. They often flew together and, when the old ladies weren't with them, swapped airport waitresses and racked up sack time in the Mile High Club. But the safety rules continued to go unbroken; for the most part. Either Chuck or Jeski always remained sober enough and alert enough to fly the two of them back home.

For a while, it looked like Chuck was going to outgrow Jeski, too. He was probably earning twice as much every week as Jeski, and Chuck's expensive tastes started cutting into Jeski's baby bootie fund. Not that Jeski minded that so much but his wife sure did. But everything was smoothed over when Daisy, Jeski's wife, became Silly's best friend. Then, when the baby got sick, the friendship deepened even more. And something else started to happen, too; with Silly.

The four of them started getting together every Saturday night: Chuck, Jeski, Silly and Daisy. The guys talked planes and the girls talked babies. Silly was expecting her second, Daisy her third. Sometimes they all played bridge until Chuck got so angry one night over Silly's ineptitude that he tore up the cards and dumped a Bloody Mary down the front of her new maternity dress. Before, Silly would have ran to her room and wept bitterly. Now, she just changed her dress. That's the way Hank described it anyway and there was no reason to doubt him. From then on, the foursome either went to the Tomahawk or talked and drank in front of Chuck's new Harman Kardon stereo. No more bridge.

"Gail's pregnant again," Hank Jeski told Chuck quietly. The wives had left the kitchen and continued their chatter in the living room.

Chuck's eyes narrowed. "The Redhead? Whose is it this time?"

Hank faked a jab at Chuck's stomach and laughed. "Who knows? It might even be Jim's, her old man's."

"Five'll get you twenty the kid has hair on his chest and a dimple in his chin the minute he pops.

"Nahh," said Hank, squeezing the dimple in his own chin. "She'll end up having another abortion. Anyway, her old man's got some college chick right now. Doe-eyed little quail, long black hair. Kind of skinny though. He's been feathering her nest for a couple months now. She even got him to enroll at State. Part time of course."

"What's the Redhead say about that?"

"She ain't none too pleased, I can tell you," Jeski said. "Scuttlebutt says a divorce is in the works."

Chuck was silent for a moment while he poked at an ice cube with his index finger. He watched it slide down under the amber whiskey and then clink back up against the side of the glass. "She still playing around?"

"You still got the itch?" Jeski laughed.

Chuck shrugged. "Just curious."

"Sure you are." Jeski glanced toward the living room. The girls were still talking. "She might not be so bad if she'd take a shower once in a while and chisel off some of the makeup."

"I could stand it for an hour or two," Chuck grinned. He lit a cigarette and strolled to the half-open window. He looked out into the blackness where the long hump of Bald Eagle Mountain was barely distinguishable from the cloudy sky. A wet spring breeze washed in over the windowsill: a delicate intangible stream. Absently, Chuck nodded and grunted as Jeski swung the conversation back to flying. He looked up at the mountain for a long while and was about to say something when Daisy burst into the kitchen.

"Chuck, something's wrong with your baby," she cried. "She's not breathing right and her color's funny."

Jeski was half out of his chair before Daisy could finish. He rushed past his wife and disappeared into the living room. His footsteps could be heard echoing down a hallway. Daisy started to follow him and then stopped. She looked back at Chuck who was still standing by the window. "Chuck?" she said. "Did you hear me? Your baby's sick."

Chuck turned around, crushed out his cigarette in a large glass ashtray and said. "I heard you."

"Oh," Daisy said. "I thought ..." She turned away uncertainly and then, remembering, rushed after her husband.

It was normally a fifteen minute drive to Valley Memorial Hospital when the traffic was light. Jeski made it in eight. By the time they screeched to a stop in front of the emergency room entrance the baby had turned a sickly blue color and was gasping for breath. Daisy was hysterical, Jeski was running around, guiding elbows and slamming doors. Chuck was yelling at Jeski to shut his wife *up*! But it was Silly who carefully wrapped the baby in the soft pink blanket, held it against her shoulder and carried it inside.

The plump nurses bustled around the small room trying to look efficient. They dispatched an elderly volunteer to search for the doctor. After five minutes of sobbing, unpersuasive murmurs, curses and confusion, a rumpled young man with a stethoscope bobbing on his white-coated chest came padding down an empty corridor. He nervously adjusted his glasses, smoothed down his ruffled hair and cleared his throat officiously. Before he could say anything, Chuck tore the baby from Silly's arms and thrust it toward the startled doctor. Another bumbled scene followed as the two nurses and the volunteer looked for a fresh bottle of oxygen. The young doctor shouted orders and rammed needles into the baby's arm. Silly sat quietly in a battered chair, eyes closed, hands folded across the high mound of her abdomen. Chuck stood beside her, one foot propped on a knee-high radiator. He hunched over, leaning on his knee, his eyes squinting, an unlit cigarette dangling from the side of his mouth.

Within thirty minutes the baby was dead. The doctor expressed his sympathies and assured them, briskly, that he and his staff had done everything they could for the baby.

"The heart stopped," he said soberly. "We tried several times to re-start it ..." His hands went up helplessly and then fell to his side again. "It happens sometimes," he said. He took off his glasses and wiped them with a tissue. "I'm sorry," he said. "The nurses will tell you what to do."

Jeski made all the arrangements with the help of Silly although Chuck went with them to pick out the tiny casket. Chuck also made a few phone calls. Other than that he did little the next few days but smoke and sit. When Jeski told the doctor about Chuck's grim moodiness, the doctor prescribed some mild tranquilizers and pronounced the symptoms quite normal, "considering the circumstances."

Three days after the funeral Chuck decided to fly to Altoona for coffee, mostly to be in the air again. He tried to persuade Silly to go along but she declined, as he expected she would. "You go," she said. "It'll do you good to get away."

At the far end of the runway, near the river and almost out of sight of the control tower, Chuck throttled back the Cherokee and waited. A dull black car pulled in behind an abandoned barn near the road. A few minutes later a red haired figure dashed along the bank of the river from the trees to the runway and scampered into the plane. A metallic voice crackled on the radio and seven

niner whiskey swooped up and over the city with a whining snarl.

* * * * * * * * *

Their second and now only child was almost a year
old when Silly—now called Priscilla by almost everyone
including Chuck, found out she was pregnant again. On
the same day, Chuck reached the top of his roost. Business at the factory had been falling off again. Sales were
faltering and layoff slips quickly wiped out most of the
student pilot program. The staff of instructors was going
to be cut from five to two. Chuck was not one of the
two. But thanks to the sheaf of tickets he accumulated
Beth Miller found a place for him as a company pilot.

He'd be on call much of the time, she told him.
And he might have to fly in some bad weather occasionally. Most of the trips would be to Florida or Texas,
where the company had two other smaller factories. But,
Beth reminded Chuck, he could end up flying anywhere;
wherever the brass wanted to go. But the pay was good
and he'd be building up his hours.

He leaped at the job.

About the pregnancy, Chuck had mixed feelings,
according to Jeski. Kids cost money and they make a lot
of noise. On the other hand, having another baby might
make Priscilla docile again and also keep her busy.

"A busy happy wife is definitely an asset," he told me the day I ran into him at the airport. He couldn't understand why I wasn't married yet. "Or maybe I can," he said. "The word gets around."

I ignored his sly smile. "Sorry to hear about the other baby," I said.

"Yeah," he said. "Priscilla took it hard. You know how women are. She's coming out of it though. The doc told her she'll be dropping this one in about four months."

"That's great. How's the new job going?"

"Not bad," he said casually. "I flew the Old Man to Washington last week. He and that domed baboon who runs the plant."

"Tinkler?"

"Yeah. McMasters flew down himself the day before. The three of them are trying to rustle up a government contract."

"You been flying much? I mean on your own."

"Starting to. Didn't for a while because of Priscilla. Took one trip to Altoona. Somebody said they saw me down there with Gail. Somehow the word got back to Priscilla." He shook his head. "I had a helluva time explaining away that juicy little rumor. "Priscilla, honey," I said, "you know these clowns around here, they love to make up a lot of garbage. Especially about somebody they don't like. They're jealous, that's all. It makes them feel good to spread rumors. Especially the women. They're the worst."

Chuck studied me through narrow slits for a moment. "You know how it goes. Don't you old buddy?" Then he slapped me on the back and grinned broadly. "You know what? You and me are going to have to get together out at the house sometime, slurp up a few, talk about old times."

"She didn't buy it," I said.

"Huh?" The color rose in Chuck's ears. He shrugged it away and looked out over the runway. "Funny thing," he said, almost to himself. "Since the kid died, maybe even before that … I don't know. I used to be able to tell her anything. Now …"

He looked back at me quickly, his face blank. He glanced at his watch. "I have an appointment," he said formally. He looked up at the big round clock on the wall and then flashed a thin crooked smile. "Good talking to you," he said and abruptly started walking away toward the hangar.

"We'll have to get together," I called after him.

"Yeah, right. I'll give you a call. Sometime. Slurp up a couple."

He waved and was gone.

* * * * * * * *

A few months later I was looking over the bid sheets that were tacked up next to the water fountain. I had left the upholstery department after things started to get out of hand with me and a certain married person. I was now soldering wires on the day shift. A whiff of delicate perfume floated my way. A young woman had come out of the administrative office and was walking toward the fountain. I glanced at her for a second and turned back to the bid sheets.

"Excuse me," she said. "Aren't you one of Chuck's friends?" Her voice was firm but friendly, and very warm.

She was wearing a well-tailored rich brown maternity dress and a simple broach. Her dark hair was different. It was either longer or shorter, I couldn't remember which. She seemed taller, stronger somehow, although her figure was as trim as ever, except for her abdomen. I couldn't believe the change and yet I knew it was her.

"Priscilla," I said. She smiled at my recognition. The glow of pregnancy fit her very well. She was beautiful.

"You came to our place one night after work, didn't you?"

I nodded. "That was quite a while ago. You're sure looking great."

"Thank you," she said simply. "How are you doing?"

"Fine. I saw Chuck at the airport some time back."

"Oh? I don't remember him saying anything."

"He probably forgot," I said. "He told me the good news." I glanced at her stomach and smiled.

"Yes, we're happy about it. At least I am." She laughed. It sounded forced, almost painful. "I don't suppose it means as much to a man as it does to a woman."

"Well, I don't know about that."

"You ought to come out to see us sometime. Did you know we bought a home over on the island?"

"Yes, I had heard that. Sounds like a nice place."

"It is. A bit large maybe. So it really keeps me busy. But we'll be needing at least one of the extra bedrooms pretty soon." She smiled and patted her stomach. "Chuck always wanted a big house anyway. He hated that trailer we lived in. Remember that?"

"The biggest and the best of everything," I grinned. "That always seemed to be one of Chuck's mottos."

Priscilla bobbed her head at the water fountain and came up, still smiling, her lips shiny with wetness. "Still is," she said.

"Did I see him in a new car a couple weeks ago?"

She groaned. "Don't mention that car. He's sick about it."

"What happened?"

"We only had it about two weeks when he ran into a stop sign. In broad daylight!"

"Anybody hurt?"

"No. Luckily he was by himself. Got a scratch on his hand but that's all. My ears are still ringing, however. It was only a bump on one fender but Chuck really raised the roof. You know his temper."

"How did it happen?"

"Don't ask me. And whatever you do, don't ask him. He insists there was something wrong with the steering. He took the car back to the dealer and really tore them out. They checked the car from bumper to bumper but couldn't find anything wrong. Of course that didn't sway Chuck's opinion one iota."

"I don't suppose it would." We both laughed. The buzzer sounded and I heard a couple yells. I looked up at the railing that surrounds the wire room loft. Three guys were hanging over the railing, grinning down at me.

"Time to work," I said to Priscilla.

She ignored the catcalls and searched my face with warm wide eyes. "You will come out to the house some-time, won't you?" She placed a hand delicately on my arm. "Chuck's away a lot," she said slowly, "but stop in anytime."

"Fine," I said, and then smiled.

She pressed my arm and turned away. "See you then," she said, glancing back over her shoulder.

I started up the stairway to the loft. "You know'em all, don't you?" one of the guys cackled. "Even the pregnant ones."

"Why not?" I said. "No worries if they're already pregnant."

The guys guffawed and jabbed each other in the ribs. One of them, the inspector, shifted his wad of snuff from behind his upper lip to behind his lower lip. "Who is she?" he said. "Or is that classified … information?" He enunciated the words and then spat into a cardboard barrel.

"Chuck Cornelious' wife," I said. "He's a company pilot."

"Well la-dee-da. Getting up in the world, ain't you?"

"Sure," I said. I pushed by him and went back to work. The same inspector climbed on my back all afternoon, rejecting nearly every wire harness I put together. I ended up dumping a pot of hot solder on my foot and had to be on sick leave for the next two weeks.

* * * * * * * *

The group had come apart. When Jeeves graduated from State he quit the factory and got a job teaching history at Nittany Junior High. He started selling life insurance on the side. Chuck was flying all over the country. And I was caught up in my own maze.

Only Jeski and Don were holding down the booth at Pollard's. Jeski was trying to convince Don he should take up flying. Don was trying to convince Jeski to take up bowhunting. One Friday night about two-thirty both of them came slamming up the steps to my apartment and pounded on the door.

"Get up in there, boy," Jeski drawled. "We know you're awake. Saw your fuckin' light."

From the table where I was sitting I could reach the light switch and the door knob. I snapped off the light and waited in the darkness.

"Too late, boy. We already saw it." A boot kicked at the door and joggled the locked doorknob.

"Okay, okay," I said, flicking the light switch back on. "Don't wreck the door." I swung it open and they marched in, grinning and cursing.

"What's all this shit," Jeski said. He was looking at the sheets of paper strewn across the table. "You writing a novel?"

I closed my notebook and gathered up the papers. "What's happening?" I said.

"Booze," said Don. "Chicken musta got his head chopped off." He giggled. "Goddam place closed for some goddam reason. You got any beer?"

Jeski fell across my narrow bed on his back. He cursed at the ceiling. "Kee-rist what a night." Don backed up to the sink and tried to heave his short stocky body up on the counter. He slipped off three times and gave it up. He poked around inside my refrigerator and brought out a half empty bottle of Governor's Club. "You been holding out on us," he grinned.

I shoved my papers into a drawer and closed it firmly. "So what have you guys been up to?" I got out three glasses, a tray full of ice cubes and then splashed in some bourbon.

"The usual," said Jeski. "We were on our way to the Texas when we saw your light. What do you think of this guy?" he said to Don. "Tried to turn the light out on us."

Don belched and giggled. "Damned if I know. Always was a mysterious bastard. Wannabe writers usually are." He downed the bourbon and poured some more. "Here," he said, holding his half-filled glass out to Jeski who was still on his back. "I'll take yours."

Jeski swung his feet off the bed and sat up. They switched glasses, Don's filled one for Jeski's empty. Jes-

ki downed his in two gulps and held the glass out for another refill.

"I applied for a job with the FAA," he said to me.
"Control tower. Have to take some more tests next week.
Passed a couple preliminaries already."

"Stressful work," I said.

Jeski shrugged as Don splashed more bourbon into
his glass. "I can handle it. Keep your cool. That's all
you gotta—"

He stopped in mid-sentence. "Damn, I almost forgot! Hey, Stalling, we almost forgot!"

"Forgot what?" I said.

"Cornelious, for chrissake. That's why we came
up here. Didn't you hear about him?" Jeski forgot about
the refill and clunked the empty glass down on the floor.
He vaulted to his feet waving his arms around, his dark
eyes bright and intense. "He really got his ass in a sling
this time. Man oh man. He is done for, the bastard. Isn't
that right, Don?" Don stared down into his own empty
glass.

"What happened?" I said.

"Where've you been for chrissake, in a closet?"
Jeski said. "It's all over town. He's got ... what the hell
is it? Don, you know all that shit. What's he got?"

Don's bulging forehead jerked up and he peered at
me through smeared glasses. "MS," he said.

Jeski snapped his fingers. "That's it. I gotta re-member that. I'm always getting it mixed up with mus-cular dystrophy. Anyway, the bastard is grounded. The FAA pulled his tickets quicker than shit." He paused for a second, looking at me. "Don't get me wrong. I feel sorry for the poor bastard."

"You sure?" I said. "About the MS."

"Hell yeah," Jeski said. "He told me himself."

"How did he find out?"

"Oh, hell, it's a long story," Jeski said. He grabbed his glass from the floor, splashed in some more bourbon and gulped it down. "He got this red Jag convertible, see, went all the way to Philadelphia to buy it. I don't know how the hell much it set him back but plenty. Two weeks later he bent the thing on a stop sign. Just plowed right into the freakin' thing. In the middle of the after-noon. Sunny day. No traffic."

Jeski's voice got louder. "Then he started having trouble with his eyes. Blurred up on him while he was touching down one day. Almost clipped the tail off a rag wing. Shook him up plenty."

"Maybe he just needs glasses," I offered.

"Yeah, that's what he thought. And being the straight arrow jock he is, there wasn't anything to do but check it out with the doc." Jeski stopped and shook his head. "That son of a bitch is really on his ass."

"Doc sent him to Geisinger," Don said, peering at me. "They gave him every test they had. Isn't that right, Jeski?"

"Hell yeah," Jeski said. "Every damn test in the book."

"There's no doubt?" I said.

"There ain't no doubt in the FAA's mind, baby," Jeski said. "That bastard's freakin' flying days are freakin' *over*!"

* * * * * * * * *

They were sitting in a booth by the window at Janet's. I had just come down for a cup of black rancid coffee to clear my morning head. They hadn't seen me come in and that suited me fine.

"You should have been there," Eileen was saying to her sister, Gail. Gail was looking into a small round compact, fingering a red curl across her forehead to cover a slight scar above her right eye. "All that beautiful slimness?" she went on. "Gone. It was nothing but knobby gristle from head to toe."

Still staring at her own image in the compact mirror, Gail arched the thin line of her eyebrows and ran her tongue across the front of her teeth.

"I didn't think it worked *that* fast," Eileen continued. "My uncle Ray got it ten years ago and he's still hanging around.'

"Where'd you see him?" Gail asked. "Did you talk to him?"

"No. His wife was with him. She just parked their Jag outside the bank."

"Did he see you?" Gail closed the compact with a snap and dropped it into her bag.

"I don't think so," Eileen said. "I was across the street and he wasn't looking around. His wife is really cute now, you know?"

Gail nodded. "I saw her at the Tomahawk a couple times when me and Bob were there. I thought she was kind of mousey at the time. Wondered what he saw in her."

"Not any more," Eileen said.

"I know. Did I tell you? I saw her a couple nights ago. What's that guy's name? The one with the sexy hair all over his chest?"

"Jim?"

"Mmm," Gail murmured. "That's the one. She was waiting in his car outside the Harvest Moon Motel."

"You're shittin' me!" Eileen exclaimed.

Gail smiled. "Maybe they just stopped in for a coke."

"Sure," Eileen said. Her eyes sparkled. "So *that's* how it is."

"Anyway," Gail went on, "how was he? I mean, how'd he look? Chuck, I mean."

"Next to her? Like a scarecrow. You'd think she picked him up at the Salvation Army. Needed a shave, pants flopping around his legs. She had to help him out of the car, can you believe that?"

"That kind of shit is spooky." Gail flipped a strand of long red hair back over her ear and swallowed some coffee. "Did he say anything?"

"Not that I could hear. She was doing all the talking. Not loud, exactly, but firm and patient. Like she was talking to some *re*-tard who was getting ready to throw a tantrum."

Eileen sighed and looked out into the street. A bearded giant in a plaid hunting jacket was looking in. She wiggled her fingers at him and grinned. When the man moved on she turned back to her sister.

"I don't know," Eileen said. "The guy has really changed. Obviously. For a minute I thought he was going to start bawling right there on the street."

"Chuck? Really?"

"Yeah. That's what I mean. He's at the bottom and going down. Shuffled like an old man. I don't know," she said again. "The time I was with him, the first time, I'll never forget it. He was jumping from one bed to the other, not a stitch on. A regular randy bull, but slim, you know? Legs like marble. Today, he can't even go up the bank steps without tripping. He would have landed on his face if she hadn't grabbed him. I almost started bawling myself."

"It's not worth it," Gail said.

"I know. I saw him a couple weeks ago, too. At the Texas of all places. Talked to him for a few minutes. Of course neither one of us said anything about what happened to him. Elephant in the room kind of thing. I had just heard about it the night before. Bob said it was all over the plant. He looked bad even then, although not as bad as today. But that didn't stop him." She shook her head. "Un-fuckin' believable. Right there in the Texas he tried to set something up. But I mean, really? Just the thought of it turns my stomach." She shuddered.

Someone cranked up the juke box and for a few minutes all talk was buried under the silver pleadings of Joan Baez. I dumped some more sugar in the inky coffee and smoked another cigarette. The head was starting to clear when the record finally ended. The two girls were getting ready to leave.

Gail finished her coffee. "Well what can you do? They come and they go. One way or another, they always go." The girls allowed a moment of silence to pass then Gail said. "So what are you doing till Bob gets home?"

Eileen looked at her watch. "I've got a hair appointment at one and he's working till eight tonight. I told him I was going shopping with Fran and wouldn't be back till nine or ten."

"Where *are* you going?

"Oh I'm going shopping all right. In a manner of speaking. Fran has this friend, who has this friend. He's new in the area, just started with the company."

Gail looked up with interest. "In the factory or admin?"

"Neither," said Eileen, a lilt in her voice. "He's a pilot."

"Well fancy that," Gail said as the two of them slid out of their booth and pulled on their windbreakers. "So … you going to introduce us?"

Eileen grinned. "Maybe yes, maybe no. We'll have to see how things play out."

After the girls left, I toyed with the nasty grey mass of sugar at the bottom of my coffee cup and then crushed my cigarette into it. The bus wouldn't be leaving for another fifteen minutes yet but there really wasn't any point in waiting.

I picked up my battered suitcase and paid the check. Someone put another dime in the slot. As I went out through the door a hard-faced young girl with black hair brushed past me coming in. She smiled vaguely but kept on going. The last thing I heard as I started down the street was Joan Baez again: *"Sagt Mir wo die Blumen sind."*

Where indeed, I thought, and gripped the suitcase tighter.

######